# THE UNBURIED DEAD

CRAIG DAWSON

*To everyone I stood behind a counter with.*

*Enough stories for a thousand books.*

# 1

Jackie Stark took one last look in the mirror before leaving the house to go and lay her husband to rest. She did this every time she left to go somewhere, a habit of vanity that had long since become a kind of ritual. Tidying stray strands of hair from her eye-line to behind her ear, and a forensic check on her make-up. She took a little longer with this routine today. She was going to be the centre of attention, and any imperfection could be – would be – judged, and she was damned if she was going to add to the whispers and gossip that would be swirling.

She smoothed down the imagined creases of her black skirt, and slid her arms into the sleeves of her long dress coat, which was also black. To offset, she had chosen a red neck scarf; a flash of colour to break the monotone, a concession to fashion, and an attempt to transmit some attitude. She knew how important it was to be strong today, in the crucible of opinion. Every action would be scrutinised, and assessments made by all those there today. Was she holding up ok? Is she going to be able to get through this?

Her eyes looked tired. Her make-up couldn't distract from the reddening around her eyes, a combination of exhaustion and worry. The last few weeks had been a torture, from the shock of the news, to the pinball options of what to do next. So much to think about, and to balance, and there she was in the middle of it all, struggling.

Jim Stark was dead. Taken from her in the middle of the night, a week or two ago. The days mashed into each other. She was told hours after he had died, by a too-young policeman who she could have sworn had a smirk on his lips when he rang her doorbell at 7am. It wasn't unusual for Jim to be out all night every once in a while. It was a consequence of what he did to put a roof over their heads and food on their table. Jim Stark was the most powerful criminal in the city. And he had been shot in the head.

She felt that the facts of that night had been deliberately kept from her. She couldn't shake the feeling that the ever-changing cast of police personnel who visited her were more interested in trying to draw insights into Jim's business rather than any duty of care in telling her exactly what had happened. Instead, she had to piece together her own conclusions from the scraps that she could glean from their careless talk, or, in time, from the sheepish and dutiful Stark employees that turned up at her door to pay their respects.

Jim had cast a long shadow over the city, and, even in death, he demanded deference, though as the days started to add up to become weeks, Jackie couldn't help but feel that this was changing. Jim would tell her everything, despite never expecting her to get her hands dirty herself. They had always had complete honesty between them, but he had been strict in ensuring that there was nothing – no signatures, no presence at meetings – that would tie her into anything. Plausible deniability. Play the dumb trophy wife to the fierce and ruthless villain. But she knew where the bodies were buried. Literally.

She learnt that Jim had been killed by a married couple, of all things. What she had learned was vague, gleaned from some of the faces from the business that hadn't melted into the shadows. Stories and whispers, truths and half-truths, with Jackie left to sift through to try and piece together what really happened the night her husband was killed. This couple had run from the city, and from Jim, because the man had refused to do as he was told, wouldn't bend the knee and swear loyalty to his king. So, Jim had sent word to anyone who could listen that this couple needed to be found, and eventually, find them they did. Some comatose backwater on the other side of the country.

Jim had sent his best to deal with them, and the chase had led all the way back to Liverpool, until it all came to a head in a non-descript office building that Jim owned, down by the river. The building was set up to be a venue for execution. Jim and his best, surrounding the place, their quarry inside. A perfect place to tie off the loose ends.

But something had gone wrong. Horribly wrong. Jim and his boys never made it home that night. Instead they were the ones cut down, shot dead like ducks on a range. Her husband taken from her by a couple of nothings who didn't know their place.

After that constable had broken the news to her, his eyes twinkling even whilst Jackie had wailed and sobbed, she had fallen into a fog, unsure which direction to strike out for first. She had to play her role, of course, as the dutiful wife robbed of her devoted husband, who had somehow been drawn into some vicious mob war for whatever reason. And beneath that façade, she knew that across the city, as word spread, there would be the igniting sparks of ambition amongst the dogs who had fed at Jim's hand. So many angry, desperate little people who all wanted their place in the sun, who Jim had kept in line through force of will and the threat of ultimate sanction, who would want to fill the vacuum. They knew that a space needed to be filled, and they would damn sure want to make sure it was them that filled it.

Jackie also had to endure the simpering from well-wishers with good grace, a revolving door of doe-eyed wives who would hold her hand, and pat her wrist, their fingers clad in over-sized gold rings. The golf club clans who Jim had used as a pathway to respectability ticking off their obligation in dutiful visits one by one, all hoping for some crumb of tittle-tattle to take back to the Nineteenth Hole. How was she? Did she cry? Did she wail? Jackie performed as best she can, her anger ensuring she gave them enough, but not too much.

And then there were the Stark associates. The most trusted, and most loyal, had all bled out on the forecourt around that office building, so it was a few from the next level in the hierarchy who made the journey to her front door. It was in these meetings that Jackie knew she had to be immaculate. She expected the socialite wives to be assessing her, but the worst they could do to her was embarrass her, or patronise her. The Stark employees, if that was the word, were a scrum of the hungry and the corrupt, and they would be assessing her for completely different purposes, not least to see whether it was worth measuring Jackie up for a shallow grave behind the motorway, either through naked ambition or self-preservation. Could she be trusted to keep quiet, or did she want to take her place at the top table, now her husband had left the stage?

In addition to those groups was a third, equally perverse. The police. Jim Stark was known to them. He had been for years. But a mixture of *omerta*, pure fear and care to be one or two steps removed had always allowed him to operate without fear of interference. But it seemed all Jim had managed to create was a house built on sand. With Jim gone, the police swarmed, maybe not even daring to dream of some great breakthrough, and a closed case that would be the source of back-slaps and shared brandies for years to come, but instead happy to settle for a subtle twisting of the knife, or a gleeful kicking of the shins, safe that the ogre had been toppled. They visited day after day, their attitudes oscillating from obsequious, sarcastic concern, to aggressive, finger-wagging accusation. "Sorry for your loss" soon became threats of imprisonment, if Jackie didn't tell more, tell all, tell everything. But she wasn't weak. She built her wall of denials and never let it crack.

The face in the mirror looked back at her. It seemed gaunt, and severe, and old. Haunted by her own reflection, with drawn cheeks and pursed lips. The funeral car was waiting outside, her grandchildren waiting in the back seat for her, keen to hold onto Nannie Jacks, hoping that she would have some magic words for them that would bring Grandad back to them. The cold face in the mirror looked back at her. There, just ever-so-slightly, she could see a flicker of spirit in her eyes. An ember that she was nursing, encouraging, willing it to take. It was all she had.

She knew she had precious little time to deal with all of this. Her concerned family needed to be led, and this role of hers as dutiful wife, mother, grandmother, needed to be played to perfection. And through all of that, she had to come up with a plan. Because there were some things that she had decided in that first long, cold night after she had been told that her husband was laying on a mortuary gurney staring at the ceiling with dead eyes. She was going to take control of the Stark business. And then she was going to find Tony and Eleanor Grace and kill those motherfuckers once and for all.

# 2

She couldn't have recalled the trip to the crematorium if she'd tried. Her mind was wandering, stress-testing potential decisions and weighing up likely outcomes, all whilst outwardly she maintained that image of calm and poise that she had worked hard to cultivate over the recent days. Occasionally, she was yanked back to the here and now by the hand-squeeze of her granddaughter, sat to her right in the back seat of the funeral limousine, an image of childish perfection in shiny shoes and a simple black dress and coat. Her grandson was to her left, a couple of years older than his sister, and old enough to think of any show of emotion as weakness or unbecoming. But Jackie could see that underneath the sullen exterior he was trying to project, was a lost little boy struggling to keep his lip from trembling.

Late autumn was becoming winter, and the weather was crisp, the sky grey, and any memory of summer warmth and happiness was replaced with a bleakness that matched her mood. The procession of limousines, led by the funeral car, queued at a turning, indicators all blinking to turn across oncoming traffic, through looming gates, and up a gravel path towards the crematorium building that stood on a hill, looking out across the city. As the cars turned, and drove slowly towards the red-brick building, Jackie couldn't help but look out through the tinted windows at the scrum of mourners who had come to pay respects, gathered at the top of the drive. So many of them. So much small talk to endure, simpering looks to tolerate, awkward silences to puncture. She sighed, took a moment to refocus, and squeezed the hands of both grandchildren sat either side of her.

"Here we are, then," she said. "Time to say goodbye to Grandad."

Little Megan looked up at her, already sniffling. Toby, on her other side, was gnawing at his bottom lip, doing his best to "be a man", whatever that meant. She sighed again. It was the consequences of machismo that brought her to this place, Jim being Jim, insisting on managing these things himself, when he should have just delegated and let someone else be the one in the cross-hairs.

The car pulled up at the door of the crematorium, and the door was opened by one of the undertakers, frock coat and top hat, and genuflecting deference. He gripped the brim of his hat, as he held the door, as Jackie ushered Megan out of the car, before turning back to indicate that Toby should follow. From the next car back, their mum, Jackie's daughter, had gotten out of her limousine, indicating to the children that they were to stay with Nannie Jacks. The entire cortege got out of cars, and, to avoid making any kind of awkward faux pas, instead started straightening outfits, or patting down stray hair, until someone made the first move inside.

The undertakers, now the cars were empty, moved to the back of the lead limousine, and opened the rear door. Jackie felt her eyes sting as she saw the undertakers reaching down to lift and shoulder the coffin – that wood box that held her beloved - because the men who would naturally have taken on this duty were all dead. Left in bloody ruin on a forecourt by the river, cut down by a sniper they hadn't planned for. Left to be boxed up in their own coffins, and wept over by their own people. Jim didn't have friends. That much was evident. He had associates, and employees. And she felt alone.

With a smooth, practiced effort, the coffin was shouldered, and solemnly carried into the building. Jackie looked away, the reality of the situation crystallised for her, catching the gaze of some of the mourners, who quietly stood apart, watching the sombre ritual take place. She regretted looking. A held gaze needed acknowledgement, and all she could do was give a wan smile of recognition, trying her best to transmit fortitude, but she was weaker than she wanted to admit, and hated that these people might see through her defences. Instead, she looked down at Megan, who had slipped her hand into Jackie's, and instead forced herself to smile, as warmly as she could muster, hoping to find some solace in the expression of a child.

Jackie felt a hand on her back, and turned. It was her daughter, Carol, keen to support her mother, and ensure her children were not at risk of becoming a burden or an embarrassment. Just checking in.

"Come on, ma. Let's get inside."

"Alright, love. Okay. Was lost in myself," Jackie whispered.

Carol rubbed Jackie's back, a gentle cue to move, and Jackie led the family inside, the other mourners waiting until they had passed before entering the building themselves, with only the crunch of gravel and the low bubble of whispered words to be heard.

The reception room was relatively small and nondescript, being just a holding area before the main ceremonial room. In front of double doors to that room, just to one side, was a sign with the word "STARK" spelled out in white letters on a black background, the letters pushed into holes on the backing, easy to remove ready for the next name to be displayed. It was all so impermanent, thought Jackie. In an hour, it would all be changed – the letters would spell out a new name, the flowers would be moved, and the ovens would be ready for the next body to be fed into it, an insatiable maw that would just devour and devour. Lifetimes burned to ash, and prince and pauper alike taken away from this unprepossessing building in little canisters. The unfairness was sickening to Jackie. This was Jim Stark. The king of Liverpool. Life and death at his command, with the snap of a finger. These people, these parasites, knew what he was, but they didn't respect him. They feared him, and the fear would soon fade, and they would try and make their own play for what Jim had built.

Jackie found that her sadness was fading now, overshadowed by a brute of white-hot rage. Rage at how her Jim had been taken from her, and rage at those who had done it.

The service passed by in a blur, her thoughts distracted from sentiment, and instead focussing on practicalities. What she needed to do first, to keep what Jim and Jackie had built between them. She was conscious to perform in the right way – remembering to laugh in the right places during the eulogy delivered by a red-faced social club drunk that Jim had barely tolerated. Making sure to attend to her grandchildren, left and right, to reassure them, and, in turn, be reassured by the affection that they gave her.

They were good kids, and they loved their Grandad Jim, but, even with that, Jackie knew that being sweet Nannie Jacks in plain sight would reinforce the impression of underestimation that she would come to rely on in the days ahead.

The curtains opened, the conveyor rumbled, and then the curtains closed again, as the coffin slid from view. The inevitable Sinatra song played out from the speakers positioned in all four corners of the room – Jim was nothing if not predictable, at least outwardly, and even in death, Jackie saw no reason to let those who didn't know the full extent of the man in on any secrets. Let them think of him as the bumbling, jovial, larger-than-life taxi boss, and not the single-minded, ruthless leader of men that he really was. Maybe they all knew the real Jim Stark? Let them all join in on this charade, then. Let's see which one of these fuckers dared break rank, she thought.

The body gone, and the service over, and Jackie, the rest of the mourning party behind her, had drifted back outside. There would be a wake to get to, once the small talk here had been dispensed with, after enough of the attendees had made sure to pay their tribute to her, but first, Jackie needed a cigarette.

She moved away from everyone, walking off from the gravel path, between the gravestones that dotted the grass in front of the crematorium building. Most of the graves were from decades ago, when burial was the preferred option for those that could afford it. Dutiful wife. Loyal husband. Carved sentiment on metre-high stone confessionals. She didn't believe a word of it. What she had with Jim was special. Trust. No secrets. The name Stark meant more than all these stone-cut names added together. Let a hard wind come and scour this whole city, and let only one memorial stone stand, with only one name. She took a long drag on the cigarette.

Footprints crunched across the gravel behind her, and then quietened as the walker stepped off the path and onto the grass. Jackie turned to see who was coming.

The man was, like most people here, dressed in black, in suit and polished shoes. But Jackie had a good eye for details, and saw the suit had the fit that only a well-tailored suit could give. He wore a gold ring on the index finger of his right hand, ostentatious in size, but otherwise, the only concession to display that he gave. If Jackie had attempted to describe him to someone else, she would have struggled beyond the obvious – he was maybe mid-sixties in age, of average height, and average build, and clean-shaven. His hair was dark, with his temples greying slightly. He could've been anyone, but if it wasn't for the suit, Jackie would've instinctively thought it was one of Jim's employees – an accountant maybe? - come to pay respects.

"Mrs Stark?" said the man, in a honeyed voice.

"Yes?" Jackie said, in return. She took another drag on the cigarette, refusing to interrupt this small pleasure for some stranger.

"My name is Solomon. I was an associate of your late husband."

"Oh, I see. It's kind of you to come, Mr Solomon." Jackie offered this as a dismissal. The man had paid his respects, and could leave now with her blessing, duty fulfilled.

"I need to speak to you in private at your earliest convenience, if I may. It's regarding some arrangements left by your husband in the event of such a tragedy," Solomon said, his mellifluous voice at odds with what Jackie might've expected from one of the attendees here to pay respects to her.

"Arrangements? A will? Oh, I think that's in order, Mr Solomon. My husband was very thorough regarding that sort of thing." Jackie remained polite, but was hardening her tone thanks to her wariness regarding any kind of grift. She was who she was, after all – no mug.

This Solomon moved closer, in order to be more discreet. There was no-one close enough to possibly hear them speaking, but the gesture was important for his audience of one.

"Of sorts, Mrs Stark. Your husband was aware that there were consequences that could potentially affect those he cared for in the event of any...occupational hazard associated with the business he undertook." The words came out smoothed, as if from a fine lathe. "I understand that a more conventional will was prepared, but I am instructed to inform you that...other arrangements were also made by your husband."

"Other arrangements?" Jackie said, still carefully manoeuvring her way through this conversation. She looked over Solomon's shoulder, and saw her family clustered in front of the double-doors of the crematorium, waiting for Jackie to return to them so they could all leave together.

"Your husband was a very careful man, Mrs Stark. He knew that if anything were to happen to him then that could compromise your lifestyle, at best, and your safety, at worst. He ensured that steps were taken." Solomon had clasped his hands together as he spoke, shoulders rolled forward, affording all due deference.

"What kind of steps?" Jackie said, the cigarette forgotten about now, burning down to ash in her fingers.

"I will need to talk you through it in more detail, Mrs Stark. But, in essence, a great deal of money, and my services on retainer, in order to ensure that your position, and your business, are unthreatened during this time of flux."

Jackie stared at the man, looking him up and down. This was unexpected. She might've known Jim would've kept some things from her, but all this? A mystery man delivering riddles, at the graveside? It seemed implausible. But, as Jim had always said, let it play out. Let them show their hand. And so, Jackie decided to see what this man had to say for himself.

"What kind of services?" Jackie said.

"Mrs Stark, my job is to arrange things. And one of the things I can arrange is the employ of others, with different capabilities. Do you understand what I mean? Others who can fulfil all manner of requirements for businesses such as yours," Solomon said, the implicit meaning clear.

Jackie dropped the now-expired cigarette, and instinctively ground it under her sole. She reached inside her handbag for another, and looked away from Solomon as she lit it, taking in the sight of the graves and the trees all the way to the gates at the entrance to the crematorium grounds. Another man was stood by the gates. A thin, grubby man, with a rodent face, and a cap pulled tightly down over his eyes. He looked familiar to her. Looking at him gave her a feeling of repulsion, which brought with it a feeling of recognition, the two impressions inextricably linked – she had seen this man before somewhere. Sometime. But when? And then she remembered. This was someone that had come to meet Jim, a day or so before he was killed.

"Mr Solomon?" she asked

"Yes, Mrs Stark?" Solomon replied.

"There's a man by the gate over there. I need to speak to him. Is that something you can help me with?"

"I understand, Mrs Stark," said Solomon, who turned ninety degrees and snapped his fingers. From behind one of the trees, another man, much bigger than Solomon in both height and stature, stepped out. Solomon pointed at the man stood by the gates, and the larger man nodded, and strode off in the direction he was told.

# 3

Cold Cut wasn't sure why he had come. Jim Stark was a terror to him, a bogeyman that kept him awake at night, and crouched in every dark shadow, waiting to creep up behind him and turn his whole world black. Cold Cut walked a different city to most – that parallel place that had the same shape, and the same streets, as the one that those *normal* people inhabited. His city, though, was a city of subtle looks, of handshake deals, and of sharp ends. If you grew up in that world, you understood how survival was predicated on what you had to offer, and how long you keep your mouth shut. And stretching from the east and west of this world, was Jim Stark, and the organisation that he had built up to loom over the city.

Cold Cut had heard the name for as long as he could remember. Sure, Cold Cut was ambitious, but in a feral, desperate way. He could only see the next step up, to just lift himself from the pack that he so despised, jostling for the same street corner scraps. Cold Cut wanted to be more than those he mixed with, if only to just receive the respect that he felt he so deserved. Jim Stark wanted much, much more than that – he wanted everything – and Cold Cut feared a man who had the vision and ruthlessness to pull away so far from the street-level it was as if he was living on a different planet.

The Stark business found its way into everything. Cold Cut had worked for them – of course he had. It was harder to avoid Stark than not, and even if you could scratch out an earner that didn't owe some fealty to Stark, you ran the risk of drawing the worst kind of attention. The Mersey was getting shallower, they used to joke. Every time Cold Cut had found himself doing a favour for Stark, he did all he could to make sure it was done quickly, quietly and without drama, until he could step away from the glare of their assessment and get back to the grubbiest of lives.

He had made one mistake. A Stark job went south, whilst he was the lookout. The Stark reputation was not easily earned, and Cold Cut took no chances, and got out of town as soon as he could, a survivor's instinct driving him hundreds of miles away. He escaped into a purgatory, in a strange town, trapped with family who he despised, and despised him in return. Only through pure chance was able to barter a favour with Stark, and buy his passage back to his city, bittersweet when he discovered he wasn't missed in the first place.

The currency of his return was him finding Tony and Eleanor Grace. The couple who had crossed Jim Stark, and left the city to start a new life. Some ridiculous odds rolled in, and Cold Cut had stumbled across them down in the arse-end of nowhere, to a small village huddled on the drear coast of Norfolk, a chance circumstance he found almost impossible to comprehend. Cold Cut had sent word, and Stark had sent killers, and somehow the Graces had escaped all of them, heading back to Liverpool. Stark had backed them into a corner, and the Graces had pushed back, and a few days after they had returned, the Graces had left bodies on river-side cement, and Jim Stark with a bullet in his head.

Cold Cut was there that night. He didn't see Stark die, but he saw plenty of others cut down. Bang, bang, bang, the shots had rung out, Cold Cut watching as men he knew well enough to shrink from, were executed without a bullet wasted. It was a charnel house, and Cold Cut had seen it all, cowering in a car, as the Graces had sprung their trap.

They hadn't killed him, though. When the night had emptied out to quiet, they had walked past him, looking at him only long enough to judge him as not worth worrying about. His feral ambition was quieted for just that moment – despite his hard-scrabble life to be more than he was, in that moment, he was endlessly grateful that he had never managed to be anything more than pathetic. If he been something other than that, then he would have joined the butchered a few hundred yards from where he was sitting.

The Graces had walked into the night, evaporating like marsh-land phantoms, leaving a heavy silence behind them. The city had held its breath for a few moments, until the reality of it all had snapped back into place, bringing with it sirens and new threats for Cold Cut to dance around. He had left the scene at pace, scurrying back to his flat, where he spent the night unable to take his eyes off his front door, amidst the damp, the fag-ends and the old pizza boxes.

Stark had to be dead. Everyone had said it. The bodies of his men made it impossible to doubt that. That the Graces had left as they had, walking tall and not looking over their shoulders, was further proof. But, even so, Cold Cut still couldn't quite believe it. So that's why he had come. Come to see if the old man was really going to be made ashes, his transformation from God to mortal complete.

He watched from a position further down the road, as the funeral cortege had turned in, a pile of cigarette butts around his feet, as he chain-smoked one after the other, his yellowed fingers shaking. He didn't like being out like this, exposed, and he certainly didn't like being as close to anyone who had any real connection to Jim Stark. But he had to prove to himself that Stark was gone, for good, and he could start to think about his place in the eco-system he existed in.

He had moved to the gates to see the mourners filing in, Jackie Stark at the head of them, like some queen to be treated reverentially. He remembered meeting her, albeit briefly, when he was taken to Jim Stark's house. Even now, visiting Stark's house seemed almost more terrifying than the night when the gunshots rang out. He expected his spectres to haunt dark alleys and lonely tenements. That the most feared man in the city lived in a bland house on some homely cul-de-sac. Hiding in plain sight. He had been ushered in, Stark all smiles and good graces, past Jackie Stark and the two kids that Cold Cut could see were hovering around Jackie at the crematorium entrance. It was only once he had been taken to a conservatory at the back of the house, that Jim Stark had removed the mask, and revealed the real Stark, brutal, efficient and ultimate. That the fearsome could appear so mundane had left Cold Cut unsure of his footing ever since – what other things were hiding behind plain smiles and friendly eyes, wherever he looked?

He had one last cigarette to smoke, as he lurked by the gates. Rolled as tightly as a toothpick, stretching out hard-bought tobacco for as long as he could. He would just smoke this one last cigarette then go, comforted to know that at least one of his demons had been sent back to hell. The mourners had filed out, and, even from here, he could hear that the conversations had gotten louder, as if those in attendance had themselves also been reassured that Jim Stark was not coming back. Cold Cut found his thoughts drifting, the nicotine hit calming him, achieving critical mass of tar and chemicals with each rough breath. In and out, in and out, smoke circling his head, and him turning his attention to the more prosaic. What to eat later. Who to tap up for owed money. Who to beg for a furtive backdoor fuck. Stark had gone, and he didn't need to worry about that world and those that lived in it, a few hundred yards away.

He didn't even notice the man walking towards him. The man was a shape at the corner of his vision, a cataract in a black suit. Cold Cut hadn't recognised anyone from the funeral mourners, other than Jackie and those two kids, and had judged himself safe. It was only when the man had placed a heavy hand on his shoulder that Cold Cut realised that he hadn't managed to escape Stark, even after death.

# 4

"Do not try and run. Do not call out. My employer has asked me to take you to him, and I strongly advise that you do as you are told, with no fuss."

The man had spoken to Cold Cut in a plain voice, with just the merest trace of an old accent jostling for attention between each syllable. He was much bigger than Cold Cut, though that in itself was not unusual. Cold Cut's whole life had been spent around people much bigger than him, usually physically, but also in terms of status. Deference came easy, his viciousness hiding in the reeds, ready to for him to unleash it if he was ever confident enough that he had the upper hand, rare as it was. But not here.

The man's fingers gripped him firmly, as Cold Cut was led through the gates, and into the crematorium grounds, towards another smaller man, and there, next to him, Jackie Stark. Jackie Stark who was staring right at him. Jackie Stark who had remembered him.

Cold Cut felt sick. His thoughts were drowning him. That fierce and frequent sense of injustice – why him? – was shouting loud, angry that he had, yet again, managed to fall into a situation he would have much preferred to sidestep by a hundred miles or so. And in addition to self-recrimination, another voice joined his internal choir, a voice of lizard-brain survival, quickly trying to work out what was going on, and how best to get himself out of it, as it had so many times before.

Everything seemed louder. The crunch of footsteps on first, the gravel path, and then the remainder of autumn leaf-fall. The rush of traffic on the road behind him. The roar of the blood in his ears. Despite his naked ambition, Cold Cut was comfortable being a bottom-feeder. He accepted that those above him had rewards that he wanted, and a lifestyle to covet, but they also usually ended up in places like this sooner than they otherwise expected, burnt in wood boxes, one after the other. People higher than him – much higher than him – always wanted something, and it was never a good something. It was always a sharp conversation, with sharp consequences, and the squalid safety of his life taken from him. What did Jackie Stark want with him? What did she know?

“Nannie...?”

The little girl had detached herself from the main group clustered around the doors of the crematorium building, still going through the “see you in a bit” social niceties before they presumably decamped to some function room somewhere. Cold Cut, Jackie Stark and the two men all turned, and looked down at the little girl as she spoke. Cold Cut felt detached from himself, the surreal intervention of the child distracting him from the acute situation that he was in. What could he do? He wasn’t brave enough to try and make a break for it, and yet, not completely sure that being stood in plain sight would be a defence for him. After all, his previous dealings with anyone associated with the name "Stark" had shown him that standing in the open wasn't the defence it should have been.

Jackie Stark crouched down, so her face was at the same height as the girl's. A warm smile spread across Jackie's face, and the little girl's wariness eased, despite her uncertainty around these other grown-ups.

"Nannie, mummy wondered if you were ready to go?"

Jackie looked over the girl's shoulder into the group of people fifty yards or so away. A woman met Jackie's eyes, and waved to her, then pointed to her wrist, indicating that it was time to move on. Jackie waved back, and held her hand up, indicating that the woman was to go ahead.

"Look, my love. Nannie is just going to stay and have a talk with her friends here, and then she is going to come and follow you. You go and make sure your brother behaves himself for mummy, and Nannie will follow afterwards. Okay? Can you tell mummy that I'll come along in a moment?"

"Okay, Nannie. I'll tell mummy," the little girl said politely. She looked at Cold Cut, her face unsure and wary of him, before turning to the other men stood next to Jackie. The smaller man smiled warmly, eyes twinkling, which drew a smile from the little girl.

"Tell her Nannie's friends will make sure she gets there okay. Will you do that, Megan love?" Jackie spoke to her grandchild as if she was issuing important instructions that only the little girl could achieve. It worked.

"I will, Nannie. Bye." The little girl turned away from the group, and skipped away, back to her mum, pausing only to wave back to Jackie once she had made it halfway back to the main party.

The interruption over, all pretence could wash away, and Jackie stood up again, the thin veneer gone and replaced with a severity and certainty of purpose that nailed Cold Cut to the spot. Yet again, he had found himself under a microscope, and certain that he needed to tread exceedingly carefully to make it out of here, at best, without obligation, and at worst, on his own two feet. Actually, that wasn't the worst outcome, but he refused to let his mind dwell on that possibility. It was important that he concentrated, then he could make his way back to the peripheries, where he was most comfortable.

"I remember you," said Jackie, staring at him, barely able to prevent her nose from wrinkling. She stood in front of him, immaculately dressed in black, her outfit complimented by expensive jewellery and perfect make-up. He cowered nervously, dressed as usual in grubby tracksuit and worn trainers, nicks, tears and stains on his clothes from top to toe. She didn't take her eyes off him, her intense glare scaring his eyes away from hers.

"Do you remember me? I'm sure you do," Jackie continued, demanding an answer.

"I..I.." Cold Cut stammered, any pretence at deception or ignorance curling up and dying like a feeble green shoot under a desert sun. He gulped. "Yes, I remember, Mrs Stark."

"You came to our house. You were brought there, to talk to Jim," Jackie said to him, in a firm voice. The two men were also staring at him, the larger man a half-step behind Cold Cut, an open door that would slam shut if he made even the slightest intimation that he was going to run for it.

"I'd like to have a little chat to you about that. You don't have anywhere to be, do you?" Jackie demanded a positive answer. A negative would do nothing but risk her irritation, and Cold Cut wasn't stupid. He knew well enough that he should play along, and show respect.

"No, no, of course not. No problem, Mrs Stark."

Jackie Stark turned to the smaller man, who was still looking at Cold Cut, before flashing a quick look at the larger man - stay on your toes, it said – and then to Solomon, his face unthreatening and inscrutable.

"Mr Solomon, I wonder if I could trouble you to help me find a quiet room to talk to this...friend of ours for five minutes or so?"

Mr Solomon pursed his lips and nodded, then turned on his heels, and walked steadily back to the crematorium building, past the one or two stragglers who had not yet left, still engaging in small-talk on the steps, incongruous laughter occasionally breaking out in this sombre place. Solomon opened the double doors, and disappeared from view for about a minute, before the double doors opened again, and he beckoned for them to follow. Jackie Stark immediately strode off, keen to get inside, and to get to the nub of the matter. Cold Cut felt the heavy hand squeeze almost imperceptibly on his shoulder, an indication that he should follow her, and that any deviation from that might result in a far more *perceptible* application of pressure.

Cold Cut moved towards the building, like a man marched to the gallows.

# 5

Jackie entered the building, and looked for Solomon. He had moved further into the building, and was holding open another set of double doors, that led away from the reception area, into a part of the building that was set aside for "staff".

As Jackie moved through the double doors, she noticed that Solomon's associate and Cold Cut had also made it inside, with the smaller man being led towards the open doors.

"There's a meeting room just along the hall, Mrs Stark," said Solomon, indicating for her to continue down the corridor for a few yards with his hand.

"Whoa! I'm sorry, there. You can't come down here," came a voice from further down the corridor. One of the staff, in a smart, but off-the-peg suit, had noticed the group, and was walking towards them, hands up as if warding them. "Just back through there, to reception, please."

Mr Solomon walked towards him. Jackie didn't hear the conversation, but it was quiet and one-way, with Mr Solomon moving towards the man, close enough so that only the two of them were party to what was said. Jackie couldn't help but stare at the two of them, maybe fifteen paces down that corridor, the man from the crematorium facing her, leaning down towards Mr Solomon to ensure he caught every word said. Jackie couldn't parse what was said by Solomon, but she saw the man's face change expression – first, defensive, then it paled, before finally, it settled on a look of affrighted acceptance. This man Solomon was impressing her. She didn't know how Jim had found him, or exactly what was the extent of his obligation to her, but he was a man capable of opening doors – literally, and figuratively – and she was more than happy to continue to let him lead the way forward, with the promise of answers to come.

Mr Solomon turned back to the three who were hovering around the entrance to the corridor, with a broad, magnanimous smile on his face.

"My friend here was mistaken. He has allowed us to take one of the consultation rooms for a short spell, in order for us to have some privacy for our conversation."

The employee had regressed into some sort of schoolboyish demeanour, shuffling from foot to foot, and looking at his shoes. He mumbled something to Solomon.

"No, no," said Solomon, "we have no need to refreshments, but it is very generous of you to offer. Just some peace and quiet will be all, thank you."

The employee took this as his cue to retreat, and walked away from the group in the opposite direction, to busy himself in some other part of the crematorium, away from these people – this person – who had clearly said something that caused him real fear. Mr Solomon beckoned for the group to approach, his associate and Cold Cut first, and Jackie behind them. He opened a side door and then held it open for the three to pass, into an austere little room, with cheaply cushioned faux-leather chairs around a rectangular formica table, two on each side.

Solomon's man pulled a chair out, and steered Cold Cut to sit. Once Cold Cut had taken his place, the man pulled the chair out next to Cold Cut, and moved it back, so he could sit just over Cold Cut's shoulder, between him and the door. Solomon pulled out one of the chairs on the other side of the table, and indicated for Jackie to take a seat.

She sat down, glaring at Cold Cut, who refused to meet her eyes, darting his gaze this way and that. Anything but look directly at anyone, a trapped animal. Solomon sat down next to Jackie, and rested his hands on the table.

"Mrs Stark," he said, in his honeyed voice, "we have as much time as you require. Please do feel free to ask any question you like, and we will ensure that this gentleman is honest with you."

The threat was implicit, and fell heavy, as if Solomon had dropped a butcher's knife on the table. Cold Cut wasn't distracted enough to miss it. Quite the opposite.

Jackie sighed, then reached into her handbag and rooted around for a cigarette. Once she had found one, she put it to her lips, and flicked her lighter open, igniting the end. A deep drag, an exhale of smoke, and then a tap of a finger, dislodging the fresh ash from the cigarette end onto the cheap carpet beneath their feet. Only then did she speak to Cold Cut.

"I recognised you. From that night. You came to our house with the man who did all of Jim's..." she paused for a moment, searching for a euphemism, "...heavy lifting. So I knew it was important."

Cold Cut nodded. He remembered. How could he not? A summons from Jim Stark himself, to his house no less, was not something he would ever forget. Jackie continued.

"I want you to tell me everything that was said. Because I know that what you talked about that night helped put my husband into that fire back there. And I'm not happy about that." She took another drag. "Not happy at all."

Jackie was struggling to control her emotions. She felt like she was being assaulted from all sides, with grief looming over her like a backalley mugger, but also anger, shame and no little fear. She had been in Jim's world for long enough to know that weakness was the ultimate sin, and even if she felt it, even if only slightly, like a child pulling at the hem of a skirt, it had to be ignored, or she would be dismissed, waved away, or worse, torn apart by the relentless ambition of those orbiting. She poured all her concentration onto the little rodent man facing her, and found that this was all she needed to keep the low flame of indignation burning blue.

Cold Cut was scared of Jackie Stark just because of the power of her last name. That name had weight, and clearly had been cashed in to bring the two men into this equation as well. He'd swum long enough in these waters to know exactly what kind of people he was stuck in this room with. Jackie had the money and the power, the little man was the contractor, and the big ape behind Cold Cut was the no-nonsense, didn't-need-telling-twice muscle, who would snap every one of Cold Cut's fingers as nonchalantly as if he was pulling takeout chicken off the bone. He wasn't planning on letting one falsehood fall from his lips. After all, it wasn't his fault that Jim Stark was dead, was it? Was it?

Jackie leant across the table, with Cold Cut unable to fight the urge to shrink back into his chair. As soon as he recoiled, he felt that heavy hand back on his shoulder again, straightening him in his chair, demanding he give the lady opposite his full attention.

"Tell me what you talked about. Tell me about the people who killed Jim. Everything," Jackie said.

Cold Cut started to speak, but found nothing in his mouth but dust. Jackie segued into good cop.

"Do you want a smoke, lad?" she asked, pushing the cigarette packet across the table to him, the lighter pushed inside, snug against the remaining cigarettes.

"Thanks, thanks..." Cold Cut managed to stammer out, before reaching for the packet, and pulling a cigarette out, carefully, as if it was porcelain. The lighter found flame after a couple of attempts, and he lit it, focussing on the flame rather than anything else. Precious seconds before reality found gear again.

He puffed the smoke out. Then he started talking.

# 6

Tony Grace drove. It gave Eleanor the opportunity to strip out of her fatigues, and clean her face of camouflage paint with the wet-wipes that she had pulled from her hold-all. Everything about that night was planned and discussed to the smallest possible detail, and getting away clean was as important as any other facet of the plan. Neither of them could know exactly what was going to happen before they left for their confrontation with Jim Stark and his crew, but their survival depended on them planning for both the best, and the worst outcomes.

They were both alive. They were both unhurt. And Jim Stark was dead. But that was as far as the good news went. Everything else was turmoil, yet again. They thought they had found their peace in Norfolk, and a life that bordered on soporific, where violence and drama seemed otherworldly and foreign. Yet it had crashed back into their lives again, making mockery of their comfort. Their "forever" home had become a battleground, and even now, having killed the men responsible for making it so, it still felt like their future had been obliterated, leaving them with dust.

Neither of them spoke as they made their way from the city. They had found the plainest car that they could, swapped the numberplates, and parked it as close to the rendezvous with Stark – their Thermopylae – as they dared.

Even after the chaos of the violence had subsided, it still cast a long shadow over them. Had they considered every angle? Could they make it back to the car without arrest, or worse, a second wave of assailants appearing from behind the next street corner? The desire to break into a run was fierce, and difficult to resist. They both found themselves breathing slowly, and counting each pace until they were in the relative safety of the car.

Even driving out of the city felt terminal. The second-nature act of driving felt unwieldy and dangerous, as if there were new obstacles that were being thrown in front of them to leave them exposed. Traffic lights that took too long to change to green, or parked cars that looked ready to suddenly veer out, crashing into them. Despite what had happened to their boss, the CityArrow cabs were still out and earning, the news either not filtering down to the drivers, or any whispers waved away. But to Tony and Eleanor, it was as if the city had been jolted awake, and every cab was a pair of eyes searching for them.

The concrete grip of the city squeezed tightly around them. Tony drove slowly and cautiously at first, until he realised that *too* slow and *too* cautious was as conspicuous as pedal-flat careering. He squeezed the accelerator, pushing the car to the speed limit, but no more. Doing his best to drive as close to illegality as the other cars on the road, especially at this time of night. Half-an-hour passed with the speed of an ice age, but, eventually, the looming buildings gave way to broader vistas and wider roads. They had left the city.

The hypnotic rumble of steady speed gave them some comfort. Enough that they felt able to talk to each other. Eleanor had cleaned her face, and had unzipped her all-in-one fatigues to her waist, revealing the plain t-shirt underneath. She had let her hair down from the tight ponytail, hoping that small details changed would radically alter her appearance, just in case. For now, there was nothing else to do but drive, and talk. She reached over to Tony, and gently squeezed his knee, pulling him back from whatever crucible he was burning himself on.

"We're going to be alright," she said, the tenderness of her touch matched by the tone of her voice.

Tony sighed. It was a release he needed.

"Are we, though?" he said, finally. "What are we going to do? Where are we going to go?"

Eleanor gave his leg another squeeze, and then moved her hand to push back some hair from her eyes, a nervous habit when she was thinking carefully about what to do or say.

"The plan is sound. The worst thing we can do is second guess it. We're not at that stage yet. Let's drive north, like we said, ditch the car, then get a train."

Tony knew to challenge the plan was foolish, but now the conversation had started, his worst impulses took over.

"Is a train really a good idea? We're going to be trapped on it," he said.

"I know, but it's a risk worth taking. They will only be thinking about the roads, and a short train trip will let us reset, and get back to the roads from a different starting point. That's if they have even got themselves together to look for us."

"Someone might," Tony said, quietly. Embarrassed to persist, but unable to help himself.

"Someone might. But we can't do any more than we are doing. We could split up, but I don't want to do that. We could go to ground close to Liverpool, but being close to the city just doesn't seem sensible to me. Not now."

Eleanor took a sip of water from a bottle she had brought with her, then passed it across to Tony for him to do the same. He knocked back a swig, and passed the bottle back, so Eleanor could screw the top back on, and put the bottle in the map pocket of the door. Eleanor spoke again. She knew what Tony was like, and how he needed conversations like this at times of stress to maintain his conviction.

"We'll find a hotel near a town, get some rest, and walk into town in the morning to catch a train. Local trains. Bounce to a bigger station somewhere east, and then start to go south. I think they would expect us to go back east, or back south first, so this is the least risky direction. Just wrong-foot them in case they are out on the roads looking for us."

"Yes, makes sense," Tony said, saying it out loud to make the decision solid. He was aware of his worst impulses at times like this, but couldn't help himself. It was why he loved his wife so much. They meshed. She supported him, understood him, and led him to the light. In turn, even soft challenges like this helped her continue to challenge her conclusions. Between them, a plan would be finessed.

"How much money of we got left? Cash, I mean?" Eleanor said.

"A grand or so, maybe a bit more," Tony replied.

"How many days do you think that will give us?"

"I think we can stretch it, with everything we've got, for ten days, maybe a fortnight. If we're careful."

"So, let's work our way through that lot, keep our heads

down, and see how long we can make it last," Eleanor said. "The longer we can wait, the better."

"And then what?" Tony said. "Where are we going to go after that? We can't go home."

Home was back east. The life they had built from the rubble they had been left with the first time they escaped Liverpool. Their safe, quiet life that became a comfortable reward for all the drama they had experienced. But somehow that drama had followed them there, left dead bodies and burnt buildings in its wake, and presumably, questions to answer. They weren't ready to risk going back there, and face a war on multiple fronts.

"We go to the family," Eleanor said.

# 7

Cold Cut recounted the conversation that was had in the conservatory of Jim Stark's home. He could remember everything that was said, between the three men who were there – him, Stark, and his enforcer, the Red Pope, sat around on wicker chairs and glass topped tables, the suburban mundanity at odds with the hard words of murder spoken there. Jackie said nothing, and just looked at him, intently and fiercely. Her emotion was too hot to be hidden, but at least it was something plain enough to understand. Cold Cut preferred it to the implacability of the man sat next to her, this Mr Solomon, who listened to everything said without a twitch or flicker of expression. Cold Cut felt tiny beneath his unchanging scrutiny – a microbe under a microscope, and, presumably, worthy of as much affection.

Any pretence evaporated from Cold Cut in that room. There was no point in trying to negotiate, or to overstate his role in any of the events that he was tasked with recalling. One thing Cold Cut knew how to do was survive, a hard-wired impulse that had seen him well, or as well as things ever got for him, over the years, bumping along the edges of the life he had made for himself.

He told them everything, as best he could. A patchwork quilt of direct recollection and what he had gleaned from the conversations overheard over the months that Tony Grace had been involved with the Stark organisation. How Grace had started small, working doors for Stark meetings, impressing with his quiet professionalism, slowly but surely becoming noticed. Cold Cut did his best to piece together the ill-fated poker night at the same building that Stark had lost his life, when an inside job went sour, and one of Grace's friends was left bleeding, whilst another had found himself betrayed by those he had fallen in with to rob the place. It could all be traced back to that incident, with Grace then put first under a spotlight glare, and then challenged to prove his loyalty when the betrayer had been caught. Jim Stark told Jackie everything and anything about the business that put a roof over their head, and added zeroes to their bank balance, and she had heard this story before, but even so, she listened intently as Cold Cut told it again.

"It's just what I heard, Mrs Stark," said Cold Cut, in the same quiet, docile tone that he had adopted throughout this interview. "Mr Stark told Grace that he needed to prove that he had clean hands about the robbery, and when they had found the...the..." Cold Cut paused. Even saying it out loud in this room, to these people, seemed too much like betraying a confidence. As if saying it would conjure the spectre of Jim Stark out of thin air, to monster and haunt him.

"Speak plainly," said Mr Solomon. He leant forward slightly, steepling his fingers, and peering over the top of them.

Cold Cut gulped, his Adam's apple bobbing like a float on a river.

"When they found the inside man, Mr Stark wanted Grace to be the one to deal with him." Cold Cut spoke with a steady voice now, whistling in the dark to keep the wolves away. "But Grace wouldn't do it. So Mr Stark had to. And the Graces ran to get away. Mr Stark didn't like that."

He told how Stark had ordered a net to be dropped over the city, once he had realised that the Graces weren't going to fall into line. How they had escaped, and tried to carve out a new life on the Norfolk coast, putting the city miles behind them, satisfied to disappear into a warm anonymity. Cold Cut told how he had been the one who had found them, completely by chance, doing his best to be nimble regarding his own reasons for being out of the city – he had failed Stark himself, and ran, not discovering the perverse irony that he wasn't missed when he went. A disconnect between his own self-importance and his desperate failure to register as important to anyone of note.

Once he had found the Graces, Cold Cut had coveted that information like treasure, hoping to buy himself back into the embrace of the life he had expelled himself from, summoning the Stark crew like the Wild Hunt itself. They had left chaos behind them, as they roared through the sleepy coastal village, looking for the Graces. A pub was torched, a man was killed, all to scare their quarry from the long grass. But, again, the Graces had slipped away, returning to Liverpool seeking their own revenge, with Stark and his men, Cold Cut included, scrabbling to follow their trail.

Jackie Stark didn't speak as Cold Cut talked. She felt a simmering resentment bubbling up simply by being in the presence of the verminous creature snivelling and sweating opposite her. She welcomed it. It gave her something to focus on, rather than the indistinct crush of indignation she had flailed against since the police had turned up to gleefully ruin her life. Every word Cold Cut said was weighed and examined, tested and explored, as Jackie looked for any new clue or any new direction that she could follow that might help her find those responsible for killing her husband, one unsteady step at a time. By contrast, Mr Solomon, sat to her right, was implacable. How often had he sat in a room like this, with a person like this, distilling truth from the soup of words offered?

Cold Cut's tale had arrived at the night Jim Stark was killed. Thrashing around in her inchoate rage, Jackie had even found room for it to accommodate Jim. He had made a mistake. A hubristic mistake. He had believed in his own immortality, as the King of Liverpool, untouchable by anyone, walking in plain sight for so long he believed that no-one could lay a finger on him. Pushed along by his indignation, he had driven to that riverside property, so confident that his men would rid him of Tony and Eleanor Grace, once and for all, as they had done to so many others who had dared transgress in the past. But it was a trap, ruthless and cold, and that same hubris had done for them all. Tony Grace was a soldier, a good one at that. Stark's men had discovered this when they had made their investigations into him as Tony Grace started to be noticed. Or so they thought. Jim Stark was dead, shot dead by a bullet forged by his own assumptions. It was Eleanor who was the soldier, and it was her who had shot every one of the men who had turned up to that building that night, her husband as bait, and her behind a long-sight and a rifle.

"I saw it all," Cold Cut said, finally. He had decided that his best approximation of honesty was the best policy, as he was honest enough to realise that spinning lies was a recipe for disaster. At least if he told the truth, then he might stand a chance of being consistent, maybe even of value. "Mr Stark got it wrong."

He regretted using that word instantly. A tiny narrowing of the eyes from Solomon sat across from him. An almost imperceptible shift from the man in the chair behind him. And Jackie Stark, sat opposite him, pursing her lips.

"Wrong?" said Jackie, unable to smother the indignation that she felt with her husband – her dead husband – being criticised by this creature, of all things.

"Misled. I meant misled, " Cold Cut spluttered, paddling back to a safe shore. "Mr Stark had arranged for Grace to be investigated, and the men who did the work reported that it was Tony Grace who was the soldier. They didn't look closely enough. I think they just jumped to a conclusion."

"It was the woman?" said Mr Solomon, the slightest change in his voice suggesting that even he was surprised at this revelation. "She was the soldier?"

"Yes, sir," said Cold Cut. "Grace was the bait, and his wife did the work. They didn't even think about her before they went after Grace. Then she killed them all. All of them. Mr Stark was last."

Jackie pushed her chair back as she stood up, the metal legs scraping on the hard, cheap carpet. She clipped open her handbag, rummaged inside for her cigarettes and a lighter, and made to walk out of the room. The three men all looked at her as she walked. She opened the door, and just before she stepped through it, she turned back and spoke to Cold Cut.

"You know what they look like. I'm going to want to keep in touch with you. Do you understand?"

# 8

The rest of the day was a battle for Jackie. Chance had delivered this pathetic man to her, and he had dropped breadcrumbs that might lead her to her revenge, whereas before it was nothing but dead ends and angry confusion. Her desire to move forward with her revenge was an imperative, but she had other obligations. The soft duties of family, small-talking her way through all kinds of platitudes from those who had known an aspect of Jim, though none of them could piece together every facet to see the full picture of the man. Not like she could. The poker table buddies, the loyal underlings at the cab company he owned, the extended family who couldn't square the brutality of his end with the cosy memories they had of him. Then there were those who knew more of the criminal Jim Stark, lining up dutifully to pay their respects to Jackie, smart enough to keep their options open until they had a better idea of what would happen to Stark firm now he was dead. And through all of this, Jackie had to temper her responses for the audience. Tenderness with family and friends, and then steeliness and confidence for those who knew the ruthless side of Jim Stark. "Never show weakness," Jim had told her, and she clung to that advice as the long minutes crawled by for the rest of the day.

But at least she had direction now. This was a small torture, and one she could bear, satisfied that at least she now knew something that might just expose those responsible for the killing of her husband from the shadows they had melted away into. It might be hopeless, but until then, she had forward motion, and that was a comfort.

Solomon and his associate had followed her to the wake, held in a function room in one of the many old estate pubs that Jim Stark had an interest in. Jackie had refused to have the wake at home, using some excuse or other, when really it was just because she wanted to be able to leave and find her solitude in the event that the day became too unbearable for her, for whatever reason. She had looked through the frosted glass from the first floor window, and saw the black car that Solomon had followed the funeral party with parked up at the side of the road opposite the pub. She felt reassured. At was as if Jim was still looking out for her, despite...despite everything.

As the wake petered out, with the vast majority of family and well-meaning well-wishers making their excuses, Jackie had used the excuse of a cigarette break to make her way outside, and then across the road to Solomon's car. The window wound down from the passenger side, revealing Mr Solomon.

"I hope you don't mind our presence, Mrs Stark, but it's important that we maintain a presence. I'm sure you can understand," he said.

"No, no, that's fine. Do you think there's something to worry about?" Jackie said.

"We can't be imprudent, Mrs Stark. From my experience,

you should never be surprised at the reactions of certain elements of our business," Solomon said, enjoying the wordplay of his euphemism. "It's prudent to be careful."

"I understand. I had expected there to be some move on me," Jackie said. "There have been a few of them today, all condolences and patting my hand today, but I know they were just sizing me up. Seeing whether I was someone they needed to respect."

"As I would expect," said Solomon. "These are the bottom-feeders, just seeing whether their golden goose is still laying. I don't think we need to worry too much about those people. No, the ones you will need to, ahem, impress, are the more ruthless types. Those with ambition, either in your husband's direct employ, or those who simply want what he built. This is something I can assist with."

"Help how?" said Jackie. She drew on a cigarette nervously, immediately angry at herself for revealing her underlying worries.

"We will guide you through the process, Mrs Stark. Please. You have nothing to worry about. In my experience, a simple firmness is all that is required in these situations. A rolled-up newspaper on the dog's nose, as it were."

Mr Solomon extended his gloved hand from inside the car, offering Jackie a business card. She took the card, and examined it. It was black, with white embossed type, with only a phone number printed on it.

"This card is how you can get in touch with me, day or night. Keep it safe. We will always be close, but if you need to speak to me, this is the quickest way."

Jackie slipped the card into her handbag, and clicked the clasp closed. She flicked her cigarette into the gutter, and looked over her shoulder back up at the first floor of the pub, though she could see no more than the frosted windows, the room dark inside.

"I need to get back in. I can't stand out here all day," she said.

"I understand. Please go back inside, and we will be in touch in due course to discuss next steps. Rest assured the gentleman we spoke to this afternoon has been given strict instructions to make himself available should we need him. We look forward to a smooth transition through this process with you, Mrs Stark."

Solomon whirred the electric window closed, and the car was started, lights flashing on in the late afternoon twilight. She waited for the car to move away, tyres crunching loose tarmac as it moved forwards, then indicating to turn, before disappearing down one of the many side-roads that made a maze of this estate. Jackie watched the car until it had turned from view, and then walked as proudly as she could manage across the road and back into the pub, up the stairs that led to the function room on the first floor.

Most of the attendees had gone. Her grandchildren were still here, no longer able to approximate solemnity and instead giggling as they flicked ice-cubes at each other from their fizzy drinks. Jackie's daughter had given up trying to discipline them, especially as most of the audience for their fun and games had long since left the pub. Best to let them blow off steam now, as giggles were easier to manage than tears. Jackie saw that there were a few other tables still full – the hold-outs nursing pints, making up excuses not to go home, be it for the buffet they could still take advantage of, or the need to gain kudos for being amongst the last to leave. Any pretence at remembrance had long evaporated though, and instead the talk was either about some TV series boxset or the new stadium for the football club. They would've been crushed if they knew how little they registered for Jackie. Other than her family, she simply didn't care about any of these people still here. She knew their names, but this was something of a parlour trick to flatter or persuade, wielding small talk like a hypnotist's watch. Today, though, she had no energy for the pretence. *Fill your bellies, you grubbers, but don't think anything has changed. The Stark name still means something in this city.*

"Are you alright, mum?" Carol said as Jackie sat down in the booth next to her.

"Long day, love" Jackie replied, reaching for the half-drunk glass of red wine that had stood on the table for some time now. "Looking forward to a long bath."

"Ah, that sounds nice," Carol said. She let the words rest now, understanding that the silence didn't need filling, instead reaching across to squeeze Jackie's hand, which drew a smile from her mum.

The sounds of the pub became nothing more than ambience to Jackie as she let her mind drift, examining her internal tasklist point by point, weighing up each obligation as if it was an artefact to be appraised. She was the head of the family now, and had to manage this hard transition, now that her beloved Jim had left them. But she was also the head of a business, Jim's cab firm that dominated all the streets and alleys and pick-up points, and then beneath that façade, the true face of the organisation that ran the crime in this city. Potentially fatal cracks now spiderwebbed across its foundations, with not only Jim dead, but also the inner circle of his most loyal lieutenants all sacrificed at the altar of his revenge. She didn't even know who the next most senior employee in the business was, and whether the wheels were still turning, though she had seen CityArrow cars on the roads despite everything. The money must still be going somewhere. She needed to make sure it was to her.

And then, the diamond-hard pearl at the centre of this mess, was her fierce desire to see those who had taken Jim from her punished, and in the most brutal of fashions. Maybe a very public execution was the cachet she needed to remind the whole world that the Stark name would still mean something. That didn't matter as much as her desire for revenge, pure and simple.

It could've been minutes, or it could've been hours, but eventually, as her little Megan snuggled into her, exhausted from the day, she allowed herself to drift back to the here and now, and giving Megan a little squeeze, mouthed to Carol that "I think we should be making a move", happy that her grandchild had given her impetus to go home, and try and forget about all the machinations whirring around her head if only for an evening. Carol gently woke Megan, nudged Toby to attention from his handheld console, and led them both to the exit.

Jackie shooed them ahead, and picked up the children's coats, taking advantage of the opportunity to leave without having to say meaningful goodbyes to everyone remaining, individually. Instead, she turned to face the room, from the doorway, and spoke –

"Thanks for coming. I really appreciate it. Jim would've been grateful as well." She made to leave, paused, and then turned back, one last time.

"And make sure you tell everyone something. Nothing has changed. The Starks are still in business."

# 9

Eleanor was army. She may have left the service years ago, but she would be army until she died. Her unit were a family that would be there for her until that day, and her for them. Like any family they bickered and squabbled, with some closer to some than others, but any one of them would take a bullet for her if she needed them. Years had passed since she saw some of them, but their bond was one forged under fire, on that total reliance that the person next to you would go through hell to make sure you made it back alive. That didn't get waved away when you left.

Tony was with her then. He had never felt threatened by her, or by the relationship she had with her unit. He never had the ambition or desire to be "alpha", whatever that was, and loved this woman so deeply that supporting her was all the goal he needed in life.

He knew she was impressive, but then she'd find new ways to surprise him. He had had concerns that she would find it hard to find her place in the traditionally male world of the forces, but he needn't have worried. Eleanor was will and drive personified. The barriers that were placed for her were treated as if they were balsa-thin and smashed with ease, and in a short while, she was just "Grace" and any hand-wringing about capability or gender or toughness were forgotten the first time she beat the shit out of one of the training group.

Nothing builds bonds like the total reliance on another human being to best ensure that you could survive when the bullets were flying. It becomes the sort of environment where ink is applied to skin to brand that loyalty forever. Eleanor was no different – on her shoulder-blade, she had had the unit insignia tattooed, just like everyone else she served with. And even though she might not have spoken to, let alone seen, most of her unit for many long years, that ink symbolised a bond that would not – could not – be broken.

Tony and Eleanor had moved away from the motorway to a truck-stop that overlooked the main road, the cars fizzing along beneath them, north to the Lakes and Scotland, or south back along the way they had come. The headlights illuminated the asphalt, the motorway bright as if it was haunted by will-o-the-wisp dances, and the looming hills that surrounded an ominous black by comparison.

The Graces sat on the car bonnet, tearing open the prepackaged sandwiches and gritty coffee they had bought from the shop. The gloom of the countryside was a comfort. It made them feel like they too could escape into the dark, and find that anonymity that they craved, which had been snatched from them hundreds of miles away, back in Norfolk. This was a chance to take a breath, and forget about the sharp end they were living under, if only for a few quick mouthfuls of food.

As usual, Tony treated food like a means to an end, devouring his sandwich in a few bites, before reaching behind him for the coffee, taking sips despite it still being blisteringly hot. He held the coffee in one hand, and let his mind wander. A few minutes passed, then he snapped back to the here and now, and slipped his other arm around Eleanor, pulling her close. Eleanor smiled, and carried on with her food, both of them feeling strength from the other's affection.

"What do you think we do when we run out of money? Where do we go, love? Any idea?" Tony said, taking advantage of having finished his food to start the conversation again.

"Yeah, I've been thinking about that," Eleanor said, in-between mouthfuls. "I'm not completely sure where some of the lads are, and I might be being paranoid, but I'm not sure it's a good idea to start sending out messages on the internet to people. We need to vanish for as long as we can first."

"You think we might be traced? Really?"

"I don't know. I think we need to be as careful as we possibly can be, at least until we can see how the land lies." Eleanor took a sip of her coffee, before setting it down, it still too hot for her.

"I guess. I suppose it's easy to think of that lot back in Liverpool as just a mob, but we don't know what their set-up is below the leadership. We might well have cut their head off, but you don't get that big without having resources."

"Exactly," Eleanor said. "It's pretty plausible that there are some capable sorts ready to take over, or they've got money to go and get some. Whether or not they have enough to come after us I don't know, but we need to go to ground and wait."

"Yes. Heads down for a bit. We can have a look at what happens to them in time. Plus I think we could both do with seeing a pleasant face or two."

"Do we know any?" Eleanor laughed. "Friendly, maybe. Pleasant, not so much."

They both laughed at this, both flicking through a mental ID parade of faces of Eleanor's unit, the thought of them generating a barrage of memories that couldn't help but amuse.

"I'm thinking Steaky," Tony said. "Just logically seems the right call. As far as logic can ever apply to him, that is."

Like any group, there was always one. Steaky was their one. If there was ever someone who would volunteer to be the butt of the joke, or stampede to the centre of attention, it was him. Able to stroll into a pub, completely naked, yet disarm any protests with his broad smile and airhorn laugh. But underneath the brash, window-rattling persona, he was rock-solid. He was the one who would always turn up – to lend a hand, or to buy the first round.

He was the one they tended to go to, when they needed help without negotiation. It wasn't because other members of Eleanor's unit were unreliable, or unwilling, but Steaky was the one who wouldn't let anything stand in the way of his loyalties. From the outside, it looked as though that might have cost him, a couple of failed marriages behind him, and no steady job for longer than a year or two. But both Eleanor and Tony knew that Steaky wouldn't have had it any other way. His friends were everything to him, and always would be. So much so, that they sometimes worried that they asked too much of him, thinking of the sacrifices he might make to help them.

"Logically," Eleanor said. "Yeah, you're probably right. Christ. I don't like to do it, though. This is pretty sketchy territory we are trying to get through."

"I know," Tony said, "but he already knows about all this. Most of it, anyway. We've already roped him into this, so it must be better to just have one of them involved, and not the whole lot of them."

When things had come to a head with Stark, Eleanor had managed to get out of the city. A nervous train ride, made worse by them having to seperate, took her south, all the way to Stoke-on-Trent, and a knock on the door of the one person she could bank on to be in. Steaky had kept a rifle of Eleanor's safe for her, hidden away in the cellar of the terrace house he lived in.

The rifle was a symbol of the old her. The killer. The surgeon. She had hoped that by trusting it to Steaky, and getting it away from her, she could distance herself from the person she had used to be. Tony and her were building a new life – a quieter, safer life – and that needed both of them to build new versions of themselves. Pictures and medals soon became like wallpaper, but this rifle was her Excalibur, and it needed to be well-hidden. Well-hidden, but not completely forgotten.

"You're right, Tony. He's got no ties, no dependables, and he lives on his own. And it's Steaky, for fuck's sake. You know if he had the slightest clue we were debating this, he'd have called us both twats and demanded to be involved."

"That's half the problem. That daft sod could do with a break from trouble, and just find a bit of quiet himself. But where else can we go?"

"Stoke, then," Eleanor said.

"Stoke, then," Tony agreed. "Come on, then, me duck. Dunner keep me waytin'"

"You need to work on that accent. Preferably by never doing it again."

"Philistine," Tony said, and they both laughed, as they opened the car doors, and climbed in, to find a bed for the night.

## 10

Jackie waved the car away after it had dropped her off at the end of her short drive, at the house that she had lived in with Jim since it was built. She waved, but saw that no-one was looking back to her to return it. The kids either asleep or engrossed in screens, and her daughter just concentrating on getting home. Jackie felt alone. The house was dark, and she sighed as she turned the key in the door.

"Mrs Stark?" a voice spoke from behind her.

Jackie spun around, surprised. Two men had appeared on the drive, one thin, one fat, like a one and a zero made flesh. They were both in middle-age, but hard to age beyond that, cigarettes and poor living adding years to them like weight to a packhorse. The fat one was broad with it, arms like hams pouring out of his t-shirt, which struggled to contain his prodigious belly. The skinny one was painfully so. Skin almost translucent, pulled tight over his bones, making him seem like he was made entirely of sharp edges. A cudgel and a razor blade, she thought, and both of them inching towards her.

"Who are you?" Jackie replied. She knew people like this. Jim would speak to anyone, and knew everyone, that knowledge a power he could use for who knows what, but always useful to have. Any trip to the shops would always be littered with interruptions and a repeat of the same old routine – "Hello, Mr Stark" followed by her husband saying "How are you? And do call me Jim" though they never did. She rarely asked Jim how he knew someone. There just wasn't enough time in the day, and as long as they were suitably referential, she knew that his name – *their* name – still had power. Now she needed to see if that name had any power now he was gone from her.

"Well, Mrs Stark. You won't know us, but we know you," the thin one said, a voice like crushed glass. "Your fella, y'see. He did us wrong."

"I wouldn't know about anything like that," Jackie said. She felt a ripple of nausea and nerves, but pushed it down. Hyenas could smell fear. "I've had a long day."

"All of our days are long, love," said the fat one. "I'd say ours are longer than yours."

"That's right. See, your husband came after us. Came after our family." The thin one spat the word "husband" like a curseword. "He reckoned our boys had stolen from him, that's what we heard. He reckoned they needed to be taught a lesson."

"I have no idea what you are talking about, boys," said Jackie, as matter-of-factly as she could manage. The door was behind her, and she knew this was getting close to her having to chance bolting inside and trying to lock these two out, before they get any closer.

"Look, we admit our boys could be a bit pushy. A bit daft, like. But they didn't deserve what he done," the fat one said, these two taking turns in speaking like some vaudeville routine. “They didn’t know that they were taking from him, and he didn’t need to do what he did.”

“I don’t know anything about what my husband did. He’s dead and gone. Dead and gone now. Let’s just leave it be, eh?” Jackie said, a firmer tone to see if she could shut this down quickly and finally.

“Yeah, we know about that too. Sent him to the flames today, didn’t you? Too good for him, I reckon. After what he did,” the thin man said, his hands now jammed in his pockets.

“I don’t know what he did. I think you two better go.” Jackie was angry at herself. She knew she sounded weak as soon as she said this, but the words had escaped, and the two men had made their inferences. A cruel smile pulled subtly at the lips of the fat one.

“We’re not going, love. Your Jim took our boys from us. We’ve never seen them since. Since they tried to pull that job on him. Some stupid job taking down some stupid poker game, but it’s not like you haven’t got the money, right? You could’ve just let the boys go. Or just taken the money back off them. We heard they ended up in the back of one of your cabs, and then never seen again.” The fat man inched forward as he spoke. He was too close to escape from now.

“We’ve heard they were killed. Cut up and fed to dogs or something. We hear all the stories. People fucking love to tell us the stories. And the thing is? Fuck ‘em. Them boys of ours were good for nothing. But family is family. And we reckon we are due some compo for it. Reckon you need to do the right thing by us.” The thin man pulled out one of his hands from his pockets, letting the streetlights reflect from the sharp metal of the knife he was holding. “Reckon you need to get us some of that money. A lot of it.”

Jackie stumbled backwards, tripping on the raised mat that lay in front of the front door to her house. The road seemed quiet, and she heard nothing more than the muffled audience cheers from a TV gameshow from one of the houses, and a car door shut just around the corner of the cul-de-sac.

"Careful, pet," chuckled the fat man, humourlessly. He reached for her with one of his paws.

Jackie shut her eyes. She felt weak. Broken. Lost. Jim was gone, and with him, any power and respect was gone too. These two men, so far beneath her as to be ants, had found confidence they should never have had. And if she got away from these? Then there would be others. An endless procession of villains and grabbing hands, all wanting some reward or some revenge for whatever they felt they were owed.

"Mrs Stark. Please don't move." A different voice had spoken. A steady, low voice, and one she recognised. She dared herself to open her eyes.

Stood at the bottom of the short drive was Mr Solomon, and next to him, his associate, dwarfing him by a foot or more. Mr Solomon looked down at Jackie, and gave her a reassuring nod. Then he reached up to the man stood next to him, and rested a hand on his shoulder, the impetus all the man needed to come alive, like a golem given his orders.

"If you could, Mr Parker," said Mr Solomon.

The fat and thin man spun round as soon as Mr Solomon had spoken. The mouths lolled open, surprised by the intervention, before clamping shut as they prepared themselves, like cornered dogs, to snarl and rip and tear their way out of this situation. Things had changed so quickly they couldn't quite comprehend what had happened.

The knife was fully revealed from the thin man's pocket now. The fat man just made do with balling his huge fists. Both prepared themselves for whatever came next, as Solomon's man moved towards them, steadily and confidently, as unwavering as an iceberg heading towards a frigate.

Jackie found herself in a low crouch, but her eyes were open now. She drank in the scene, outlandish as it was, so incongruous to the sleepy suburbia these houses represented. The two men, nervous and angry, twitching ready to strike, and then opposite, two men dressed in black – Solomon and Parker – both implacable, Parker steadily closing the distance to within arm's length.

The knife swiped through the air. Parker dodged it with incredible speed, seeming to move before the knife had even moved. Another jab at the air from the knife, and another side-step, before the subtlest shift of weight on his foot saw Parker go from a backwards movement to a forward step, and a left hook that knocked the thin man unconscious, his head bouncing on the paved driveway after he fell. The fat man swung a massive left hand wildly, which Parker blocked with his right forearm, then arcing his left arm down to block the right hand that was thrown next. Both punches diverted, Parker took the opportunity of open defence to press home the opening the fat man didn't realise he had created until it was too late. A flurry of punches rained in on the man, Parker's arms blurring as he pounded blow after blow like a frenzied engine, first crushing ribs, before a stunning uppercut lifted the fat man onto the balls of his feet. A straight-finger jab stabbed at the fat man's larynx, his hands automatically clamping around his throat as he struggled for breath.

"Please, Mr Parker," said Mr Solomon, from behind him.

Parker turned to look at Mr Solomon from over his shoulder, before turning back to the wheezing fat man, who had tears streaming from his eyes. Parker almost toying with him, he circled the man, light on his toes, until having decided he now had the optimum position, smashed his palm into the man's nose. The fat man dropped like shot game.

Mr Solomon walked forward, his immaculately polished shoes clicking on the paving. His gloved hand reached down, and Jackie took it, allowing him to help her to her feet, and to composure, after the thirty seconds or so of surgical violence she had witnessed had finished. The sounds of the street rebounded back to the usual quiet mundanity. It was over so quickly it was as if it had never happened, the two slumped bodies the only evidence.

"Shall we go inside, Mrs Stark? A cup of tea seems to be very much in order," said Mr Solomon, indicating to the door with his other hand.

Jackie turned the key in the door, and allowed herself to be ushered in. Solomon had his hand resting delicately on the small of her back, gently steering her forward, inside the safety of her home and away from the driveway. Jackie turned to speak to Solomon, but before she could find her words, he spoke to her.

"Please. My associate has this all in hand. I told you that we have been tasked to support you, Mrs Stark, and that is what we will do. Please allow Mr Parker to straighten things out with the gentlemen outside, whilst we take a moment to regain ourselves."

Jackie turned to close the door, Mr Solomon now patiently waiting in the hall of the house. As she shut the door, she looked out, onto her driveway. Mr Parker stood over the two men, making some silent calculation, before reaching down, pulling the fat man up to his feet by his armpits, before throwing him over his shoulder as if he was nothing but an old roll of carpet. She closed the door with a click.

## 11

Cold Cut rubbed his neck. It was the middle of the night, and he couldn't – wouldn't – sleep. His mind was fevered and hot, and he was angry at himself for falling back into the clutches of a world that he thought he had escaped. He had made it back to Liverpool, and back to his squalid flat, after months away hiding from Stark, not knowing that he wasn't missed in the first place. The flat was as horrific as he remembered it, only needing a few crumpled twenties and a wrap or two of coke to persuade the landlord to let him back inside. His eyes stung, and as he ran his fingers around his thin neck, dwelt on a painful boil that had developed on the nape of his neck. Sharp pain jabbed up his spine as he prodded at it, yet another minor torment he would have to put up with.

He had been allowed to leave by the big ape who had loomed over him, back at the crematorium, but not before he had been forced to hand over his driving licence and his bankcard, the man taking photos of them on his phone, before handing them back.

"Don't think about running away, little man," the man

had said at him, any professional tone forgotten as soon as he was out of earshot of the Stark woman. Cold Cut almost allowed himself a smile, as the mask slipped, reassured that despite all the airs and graces, this man was just as much a thug as so many of the others Cold Cut had dealt with over the years. The man had held his hand out, and spoke again – "Phone."

Cold Cut had given his phone to him, and the man had used it to dial a number. Inside his jacket pocket, a muffled vanilla ringtone rang out, as the man used the call to save Cold Cut's number to his own phone. The phone was handed back, and Cold Cut was allowed to leave.

A rattling sigh escaped from Cold Cut's lips, back in the flat. He looked around his living room, such as it was, with fresh distance, allowing the familiar to be assessed with new eyes, once again feeling dyspeptic at the shithole life that boxed him in. Mouldy walls, piles of detritus teetering here and there, and the pervasive smell of old cigarettes that enveloped everything.

He rubbed his neck again, and one or two further stabs of pain from the boil cut through any tiredness. His rodent-like instinct for survival found a scrap of optimism, and clutched onto it with desperate claws. Maybe, just maybe, there was a way to make this an opportunity, just as he had hoped his last interaction with anyone named Stark would have been. He knew the rules of the game – to climb the ladder was a game of transactions. What can be offered? What can that be traded for? He had knowledge they wanted, and if he said the right things at the right time, and somehow offered up the Graces on a platter to Jackie Stark and whoever those two men were, then maybe there would be a reward at the end of it. All he needed to do was find some way of leading Jackie Stark to them. But he needed to find the Graces first. Or some clue as to where they were now.

He lost himself in a thousand-yard stare again, back inside his head, looking for direction, or a hint, or even the barest suggestion of a hint, that he could follow. Because as much as he knew that information could be traded for his benefit, he was more aware that uselessness and failure would only be traded for punishment. He jabbed at the boil now, keen to let that pain burn him to some kind of enlightenment, wherever it was hiding.

The night sounds of the street drifted in through the cracked window that looked out over the main road. The rattle of thrown beer cans, the cackling of the late night drunks, weaving their way home, the dull rumble of the incessant traffic, even at this late hour. The city was still awake. Cold Cut reached down to the chipped and scratched coffee table that had followed him from his last three bedsits, and grabbed for his phone. He scrolled through a long list of contacts, all first names or nicknames, until he found a chat group of messages that he hadn't dared use for months. Three names that he used to lord over, who had side-stepped Cold Cut on their way to their own next rung on the ladder. Three names who delighted in their new status, keen to ensure that Cold Cut knew exactly where he now sat in the hierarchy of the streets. He hated them for it, even though, somewhere in the part of his brain where any self-reflection still wheezed and coughed for life, he knew he would've done the same in an instant. He needed them again now, and hated himself for needing anyone, let alone those who he used to monster and cajole, the tables now turned.

Acer, Belly and Cosmo. Three ridiculous names for three ridiculous men, happy to never stretch themselves beyond an approximation of adolescence, always uniformed in tracksuits and trainers despite all of them being in their late 20s. Once he might even have considered them his "crew" – the first to be called if there was a deal to be done, or some work to be bartered for, but always aware that any loyalty was gossamer-thin. And so it had proven. Cold Cut had asked them for a favour, dangling some drug deal reward in return for them carrying out a bit of legwork, but they had sidestepped him, and gone further themselves. They had found Tony Grace when Jim Stark was looking, and traded in any grubby drug deal for the kudos and potential of recognition by Stark. And then they had cut Cold Cut adrift, when he was desperate to redeem himself with Stark and his organisation. That hope he had relied on was snatched from him, and he had felt he had no choice but to leave town. And now, he was going to go back to these betrayers, these back-stabbers, to once again ask them for something.

It was unbearable. To have to prostrate himself to them after what they had done.

"It's worth it. It's worth it," he whispered to himself, trying to calm the indignant voice within, ashamed at himself. He started typing.

Cold Cut – "NEED A JOB DOING"

He had typed the word "favour" but deleted it. At least by using the word "job" he might fool himself into this being some kind of demand, rather than an appeal to a better nature he knew they didn't have.

He checked the message details – all three of them read the message almost instantly. But no reply. He stared at the screen for a few minutes, finding himself frustrated that they had the temerity to not reply as soon as they had seen it, and then even more frustrated when he realised he was in no position to push. They were talking amongst themselves, weighing up why Cold Cut was getting in touch with them now, or worse, laughing at how he was reduced to asking them for something in the first place. He stared into space, in the gloom of his flat, bristling. After a long five minutes, the phone lit up. A reply.

Acer – "LONG TIME, CUTTY"

Belly – "NOT SEEN YOU AROUND. HEARD YOU HAD RUN AWAY"

Belly, as always, following someone's lead. A blunt force when compared to the sadistic needling from Acer and Cosmo.

Acer – "WHAT'S THE JOB?"

Cosmo – "WE'RE BUSY. DON'T WORK FOR YOU"

Cold Cut seethed to himself. This was humiliating. And then, he gambled.

Cold Cut – "OK. NO PROBLEM. WILL ASK SOMEONE ELSE"

He had set his trap. He put his phone down on the table, pulled himself to his feet, and walked into his tiny kitchenette to boil a kettle for a cup of tea. He didn't really want a cup, but knew he had to give himself something to do to ensure he didn't run the risk of spoiling his play by being impulsive or impatient.

The kettle light illuminated the room with a faint blue glow to indicate it was boiling. Cold Cut dug out the least-dirty cup from the cluster of crockery that congregated around the sink, and scraped a soggy teabag from the draining board to reuse. He heaped a couple of teaspoons of sugar into the mug, then poured the hot water. Milk now. He opened the fridge door, lighting up the room as the light shone out from a mainly empty unit, before the room darkened again, as he closed the door again, carton of milk in hand. He couldn't resist looking over his shoulder at the table in the other room, a smile playing on his lips as he saw his phone screen had lit up with messages.

He stirred his tea. He was never going to be someone who was driven around in limousines, or dressed head to toe in a sharp black suit, but he was confident that he had enough about him to get ahead of the likes of Acer, Belly and Cosmo. This was a matter of professional pride to him, and them thinking they had bested him before was a situation that Cold Cut simply couldn't allow to continue. They simply couldn't resist losing their composure to find out exactly what would cause Cold Cut, a man they felt had been humiliated, to come back to them and risk making it worse.

Cold Cut sat back down in his chair, sipped his tea, and to an audience of no-one, attempted insouciance as he picked up his phone to open his messages.

Acer – "WHAT'S THE JOB?"

Acer – "JUST TELL US WHAT THE JOB IS"

Belly – "DON'T BE A TWAT"

Cosmo – "WE COULD HELP"

Belly – "MIGHT HAVE TIME. IF IT'S GOOD JOB"

Acer – "JUST ASK, CUTTY"

Cosmo – "C'MON MAN"

Good. Pleading. The result he was after. Any pretence of superiority cracked by their animal desperation to know something, or have something. He took another sip of tea, unable to resist a further perverse delay in responding, before he started typing, confident that the balance of power had shifted back to where it should be.

Cold Cut – "IT'S A STARK JOB. VERY IMPORTANT."

Belly – "STARK DEAD. OLD NEWS."

Good old Belly – never let it be said he didn't have a thought he didn't speak out loud.

Cold Cut – "JIM STARK DEAD. STARK NOT DEAD THO"

Cold Cut – "STARK FIRM NEED TO FIND KILLER. I KNOW WHO KILLER IS"

Cosmo – "STARK FIRM GOOD AS DEAD WE HEARD. WHOLE THING OVER."

Cold Cut – "STARK WIFE IN CHARGE NOW. SHE GOT HELP. STARK FIRM GOING NOWHERE."

Belly – "WE HEARD NEW FIRMS MOVING IN. STARK BUSINESS GOING DOWN."

Cold Cut sipped his tea again.

Cold Cut – "STARK GOT MONEY. LOTS OF IT. BOUGHT HELP FROM OUTSIDE."

Cold Cut waited. He needed this to be persuasive.

Cold Cut – "DO YOU REALLY WANT TO BET AGAINST THEM?"

A pause in replies. Presumably they had either opened up a separate chat thread, or possibly they were bickering amongst themselves in some squalid room somewhere.

Acer – "MAKES SENSE. THEY COULD AFFORD IT."

Acer – "WHAT'S THE SKETCH?"

Cold Cut – "STARK NEED TO KNOW WHERE TO FIND TONY AND ELEANOR GRACE. THEY WERE THE ONES WHO DID JIM. THEY MUST HAVE LEFT TOWN BUT THEY HAD DIGS HERE AND WILL HAVE LEFT THINGS. NEED YOU TO FIND OUT WHERE THAT WAS AND TELL ME."

Cold Cut – "NEED ADDRESS. NEED TO SEE WHAT THEY LEFT."

Belly – "WHAT'S THE PRICE?"

There it was, thought Cold Cut. The transaction.

Cold Cut – "STARK FIRM LOST A LOT OF PEOPLE. VACANCIES. WHO DO YOU WANT TELLING MRS STARK WHERE HER HUSBAND'S KILLERS ARE?"

Cosmo – "LEAVE IT WITH US."

Cold Cut smiled again, and finished his tea. It tasted disgusting, but to him, right then, it could've been a mai-tai on a tropical beach.

## 12

Jackie found that her thoughts were bouncing off one another like dodgems. No sooner had she managed to get the measure of one of them another barrelled into it, leaving her discombobulated. There was just so much to sift through. She sat perched on the edge of one of her living room armchairs, hands wrapped around a mug of black coffee, even though the house was warm. She had sat in her chair for an hour now, maybe more, but found it hard to comprehend the passing of time, buffeted along by the eddies of her mind.

Mr Solomon sat across the room from her, in another one of the chairs. He had tried to insist that he preferred to stand, but Jackie had made it clear that her invitation for him to sit was more of a demand, and Solomon was not the kind of man to risk upsetting a client, especially given how heightened the day had been. He was a man comfortable in his own silence, inscrutable as he sat, hands resting primly on his knees.

Parker had driven off in the car, the two villains who had come to strong-arm Jackie dragged up from the ground and roughly slung into the back seat, both unconscious, hands tied together with some cable-ties that Parker had retrieved from the boot. Jackie didn't ask where Parker was taking the two men, well-drilled in the concept of plausible deniability and simply having other, more immediate matters to worry about. Those men existed in the twilight depths of the city, bumping along from street corner to street corner, a million miles from the rarefied airs that Jackie and her husband enjoyed, even with that strategy of hiding in plain sight that Jim had so strongly believed in. That they had the gall to dare speak to her, let alone try and intimidate her, was troubling in the extreme. There were far bigger fish than them swimming in these waters, and if minnows like that suddenly had the confidence to try their luck, then what was to follow? How dangerous had her life become, all of a sudden, now that Jim had been taken from her?

"Mrs Stark, if you would permit me," Solomon said, breaking the long silence.

"This is to be expected. Your late husband held a position of no little status in this city, and it is natural for the less aware to believe that this...ah...vacancy would present an opportunity for them. We have seen this time and again. Please be assured, Mrs Stark, that we are well-resourced, well-experienced and are aware of the very real nature of these eventualities."

Solomon's tone was steady and measured, and reassuring. There he was, sat across from her, Jim's last gift to her. The gift of comfort in a world turned on its head, Jim's plans meticulous even after death.

"But there's only two of you,' Jackie said, "and there's a lot of people who can't wait to have a pop at us now that Jim's gone."

"Two here, yes," Solomon replied, "but, please, as I said,

we are well-resourced, and have already taken steps to ensure that all avenues are explored, and all eventualities prepared for. We have already made demands of others in our circle to attend to us here to assist in weathering this little storm, and to ensure that the Stark operation is left to continue in as near as possible a state as it was when your late husband was managing affairs. That is the responsibility that Mr Stark entrusted to us, and that is what we shall do."

Silence returned to the room, Jackie staring into the black coffee in her mug, finding it easy to trust this odd little man sat across from her. Jim had planned for this, and she had never had any reason to doubt him when he was alive, and swore that she wouldn't start to second-guess him even after his death. Solomon sat impassively, unmoving, and comfortable with quiet, which Jackie was thankful for. She had had quite enough of platitudes and small words for one day.

"You've done this before?" asked Jackie, finally.

"Many, many times, to one degree or other," replied Solomon.

"So, what happens now? What do I need to worry about?"

"There are two answers to your first question, Mrs Stark. In the short term, there may be further attempts by some of the less...pragmatic types to make some kind of attempt at clawing some assets away from you. We will do all we can to ensure that any such attempts are kept to a minimum, and to ensure that you are shielded from any unpleasantness. I am hopeful that Mr Parker may have taken steps to dissuade others from trying such actions by now, but in any case, we must always plan for the outliers."

"Furthermore, I would expect some of the more civilised

of your late husband's associates to also make their own enquiries. In my experience, these people will likely present themselves as friends at first, but we should be aware that in the areas of business that we operate, friendship is a rare condition in the extreme. We would do well to discount it as a plausible motivation."

"In more definite terms, I would suggest that we present a confident face to the existing organisation. People seek continuity as they find it a comfort. As soon as is practical, I would strongly advise organising a meeting of as many of the most trusted and capable members of the business to reassure them that all is in hand, and their own positions are no less tenuous than before. Let this be a task for tomorrow."

"Mrs Stark, please forgive my candidness, but you must be assured of this. Your husband gave very clear instructions on what was required. His family was to be protected. His business was to be maintained. And lastly, he was very clear on one other point. Simply put, the ones responsible were to be butchered like *fucking* cattle.'

There was a soft rap on the front door, and Solomon excused himself to answer it. It was Parker, returned after an hour or so away, having finished whatever errand he had been set. Jackie could hear hushed words between the two men, before Mr Solomon came back into the living room, Parker looming behind him, his thick frame filling the doorway behind Solomon.

"Mrs Stark," Solomon said, as he came back into the room. "My colleague has finished the task at hand, which I hope will act as a deterrent for any others who believe such actions, such as the unpleasantness we have experienced tonight, are a sensible way forward. I'm very aware that you are a woman of considerable fortitude, but I will ask whether you wish to see exactly how this has been addressed, or whether you would prefer to be shielded from the knowledge, as it were."

Solomon had a phone in his hand, and was offering it forward to Jackie for her to inspect. Intrigue had taken over, and Jackie beckoned to him to pass the phone over. It was sensible for her to simply not be told certain things, should the time come that she was ever needed to give explanations or alibis, but she was tired, angry and keen to get the measure of these two men, Solomon and Parker, who had manifested in her life offering solutions.

She laughed, a sound that surprised her as it escaped her lips. The phone displayed a photograph, so perverse in its ridiculousness, that she couldn't help herself. In the photo, she could see a footbridge that crossed a main road – she couldn't be certain where it was, but it could've been any one of the major arterial routes into the city from the looks of it. Other identifying details were hard to ascertain, but that wasn't the point. Dominating the centre of the photo was a sight so preposterous she could barely warrant what she was seeing. The two men, wide-eyed and panicked, were hung by their feet from the metal railing of the footbridge, hanging down like animal carcasses from a butcher's hook, over the main road. Their arms were bound behind them, their mouths were gagged, and gaffer-taped to their chests were sheets of paper, one on each chest. Parker had written a word on each sheet in thick black letters.

The first one said "NO"

The second one said "CHANGE"

Jackie smiled, passed the phone back to Solomon and finished her coffee. She put her mug down on the glass table next to the chair, and got to her feet. Solomon took his cue, moving through the living room door, calmly shepherding

Parker to the front door ahead of him, before turning to bid her goodnight with a deferential nod. Jackie saw the front door open, then close, as Solomon and Parker left, footsteps crunching on the gravel pathway adjacent to the driveway outside. Jackie followed behind, into the hallway, to the bottom of the stairs, and stared at the front door for a moment. She took a deep breath, before climbing the stairs to go to bed, Solomon's words ringing around her head.

The day had been long. Too long. But she felt Jim had been with her, his last request delivering Solomon to her. She let that thought be a comfort to her, and drifted towards sleep.

# 13

The morning was cold, the dawn mist slowly dissipating as the sun dragged itself up into the sky. Cold Cut had barely slept, which wasn't in itself unusual, but rather than any narcotic or alcoholic distraction, he had been kept awake by a nervous energy. He had been eager for the morning to come, and the prospect of news, positive or otherwise.

A text message had catapulted him from his chair, the news he had been hoping for. It had been from Acer, the practical one in that three-headed monster, nominated as spokesman.

"FOUND THEIR STUFF. THE LANDLORD BOXED THEIR STUFF BUT HASN'T CHUCKED IT." the text message read, and then a name and an address.

Cold Cut had walked, as quickly as his feeble lungs could stand, across town to the address in the text message. It led him away from any busy thoroughfares, and away from the hurly-burly of the morning commuter run, to a labyrinth of grubby, claustrophobic back streets. The city had secrets, dangerous ones, hidden mere yards from the face it showed the world, and it was on streets like this that you could find them. There was no pretence with streets like this – the rubbish piled up, the road signs were graffitied or missing, and people could vanish if they opened the wrong door, or turned down the wrong alley. Cold Cut knew these streets though – he grew up in places like this, and knew enough of the lingua franca to let him wander down here unbothered.

Just off from the tight side street that branched off from the main road, were paved alleyways, just wide enough for a car to drive down, stretching off left and right. Each alley was walled with concrete sheds, their garishly painted doors peeling and faded. Cold Cut checked his phone again, just to be completely sure he had the right address, and made his way to a green door, splashed with spatters of white paint and pock-marked with chipped gouges, a number roughly painted in the middle of the door. He knocked.

The door opened sharply, and a rough-looking man in a threadbare charcoal-coloured sweater appeared in the doorway. His accent was thick and foreign, and any conversational niceties had been strangled at birth.

“What you want, boy?” growled the man. Who was this who had the temerity to come to his door at this early hour?

“I’ve been told to come here. Been told you have something for me,” Cold Cut said, understanding quickly that he had just begun a negotiation.

“Says who? Who say this?” the man barked back, each word delivered like a slap to the face.

“Acer said I needed to come here. You have some stuff from a tenant that I need to look through.”

“Don’t know no Acer. You fuck off. Fuck off, boy.” Cold Cut ground his teeth. This was slipping away from him, and he couldn’t work out what the magic words were to get this door to stay open, and this dirt-smeared sentinel to back away. He only knew one magic word, and dared himself to say it aloud.

"Look! Wait! It's for Mr Stark. Mr Stark! Very important."

The man paused, loomed forward, resting a heavy arm on the doorframe as he pushed his face closer to Cold Cut. Cold Cut couldn't help but recoil slightly, as the man pushed his flat face into his space.

"Stark dead," said the man, and then he slammed the door shut, leaving Cold Cut stood uselessly in the alley, staring at the door, puzzling how that conversation had gone so badly, so quickly.

He walked away, his body unconsciously suggesting movement was the only way to fire up any new synapses, as he pondered on his problem. Had Acer got it wrong? Yet another prank from those three idiots, keener than ever to rub his nose in it? No, that wasn't it. They wanted the prestige and status that Cold Cut had dangled in front of them, and there's no way they would jeopardise the prospect of that so quickly, before Cold Cut had even laid his cards out. No, more likely was that this was the right place, and this burly idiot just refused to countenance the reality of the situation. People were like that, especially on streets like these. Better to resist everyone, than dare expose yourself to the stiletto knife of risk. But knowing this was one thing. Solving it was another thing entirely. How did he get into that lock-up?

He looked at his feet as he realised he had only one real option. He would have to be the one to take the risk, and he was never one to do something as isolating as that. Not normally.

He reached into his pocket, and pulled out his phone, tapping a few times on the cracked screen until he called up the call log from last night. The man yesterday had taken Cold Cut's phone from him to dial his own number, in order to log it for later reference, the threat implicit in that action. But that worked both ways, and Cold Cut realised he could use that number to contact them in return. So, he dialled the number, gulping to try and moisten his dry mouth before the phone was answered. A voice answered.

"What do you want?" it said.

"I think I know something about what happened to Mr Stark..." Cold Cut said. As soon as he said the name, the voice on the other end of the line cut in, angrily.

"No names. Ever."

Cold Cut paused, and tried to transmit an attitude of suitable humble deference just by concentrating. He regrouped, and tried again.

"There's an address. They have some things that we need to see. But they won't let me in. You know I wouldn't call you unless it was important."

Now it was the voice on the other end of the phone that paused. Cold Cut wasn't completely sure, but he got the feeling that another conversation was underway, with him left on hold until it had concluded. Either that, or Cold Cut was to be left in silence to just firmly underline the hierarchy here. The silence was so palpable that Cold Cut even checked to see if the call was still connected. Eventually, the voice spoke again –

"Text me the address of a street corner in the region of five minutes walk from the location. I will meet you there. Do not leave the area, or make any further communication to *anyone* until I arrive."

Cold Cut, relieved to be given instruction, walked back towards the main road from the back streets, texting as he walked. There was a discount superstore not far from here, with a reasonably sized car park, enough for thirty or so cars, that would be convenient to meet that man again, with the added comfort of being safe in plain sight. The superstore was like a parasite, a local fly-by-night operation occupying the corpse of a nationwide brand, long since collapsed under the weight of debt and bad management.

As he waited, he fumbled in his pockets to see if he could cannibalise the contents into anything resembling a cigarette. He was grateful of the distraction, fingers nimbly pulling things apart, and squeezing things together, until he had created some rough approximation of a smoke that would just have to do. Two clicks on his cheap lighter, and it was lit, and he drew as much of it into his lungs as he could, the soft crackle of burning paper as he did so.

A car had turned off from the main road, and circled around the car park like a shark circling a cramping swimmer. It pulled up next to Cold Cut, as he leant on the wall that separated the car park from the pavement, and the window wound down with a whirr. In the driver's seat was the big man from the crematorium.

"Get in. And put that fucking thing out," he said, pointing at the cigarette that hung from Cold Cut's mouth limply.

Deflated and resigned, like a man on a walk to the gallows, Cold Cut flicked the cigarette to the floor, and ground it under his heel, on his way to the passenger side of the car.

"Back seat," said the man, just as Cold Cut reached to open the door. He opened the back door, and climbed inside. The man adjusted the rear view mirror with a gloved hand, so they could see each other's eyes as the conversation continued.

"My name is Parker. You will not mention me to anyone

else. You will not mention anybody I associate with to anyone else. You are aware that we can find you, should we so wish. If I ask you to do something, you will do it, without complaint. Is that understood?"

"Got it, got it. I understand," Cold Cut managed to say, tingling with nerves.

"Tell me everything about why I am here," Parker said, his eyes unblinking in the rear-view mirror.

Cold Cut did his best to recount the text conversation with Acer, Belly and Cosmo from the previous night, and the information that Acer had shared with him first thing that morning. Parker didn't speak as Cold Cut spoke, instead just maintaining that stare, daring Cold Cut to even think about not being completely transparent with him.

"I know that Mrs Stark would want to find the Graces. I just want to help," Cold Cut said. He regretted attempting to paint himself as altruistic – it was a coat that would never fit.

"Help, is it?" Parker said, as aware of the fraud of the statement as Cold Cut was.

"Okay, look. I just want to show I'm useful, right? This is useful, isn't it? Don't you want to find them?" Cold Cut stammered.

"We'll see how useful this is. How useful you are. Have you been to this place?" Parker said.

Cold Cut told Parker about the foreign man, who had sent him away with a flea in his ear, door slammed behind him. Parker's eyes seemed to sparkle, Cold Cut suspecting that the prospect of confrontation was the sort of thing that Parker relished, away from the quiet servitude of his usual role. Clearly he was the sort of man that filled that position by dint of other abilities than politely opening and closing doors, or steadily driving cars here and there.

The car growled as Parker put it in gear to move off. Cold

Cut directed Parker right, then left, then into the maze of streets that beyond the main high street in this satellite district of the city. The car pulled up at the end of the alley, half-on, half-off the pavement, blocking the entryway for any cars that may have wanted to access the lock-ups directly.

"Out," Parker said, as he himself opened the door, getting out onto the pavement. Cold Cut did as he was told.

"Which?" Parker said, looking down the alley at the rows of decrepit doors and flaking paint.

"Green one," Cold Cut said, pointing. Parker looked, identified the door, and strode off. Cold Cut looked around, unsure whether he should follow or stay where he was, the former choice more likely to plunge him into the middle of something that might draw attention to him, and the latter likely to risk upsetting this big man striding away from him. He hopped from foot to foot nervously, unsure which choice would be most beneficial to him.

"Follow," Parker said, making the choice for him.

Parker had reached the green door, and pounded on it twice. The sound underlined how quiet this alleyway was, especially at this time of the day. Cold Cut felt something like relief. It was always better for him not to be noticed, and in the slipstream of people like Parker, and given the deeds men like him inevitably carried out, doubly so.

The door opened again, and the same man appeared in the doorway. He looked at Parker, then over Parker's shoulder at Cold Cut hovering a few yards behind him, and then back to Parker.

"What now? I said fuck off. Why you not fuck off?" said the man, the last angry question aimed directly at Cold Cut, ignoring Parker. He wasn't impressed or intimidated by Parker, his contempt and irritation writ large.

Parker didn't speak. Instead, his hand moved like a cobra strike, clamping around the man's throat, as Parker pushed him back into the lock-up, into the darkness. Cold Cut heard crashes and meaty thumps from inside the lock-up, as he carefully inched forward, feeling curiosity and nervousness simultaneously as he moved inside. His eyes took a few seconds to adjust to the gloom inside the building, the sharp winter sun replaced by the feeble light from the one light-bulb which did its best to illuminate the room inside.

The room was long, thin, and a confusing mess of shelves, piles of boxes and other ephemera stacked up here and there. A torn and dirty office chair was at the other end of the room, in front of a desk piled high with what looked like old receipts and scraps of paperwork. Cold Cut wasn't minded to examine the room in any more depth as he entered – he was too busy watching Parker relentlessly club the man with repeated punches to the ribs, each one thudding dully and powerfully. The man was flailing his arms as if he was drowning, clutching for a lifebelt that would never be within reach.

Suddenly, Parker stopped, and stood up, poised to renew his attack at the slightest hint that the man's resolve had not been completely and utterly shattered. The man wheezed hoarsely, eyes bulging as he struggled to pull air back into his lungs, hands slapping onto the concrete floor, as he dragged himself to all fours, a halfway house to standing. Parker just stood over him, making it abundantly clear that this was just a temporary cessation in hostilities, should the man have the temerity to even suggest that he hadn't accepted complete compliance.

"Take your time. Get your breath," Parker said to the man at his feet, not even out of breath. "Shut the door," he said to Cold Cut, without turning around to look at him.

Cold Cut did as he was told, closing the door to the increasingly bright morning outside, the gloom swaddling the room, with the only light coming from the single bulb.

Parker crouched down over the man, patting him on his chest, which was rising and falling in exaggerated fashion, as he fought to breathe after Parker's assault. Parker hadn't raised his voice or even quickened his breathing during the frenzy of his attack. This was nothing new to him, and Cold Cut found himself fascinated by what Parker might possibly do next, even though a significant part of him was wishing he could just throw open that door and run headlong away from this place.

"I hope you understand the position that you are in, my friend," Parker said to the man, his hand still lightly resting on the man's chest, all loaded potential, daring him to try resisting. "Now I am going to ask you a few questions, and I strongly suggest that you answer me honestly and directly. Do you understand?"

The man opened his mouth to speak, but couldn't find his words, only able to offer gasps. Defeated by his body, the most he could muster was a feeble nod of the head, eyes pleading with Parker to accept what he offered.

"Take your time, take your time. Now think very hard. My friend here tells me that you can help us locate some items. So, my first question is this – are you involved with the letting of any properties in the city?"

The man gulped, his breathing now returning to something approaching normal.

"I not landlord," the man managed to say.

Parker looked away from the man for a moment, at nothing in particular, loudly tutting, before quickly grabbing the man by his collar and dragging him to his feet. In one movement, Parker lifted the man off his feet, and back onto the desk, sweeping the piles of papers and stained coffee mugs from it with the man as he slammed him down and across it, leaving him prostrate and panting.

"Listen, fucko, that isn't what I asked, is it?" said Parker, the slightest edge of irritation now in his voice. Cold Cut was suddenly aware that another unacceptable answer from the man may turn this place into a crime scene. Even if it was just self-preservation as opposed to any love for his fellow man, he desperately hoped the man would find the right words to whatever was posed to him next.

"I'll ask again. Think carefully before you speak. Are you involved with the letting of any properties in the city?" Parker said, the last sentence exaggeratingly enunciated.

"Yes, yes. I am caretaker for landlord. He has some flats. Apartments." The man stumbled over his words in his desperation to get them said.

"Good. Better. Second question. We have been told that you have some items from one of these apartments belonging to someone we are trying to find. Do you have anything here that sounds like the sort of thing that we are looking for?"

The man opened his mouth for a second then closed it again. His lesson had been learnt the hard way, but he was nervous that the answer that he had on his lips might demand a further course of revision. Parker had hidden his violent side again, and was trying to persuade the man that it had gone for good, though Cold Cut could see from the look in his eye that suggested that he hadn't hidden it well enough.

"No, no," said Parker, "just say it. Don't worry."

Silence was not an option, and he had no better option. The man tried his luck, his eyebrows arching pleadingly.

"But there are lots of things here like that?" he said. "Whole place."

Parker grinned. It was terrifying.

"Good point. It was a difficult question. Let me try again," he said. "I want to look in every single box you've got in here until I find what I'm looking for. Think very hard. I'm looking for stuff from a married couple who left in a hurry a year or so ago. Can you help me with that?"

Parker stepped back from the man, and beckoned him to sit upright, his legs hanging over the edge of the desk as if he was a toddler sat there by a parent. The man's hands clutched the edge of the table, as he tried to find his equilibrium again. He managed to raise a feeble arm pointed at a shelving unit, with plastic storage crates arranged on each shelf, the crates all of different sizes and colours, some with lids and some without.

Parker turned to look at the shelves, then turned back to the man.

"Might be over here?" he said.

The man nodded, hardly able to look Parker, or Cold Cut even, in the eye. As soon as Parker turned back to the shelves, the man just looked at his knees, anything but look at this devil who had walked into his safe, little world.

Parker beckoned Cold Cut over, pulling him close with a thick arm. This was not camaraderie – this was control, and Cold Cut knew it. Cold Cut used the violence of the coward when he had found the need – a hidden blade, or a punch to somewhere soft before he made his run for it – but men like Parker, who he had had dealings with far too often for his liking, had a different approach. Their violence was obvious and they wore it like a badge.

"Here's what you need to help me with," Parker said, Cold Cut wilting from the physical contact. "You know about these people. You've seen them. You're going to help me find their stuff in amongst all this. Because it's definitely here, isn't it?"

The last question was the threat. The equivalent of the baseball bat placed on a table. You called me, it said, and you better not be wasting my time.

"Yeah, sure sure. I'll find it. No problem," Cold Cut said.

Not wanting to show anything other than complete obedience, Cold Cut pulled a box from the shelving, dropped it on the floor, and pulled the lid off it to see what was inside. He rooted around inside, looking for some precious indication that these items belonged to the Graces', but he knew this wasn't the box he was looking for. Some airport fiction, dog-eared and creased, some muddy trainers, and a bird's nest of charging cables. He slid the box away from him, disgusted with it, quickly pulling another one down from the shelf.

Parker had moved away, prowling the room, happy to let someone else do the menial work, especially as his preferred activities were more particular, and more painful. He was a coiled spring, all fierce potential loosely bound behind a thin veneer of control. Cold Cut made sure he was visibly concentrating on the task at hand, but couldn't help looking at Parker peripherally when the opportunity presented itself. Little, furtive glances, as Cold Cut tried to take the temperature of yet another man who he had somehow managed to let himself get under the heel of.

Parker's brow was furrowed, a knot of concentration wrinkling the skin at the bridge of his nose. He was pacing – prowling, even – up and down the length of the lock-up. The lock-up caretaker was fully docile, still sat on the desk unsteadily, his breath still forced and wheezing after the brutality of the assault. Suddenly, Parker found purpose, reached inside his jacket pocket for his phone, and walked to the door, his phone to his ear as he waited for a call to connect.

Once Parker had gone outside, closing the door behind him, Cold Cut stopped what he was doing, so he could concentrate on eavesdropping as best as he could. He glanced up, and saw that the man on the desk was staring back at him, eyes wide and desperate, imploring Cold Cut to show something – maybe some help, or support, or maybe even just some shared humanity. But Cold Cut was nothing if not a survivor, and there was no way he was going to jeopardise his own skin by taking on the ballast of another. He shook his head, and turned away, trying to pick up anything useful from the phone conversation taking place in the alley outside.

Absent-mindedly, Cold Cut reached a hand to the back of his neck, and his questing fingers found the outline of the boil that was squatting on his neck like a hot weight. As soon as he found it, he felt a sharp stab of pain that creased his eyes, and he was momentarily distracted enough by the pain, and his self-recrimination at poking the beast awake. His fingers tried to find some purchase on his oily skin, this new task a relief from the situation his life had led him into, thinking that perhaps by somehow expelling the poison in that boil, the sweet relief would permeate his entire existence.

Without warning, the door slammed open, and Parker strode back in, with fresh purpose. Cold Cut immediately busied himself with the boxes again, willing himself to be as productive as possible as Parker walked past him, and back to the man at the far end of the room.

"Now then, friend," Parker said, with heavy implication. The man recoiled as Parker approached, trying to drive himself into the brickwork of the wall at his back. "I have some questions."

"I know nothing. Am just caretaker," the man said, feebly.

"I'll be the judge of what you do or don't know," Parker said, looming over the man again. Cold Cut dared a look, and thanked whatever gods were listening that Parker was not looming over him instead. It seemed like Parker filled the room, all shoulders and shadows, the man cowering beneath him.

"So, the people we are looking for. They left the city a long time ago. Why have you still got their stuff? You are sure you have actually got it, aren't you?" Parker shifted his stance slightly, coiling that spring just ever-so-slightly tighter.

"I don't know," babbled the man. "Boss just tells me 'do this' and I do."

"Think harder," Parker said.

The man squirmed. He was bigger than Cold Cut, and was clearly someone used to intimidating others, but Parker had broken him, domesticated him, and he had no resistance left to offer.

"Things like this are worth money. Worth money to people who leave them behind. Or people like you."

"Go on," Parker said.

"Maybe there a good reason why they leave so quick. Maybe they run and pay to have this stuff looked after. Some pay cash each month, so they must have reason. Or others might come back and pay money to get stuff back."

"Ok, makes sense," Parker said, presumably to himself. Cold Cut turned his head to just check that he was not part of this conversation, before heaving another box down from the shelving in front of him, working hard to be useful.

The box was much like the others – packed with haste and without care, a lucky dip of household items. Cold Cut pulled aside the summer jacket that had covered the contents of the box, and immediately saw that he had found a treasure that might curry some favour with the big man that ruled his life right here, right now. Stacked loosely in the box, were maybe fifteen or so framed photos and mementoes, of various sizes and shapes. But the first one he saw, that had caught his eye as soon as he saw it, was the one that had convinced him, without a doubt, that he had found what he was looking for.

It was a smallish photograph, in a plain black wooden frame, faded slightly from when it was first printed. A group of people, all smiling, some standing, some crouching in the foreground. And in the centre of the picture, grinning and arms around each other, were Tony and Eleanor Grace. He'd found something valuable. Something to offer.

He stood up, and did his best to adopt his deferential pose, holding the picture in his hands like an offering.

"I've..I think..." he stuttered, angry that his words had become slippery. Cold Cut gulped, composed himself, and tried again. "I've found something we can use."

Parker turned to give him his full attention, holding his hand out to receive whatever it was this little rodent was offering him.

"It's how we find them," Cold Cut said.

Parker looked at the picture, then back to Cold Cut. His expression suggested that Cold Cut better explain himself quickly, or prepare to find himself in a similar state as the other man in the room, still labouring with his breathing, slumped against the wall.

Cold Cut jabbed at the picture, frantically.

"Look. Look!" he said, "They're standing in front of a flag. A regimental flag. It's how we find them."

Parker started to smile. He'd got it.

"Find the regiment, find them," Parker said, his teeth now bared in a cold grin, looking at Cold Cut with a predator's stare.

# 14

The next few days for Tony and Eleanor were quiet, both by desire and by practicality – the goal was to spend as little money as possible, and perhaps squeeze another night's stay out of their funds. They spent them entirely in each other's company, walking country paths and talking things through, before returning to whatever hotel or lodgings they had secured in the evening.

As the days passed, they found themselves building a fiction that they were both happy to surround themselves with. They talked less and less about their plan, once they had debated every aspect of it, until they were both as satisfied with it as they could be. After that, they let themselves believe that the wolves weren't on their heels, and this was just a simple vacation, full of old churches, riverside pubs and the crunch of leaves beneath their soles.

But it couldn't last. All they dared spend was the cash they had with them. A few bundles of notes that dwindled far faster than they hoped, even with their attempts at making every last penny stretch as long as it could. The regular hot meals were soon traded down for cheap sandwiches, and the negotiation with hotels and hostels became fiercer, all with the hope of eking out another day until they had to move on, and rely on the charity of someone else. That pinch point loomed up at them, not only as a watershed where they would have to bring someone else into their drama, but also because they didn't want this bucolic pause to be over.

They made sure to take trains that would bring them to Stoke-on-Trent by a circuitous, backwater route, even given the remoteness of their starting point. Stoke would sensibly be a fast train south from their position, but fast meant obvious, and this was the last thing they could afford to be. Instead, their route would take them first east, further into Yorkshire, before heading down to Derby, then back across to Stoke. They made sure to keep to the local services, rather than take any busy mainlines, both of them happy to give into paranoia, if it meant that that they could avoid leaving any trace of their movements, especially after what had happened to them before.

They had felt themselves so safe in the sleepy simplicity of their Norfolk lives. Enough time passed that their determination to be cautious had been eroded by their new comforts and new friends. And one tiny mistake – a photo of them pinned to a pub wall – had been the crack in the keystone that brought their whole lives crashing down around them. Never again. Not now they fully appreciated what the consequences were. Consequences that had seen friends killed, and that still might see the same delivered to them.

They had left the car behind in the car park of the last chain hotel they had stayed at, and carried their lives to the train station in the rucksacks and hold-alls they had brought with them. Eleanor had slung the rifle over her shoulder in the long bag it was kept in, keen to keep it close to her until she was completely sure that there was to be no further need for it.

Tony held the last few notes of their cash, folded over and in the back pocket of his jeans. This was all they had to see them to their safe haven. Once, they might have scoffed at the idea that someone could find them just because they had bought a coffee on a debit card, but they had friends who knew better. For the right money, whole lives were available to be bought and sold, digital avatars conjured out of zeroes and ones, leaving breadcrumbs trails for anyone who cared to look. It was unlikely, maybe astronomically so, but a photo on a wall, hidden amongst other similar photos, seemed innocuous just a few weeks ago.

Tony couldn't help squeezing Eleanor's hand as the door of the train swooshed shut, accompanied by the thin-sounding alarm to warn that the train was about to depart. It was a jailer closing a door, trapping them in this metal cell, unable to escape should they need to. But as the train grunted and heaved itself away from the station, and the stone houses gave way to the hills and trees of the English countryside, Tony let himself relax. The clanks and rumbles sang an old lullaby to him – a childhood song of seaside days out, escaping London for a few treasured hours with his mum, away from the furrowed brows and the grey tenements that surrounded him.

He gazed at the scenery outside the train carriage window. Even now, decades later, the hills of the north mesmerised him. He didn't see landscapes like this until he had grown up, and allowed himself to explore further afield than the big city. There were valleys and peaks in London, but they were made from money and ambition, and he had found himself pushed along in the eddies and swirls of the human traffic, there at the bottom. This green world had hills he could climb, that didn't care about accents or breeding or the money in your wallet. He didn't know just what life they would be left with at the end of all this, but for now – right now – he let himself stare out of the window at the comforting waveform shapes of this world.

"I'm hungry," Tony eventually said. Crushing existential worries, impending or otherwise, could wait. Tony had made a sharp reassessment of his priorities after some encouragement from his stomach.

"Seriously?" Eleanor said, turning to him, an arched eyebrow deployed like a stiletto. Her expression soon melted into a broad smile. Bombs may fall, or seas may rise, but the reassurance of her husband's appetite reminded her that however bad things were, all was not lost. Not yet.

Tony tried to maintain a poker face, but couldn't help but smile back. "Come on, look," he said. "We were out of that hotel sharp this morning, and I haven't had a thing yet. Things aren't so bad that we can't stop to have a bit of late breakfast, are they?"

Surrounded by a countryside that hadn't altered all that much in a few hundred years, the troubles that might be looking for them from around dark, concrete corners, seemed another world away. Those troubles could stay there for an hour or so. If they were careful, maybe those troubles would stay there forever, once they were convinced that things actually had changed, and Jim Stark was buried deep enough to be forgotten.

"We change train in a half-an-hour. How about we don't hurry to catch the next one, and find ourselves a nice, grubby cafe, with chipped mugs and plastic ketchup bottles, and have a big fry-up?" Eleanor said, eyes alive with the prospect. "Unless you want your usual bowl of granola...?"

Tony worked hard to keep in shape, each year harder than the last as he tried to maintain his fitness, and his waist-size. Increasingly, food became just fuel, especially as he often found himself in a life making money from jobs that required him to be that little bit faster, that little bit stronger, than the next man, despite pushing fifty. He had the discipline to wave temptation away, more often than not. This was one of those occasions where it was more "not" than "often". Tomorrow had become uncertain. "Fuck it" seemed like a perfectly valid response, especially given he had no wish to adopt piety sat next to his wife, on today of all days.

"Just this once," he said. "Because I love you. I will sacrifice my monkish lifestyle for you, my dear." He bowed his head, overegging the pudding.

"Fried eggs, fried bread, beans, bacon..." Eleanor said in a stage hypnotist's tone.

Tony rolled his eyes, dreamily.

"Black pudding..."

Tony put his hand up, to ask for a halt.

"Nope," he said. "Not for me."

"Oh, come on," Eleanor said. "It's beautiful stuff. Just pretend it's made by fairy magic. You'll love it."

"We are starting to get into some deep water now," Tony said. "I have rules. They've served me well over the years."

"Is that right?' Eleanor said, turning on her seat to face him, keen to see what nonsense the big lug was going to come out with now. He was being mischievous, which was a good sign. Any brooding was buried for now.

"Black pudding is a halfway house to offal, and that's just not going to happen. If I'm going to eat something with a face, I'm not going to eat something important. Like blood."

"Important? I reckon the pig thinks it's all important."

"Nope. If it does something useful, I'm not eating it."

He stared at Eleanor. She stared back. Both of them feebly trying to maintain their hard looks, this game of seeing who could hold back the laugh for longest. Eleanor cracked first, as always, Tony more used to keeping things inside, though once she started laughing he let himself join in. He loved her, more and more it seemed. She squeezed his hand, and he squeezed it back, then both of them cosied together and looked out of the window, just taking a break from heavier thoughts for just a little while.

## 15

Solomon had knocked on the door at Jackie Stark's house at 8am exactly. Jackie had been ready for an hour, a full night's sleep still a futile hope, her mind refusing to let her body rest. She had attempted to sharpen herself from tiredness with a long shower, adjusting the temperature like a safe-cracker gradually making the jet of water cool until she stood under cold water. That cold dragged her back to the here-and-now from her tired distractions, and she dressed herself with a fresh determination, ready to attack this new day.

The coffee helped. The quiet house echoed with the sound of the coffee grinder, whirring and crunching the beans. She enjoyed this ritual. Grind the beans, add the filter to the pour-over pot, dampen the paper, and warm the cups. It took time, and a little care, and she felt that the results made the investment worth it. Jim never took to it. For a man so used to being meticulous, he didn't have the patience, happy to spoon a heap of instant coffee into a mug rather than wait. But he'd always take a cup of the filter coffee if it was on offer, so, whenever Jackie made a pot, she always made enough for two.

It was the realisation of this that sideswiped Jackie. Another reminder of what she no longer had shot through her like a sniper's bullet. She sighed, poured a cup for her, and then poured another cup, in the hope that Solomon would take it, rather than her having to just tip it away, wasted.

"I've made you a coffee," Jackie said, as she opened the door to Solomon.

Solomon walked in, meticulously wiping his feet, one-two-three, one-two-three, on the mat before closing the door behind him.

"Really, Mrs Stark, that is extraordinarily kind of you," he said, straightening his long, dark coat with his hands as he stood in the porch. He reached a gloved hand out to accept the cup from Jackie, and took a polite sip as she turned away from him, and back to the kitchen.

"Come through," she called back, and Solomon took his cue to do without the awkwardness of removing shoes and coat, and followed her.

He took another sip of coffee, smiling and nodding in approval at the taste, a not-so-subtle compliment to his host, and his employer, before setting the cup down on a coaster on the breakfast bar. Jackie had perched on a high stool on the other side of the bar, clutching the cup with interlinked fingers.

Solomon reached inside his thick coat, and pulled out his phone, which he placed equidistantly between them. He pressed the button, and the screen lit up.

"Mrs Stark. There have been some developments. We believe we may have found a possible route to tracing those responsible for your husband's demise."

*Demise.* Not "death" or "murder". Jackie found this moleish man odd, not least the flourishes in his language when he spoke. How much of this man was façade and how much reality? Was he performing some kind of role, or was this really what he was like? He was hard to underestimate because of things like that – a transmitted sense of superiority and capability. It made Jackie feel more confident in his guidance, irrespective of how little she really knew of him.

Solomon's gloved hand pointed at a picture that was displayed on the phone screen. It was a picture of a picture. A framed photo showing a group of people mugging to camera in an impromptu huddle, some standing, some crouched. Jackie leant closer, trying to make out the faces on the screen.

Solomon zoomed the photo, and pointed again at two faces that now filled the screen.

"There, Mrs Stark. These are the people we are looking for. Tony and Eleanor Grace."

Jackie stared at them, these two smiling people, arm in arm. They looked so unassuming, so open and friendly, surrounded by friends. Her hate came easily.

It felt like the kitchen clock had stopped ticking, and the early morning clouds stopped creeping across the sky, as she scrutinised the picture. She concentrated on every laugh-line, every strand of hair and every wrinkle, as if this picture could reveal some clue or weakness that would enable her to crush them from hundreds of miles away with just the force of her anger.

Finally, she snapped back to the four-wall reality of her kitchen, Solomon patiently waiting for her next word.

"How?" she said.

"Well, Mrs Stark. This picture has given us a clue. We

believe that your husband was led to the assumption that it was Tony Grace who had the military background, but given what the rather unpleasant little man told us about the night in question, it is looking more likely that Eleanor Grace is the one who served."

Solomon continued.

"In any event, the picture clearly shows a regimental insignia on the flag which this group of people are posing in front of. I think this may well lead us to certain comrades and associates of the Graces, if our conclusion holds water. If that is the case, then we may very well have a way of tracking them down."

Jackie took a sip from her coffee. It was just barely holding onto some of its warmth, as distracted by this news, she had let it cool in her hands.

"So what do we have to do?" she said.

"Mrs Stark. As I mentioned, I have other associates. With good planning and the right motivation, these associates will be tasked with the search. I will simply tell them this – I want them to find anyone who has even the vaguest connection to the Graces, and then bleed them until they talk."

# 16

Johnny Gould, like many ex-military, was rigid in his routines. He did his shopping on the same day, he ate his meals at the same time, and he had a pint by himself, in the pub that he passed on the way home from the gym every Thursday.

He liked Thursdays. He enjoyed going to the gym. His solitary existence appreciated the change in atmosphere in a place like that – all noise and movement. He felt comfortable there, secure in the etiquette of the place, after a lifetime working out in similar gyms. And Thursday had always been his favourite day of the week – it was a half-step to the weekend, with Friday always feeling like deceleration, which he always liked to welcome with the salute of a pint.

The gym was his crutch. He was getting old, he knew, but being able to lift more weights than some half his age, or dragging compliments from others working out, gave him a little jolt of satisfaction. Life in the old dog yet. The army had hammered the requirement to be your best, and even years away from that life, he still lived by that mantra, at least when it came to getting sweat on his back. And in the same way, army life had instilled in him other habits which were hard to break, and that was the comfort of the babble of a pub, especially at night. He relaxed in the atmosphere of a good pub, and even if he was alone, which was nearly always the case, just being in a corner, watching the other punters reminded him of happier times, years ago.

He'd showered at the gym, changing into his usual jeans, t-shirt and ragged jumper which he refused to throw out, despite it being a patchwork of rough repairs and new tears. He smiled to himself when he pulled it out of his bag – the sweater was probably older than most of the people in the gym, but it had plenty of good wear left in it, he told himself, and he didn't see the point in throwing it away. He took some perverse enjoyment out of how bad it looked.

He slung his bag over his shoulder, left the gym with as warm a smile as he could manage to the receptionist, though she barely acknowledged him as she shuttled through her playlists looking for another house track to replace the seemingly identical house track currently playing through the gym speakers. The cold hit him when he opened the double doors to the outside – a rush of air that made his skin tingle, scouring the last warmth of the shower from him. He felt refreshed, and satisfied.

The night was quiet. The cold had sent most people into their cars, or their warm front rooms, and, as he walked his route, only counted one jogger pounding the pavement as opposed to the handful he usually saw.

"Good for you," Johnny said under his breath, as the jogger pushed on past him in the other direction, but the jogger was oblivious, focussing on whatever music he had cranked up on his headphones to distract him from the task at hand.

The pub was like a bright fire blazing light from the

corner of the dark street it was sat on. An old building, a pub for as long as anyone could remember, squatting in the middle of an estate like an old relative that was deliberately ignoring any hint to take itself away. The opaque windows obscured the inside of the pub, other than to allow the bright lights out into the street. An A-board stood chained to a lamppost on the pavement in front of the entrance, tied down like a vagabond in stocks for crimes against apostrophes. Two large plant pots stood on either side of the stepped entranceway, like bouncers. The pub hadn't changed in years. It was why Johnny liked it.

The rumble of conversation pitched up a few decibels as he opened the door, washing over him like a wave. The bar stretched out across the narrow room in front of him. A barman, whose name escaped Johnny, if he ever knew it, looked up, saw who it was, and nodded in acknowledgement. Johnny scanned the room, relieved to see that his usual corner booth was unoccupied, and deposited his bag there, before heading to the bar to order.

The barman had already reached up for a clean pint glass before Johnny approached, and rested his hand on the pump to pour Johnny's usual pint of IPA. The typical Thursday night routine commenced between them.

"Usual?" the barman said, preparing to pour.

Johnny, as always, looked up and down the row of pumps, taking in the logos of the keg badges displayed, as if this week would be the one where he tried something new.

"Usual, please," Johnny said, as always. The barman pulled the pint, and Johnny took the opportunity to scan the pub, mainly to avoid awkward small talk or a shared look as the pint was poured.

"Here you go," the barman said, setting the pint onto the bar towel stretched out in front of Johnny. Johnny already had the right money in his hand, again making a lie of any intention to choose a different drink, which he passed across to the barman. He took it without thanks, moving on to the next customer at the other end of the bar. Johnny didn't mind. He picked up the pint, and headed back to his corner table, carefully setting the drink down on a beer mat, before taking his seat. He sat with his back to the wall, so he could look out across the entire room.

He sighed with satisfaction. Everything was as it should be. He felt the comforting ache of his muscles after his workout, and relaxed into the warmth of routine. The pint tasted as refreshing as it always did, a small reward for him that he had convinced himself would be all he needed to repeat the process next week. He took a few moments to look over the other patrons in the pub, assessing whether there was any entertainment to be had from them, or whether he was better scanning through his phone for whatever idle distraction it would offer.

In the opposite corner, grouped around a similar table, were the five-a-side football team that were always here every Thursday as well. There were a few pitches at a nearby school, running leagues, and after their game, they always came in for a drink and a loudly fractious post-mortem. At the next table, there was a man in shirt and tie, sipping a cup of coffee and reading a book. Johnny liked to speculate why the man chose to sit in a pub, reading, rather than do it at home, conjuring increasingly outlandish flights of fancy to explain it. The next table to him were two young girls, maybe early 20s, over-dressed for a pub like this, grabbing some bottles of luridly-coloured drink before they head further into town for a night out.

A few workmen were propping up the bar – Johnny hadn't seen them before, but it wasn't unusual to see contractors, still in their work gear, in the pub. The pub offered a few cheap rooms, and a square meal, all for a reasonable price, and if there was work to be done around the town, these places offered somewhere where a saving could be made.

No drama here to vicariously enjoy, he thought, so pulled out his phone and opened one of several social media apps he wasted time on. The usual procession of motivational memes and pratfall videos filled the screen, and, after taking another sip of ale, started idly scrolling through them in some vain attempt to get current.

He was watching a video of a forklift driver pulling down an entire shelving system for bottles when he heard the double doors squeak open as someone new entered the pub. He looked up. A professional looking woman in her 30s had walked into the room, incongruous to the rest of the clientele.

She was dressed in a longish winter coat that came down to her knees, with a large satchel-bag over one shoulder. Below the coat, Johnny could make out that she was wearing a black skirt and tights, and heels, which were more about being smart than being ostentatious. Her long blonde hair was pulled back in a ponytail, which fell over the strap of her bag. He did his best to remain insouciant, pretending to be more interested in his phone, but he couldn't help watching as she spoke to the barman.

"Glass of red, please," she said. "Large." She smiled, sharing a "one of those days" expressions with the barman, by way of explanation. The barman smiled back, and reached for a bottle and a wine measure. The woman dug in her bag and pulled out a purse, and then, selected a credit card from the choice within.

"Card ok?" she said. The barman nodded pleasantly, and

walked to the other end of the bar, to retrieve the wireless credit card machine from its cradle. Like Johnny, this break in bar conversation afforded the woman the opportunity to take in the room. She looked one way, and then, turning the other, locked eyes with Johnny who had forgotten to avert his gaze as she was looking around. She smiled, warmly, and Johnny smiled back, awkward that he had been caught looking.

The barman offered the machine to the woman, who tapped her card on the unit, waited for the nod from the barman, and picked up her drink and turned to see if she could find somewhere to sit. There were a few tables unoccupied, but, for some reason, she walked directly to Johnny.

"Can I join you?" she said. Johnny couldn't place the accent, but it was southern and well-mannered, and just reinforced the impression that she wasn't typical for this place. "I'm stuck here for the night with work, and I haven't spoken to anyone sensible all day."

Johnny felt uncomfortable. His routine was sacrosanct, but he would never be so rude as to refuse a request like that. He was the sort of person who would politely wait to hold a door for someone irrespective of how far away they were. He was also the sort of person who would inwardly tut if he didn't get the requisite thanks, manners being everything to him. The frisson of new experience was appealing, but often, the safest option was the surest. She sat down opposite him, taking a lack of refusal as invitation.

"Thanks," she said. "I'm Ruth." The woman offered her hand to Johnny, who shook it politely.

"Johnny," said Johnny. He picked his phone up from the table, and slipped it inside his jeans pocket.

"Hi Johnny," Ruth said. "Sorry if I'm ruining your quiet night with yourself. Just tell me to do one if I go on too much." Johnny felt seen. He felt pathetic to have his night so perfectly summed up. It made him look predictable, which he was, but even so, he didn't like to have that truth reflected back at him. He found he wanted to work hard to appear intriguing.

"Oh, trust me, you're doing me a favour," he said. "Any excuse to get away from myself."

"That sounds a bit maudlin," Ruth said. "No need for maudlin, is there?"

"No, no. I didn't mean it like that. It's just this pub isn't the sort of place to come for engaging conversation, so I settle for the peace and quiet."

"Sounds like I've got a low bar to clear, then. Let's see how long I last until I crash into it."

"Plan," Johnny said, as warmly as he could. Ruth had raised her glass, and Johnny clinked it.

# 17

Johnny put his key into the deadbolt lock on his front door. His terraced house was on a hill, with a few steps up to the door. He couldn't quite believe what had happened tonight, but he certainly wasn't going to speak his incredulity out loud for fear of scaring things to a standstill. The door opened, and he looked back down the steps at Ruth, who stood looking back up at him, with a warm smile on her face.

She was attractive. Far more attractive than anyone he had spoken to in anything more than the most cursory fashion of late. Far too attractive than he could possibly hope for. Yes, he was in good shape, but he was late 40s now, with too many grey hairs and crow's feet to hide, and she was at least a decade younger than him, confident and positive. There was no way he was going to fold this hand he had been dealt. It might be the last best hand he ever had to play.

He stepped inside the hallway, flicked the light on, and then stepped to one side to let Ruth into the house, before closing the door behind her. She was looking left and right, politely taking in the décor and the layout, her face showing approval.

"It's nice. I like it," she said, nodding. Johnny was as thorough and diligent with his house as with all other aspects of his life. The hallway was tidy, shoes lined up in tight formation, and coats all hung on individual coat hooks. He put his keys in a keybowl on a narrow shelf above the hallway radiator, and gestured for Ruth to step into the front room.

"Here you go. Can I get you a drink?" he said.

Ruth took her satchel bag off from her shoulder, hung it over the newel at the bottom of the staircase, before doing the same with her coat. Reaching up, she pulled her hairband from her ponytail, and shook her hair down, smiling as she did it. She walked towards Johnny, slipped her hand around his waist, and stood on her toes in order to kiss him softly on the lips.

"Yes please," she said. "Whatever you've got."

Johnny felt a tingle run down his back, as if a shock of electricity was dancing down from his shoulders to the spot on his back where she had touched him. He felt young.

"I think I've got a whisky that's worth opening," he said, keen to get away, in order for him to get back as soon as possible. He smiled at Ruth, dithered briefly, then set off for the dark of the kitchen at the end of the hallway, past the stairs.

Ruth let him walk away, before walking into the front room, switching on the lights by the dimmer switch on the wall by the door. She adjusted it so the lights were low, and took the room in, drawn to the bookcase that stood in the corner of the room.

Johnny returned, with three glasses – two glasses of whisky for himself and Ruth, and a third glass filled with ice, just in case. He knew the snobbish protocols of whisky as well as the next man, thanks to several past embarrassments from his so-called betters in his forces days, but he wasn't prepared to torpedo tonight by boorishly pointing out any faux-pas. Hell, she could drink pond water out of a shoe, for all he cared.

Ruth was half-crouching at the bookcase, running her fingers along the spines of the books, presumably making some kind of assessment of him from the books he had chosen to keep, and display. He felt defensive.

"I should really freshen that lot up. I don't read as much as I'd like," he said.

"Look at you, you big pseud, you," Ruth said, pulling out a heavier book from the shelf. "Hunter S Thompson? Have you read it?"

Johnny laughed.

"Er, well. Some of it," he said. Ruth laughed.

"Ha! You fraud! They all say that," she said, sliding the book back in its place. Her finger danced along the spines again, settling on a hardback. "Now you're talking."

She pulled the book out, and weighed it in her hands, flipping it from front to back cover. Johnny had sat down on the sofa, deliberately avoiding the armchair in the hope that she would sit down next to him. He set the three glasses on the coffee table that held the middle of the room, and looked up at her, to see if he could see which book she had chosen.

"Atwood. You do surprise me."

"How dare you!" he mock-protested. "And I have read it, before you say anything."

"Fighting against the cruel yoke of our male oppressor," she said, walking across to him, book in hand, with a wry grin on her face. She looked at the simple cover again, before moving it in her hands until she was holding it by the spine.

Johnny was fighting for breath before he realised what had happened. Quicker than he could comprehend, she had jammed the long edge of the book across his throat, and with her other hand, smashed into the book spine as hard as she could, sending him reeling. His hands flailed as he slumped backwards, his eyes wide as his brain struggled to keep up with what was happening.

Ruth leapt onto him, straddling him. She still had hold of the book, but had now moved it in her grasp so the flat side of the hardback was pressed onto his face. She struck the book with her other hand again, this time breaking his nose. Again and again she struck it with her palm, scrambling his senses with each blow. He remembered an idle thought in his head, as the blows smashed, pondering who was making the feeble gurgling sound until, just as he lost consciousness, he realised it was him.

JOHNNY MADE his way back to awareness tentatively, as if his brain was being activated in careful, gradual stages. Oddly, it was taste that registered with him first – the impression of iron and rust – which was soon augmented with a crushing blast of pain, seemingly from all parts of him.

He couldn't move, and couldn't see why, his vision still smeared in a dark he couldn't shift. Cognition began to knit together and he was eventually able to make tentative efforts to assess his situation. His eyes weren't covered, and the dark was external, though as his eyes became accustomed to the lack of light, shapes began to coalesce. He was in his box room, on the first floor of his house. He could hear music coming from downstairs, a familiar chorus acting as a lighthouse with which to find his way back to his thoughts. Paul Weller. An old favourite, never far from his stereo for thirty years.

His head hurt, and his mouth felt full. He tried to turn his head, but an instant, vicious pain clamped him to the seat. His next movement was slower, testing the boundaries of the agonies that grasped him. The pain had tried to force a yelp from him, but even through the sting, he was surprised that no sound came.

He tried to make another sound, quieter this time. A simple noise to just see if he could. He couldn't. The sound that he heard himself make shocked him; a feeble, hoarse croak, gurgling thick with the blood that was in his mouth.

"Don't bother," said a voice from the fogged gloom to his right. He couldn't turn his head, unwilling to face the burn of that pain again so quickly, instead concentrating on establishing exactly the scope of his situation. He realised that he was bound, his arms and legs tightly strapped to the office chair that he kept in this box room, a hangover from a doomed attempt to turn it into an office before the boxes and bags washed over it like a flood.

He was fully awake now. It was nearly impossible for him to find a part of his body that didn't burn with pain; a kaleidoscope of agonies that ebbed and flowed with every subtle shift in his posture. The voice spoke again, quietly but still with a clarity that he understood every word despite the loud music coming from the downstairs stereo.

"I'm going to be speak very plainly to you, Johnny. And I need you to listen. Don't try and respond until I ask you to, and don't try anything else," it said.

It was a woman's voice, but it didn't sound like the woman he had come home with. The woman who had attacked him. It was an octave lower, and had the traces of a regional accent dancing around the edges of the words. He turned his head as much as he could stand, gritting his teeth as the pain came, and blood stung his tongue again. Leaning against the wall, in the half-light of the room, was Ruth, or the woman he thought of as Ruth.

The hair had changed. The woman here had short, cropped hair instead of the long cut, but even with that change, and the removal of her make-up, he could see that it was Ruth. But it was the change in expression that shook him the most. The soft edges had been ground off, and her entire expression was one of control and confidence. Her arms were crossed across her chest, and she was staring at him with cold, unblinking eyes.

"Okay," she said. "You can see where you are. What kind of situation you are in. I want you to know something very plainly – this is not a negotiation. I am going to ask you some questions, and you are going to give me some answers. If I have any suspicion that you are trying to deceive me, then I am going to hurt you. If you give me any reason to think you are wasting my time, then I am going to hurt you. I am very good at hurting people."

Ruth paused. Another familiar song waltzed up from downstairs, filling the space that Ruth had left.

"I know what usually happens now. So, instead of you wasting words and energy on trying to find some avenue to debate, which will only irritate me and lead to me hurting you, we are going to sit here quietly for five minutes, just so you can come to terms with your position. I strongly advise you to stay completely silent."

Johnny found logic, and clung to it. It was all he had.

He couldn't move and he was hurt. Escape was going to be impossible. There was no-one coming to save him – he lived alone, in his terraced house, and he had heard enough noises and loud music coming through the walls of the adjoining houses that any hope of raising enough chaos to attract attention or intervention were going to be in vain. So he was left to face whatever this woman had planned for him.

What could he uncover about her? He liked to think of himself as a hard man, who had been in enough fights in his time to think that he could handle himself, yet she had taken him down with no little ease. Using the book was clever, as it enabled her to completely over-ride any physical mismatch, and she used it scientifically, taking him down in short order. So she was capable. Trained. And had clearly been in situations like this many times before.

What did she want? Johnny knew people who didn't care much for him – who didn't? But nothing more than hot words about a parking space on the road, and a few old comrades who just didn't find his loud jokes funny, on the rare occasions they were in the same room. But no-one who would set a woman like this on him. She was professional, and professional costs money. More money than any lame punchline or parking dispute was worth.

Clearly, this wasn't an accident. This woman was here for him specifically. There was no jealous lover, or business rival. He had no interest in any of that since he left the army.

The army. It must be that. It had to be that. A foreign force, or mercenary vendetta? Sure, he had seen action, and he had definitely killed people. More than he liked to think about. But what was so special about him that would have someone organise this kind of response?

"Time's up," Ruth said. "I'm grateful you didn't waste our time. Keep that in mind."

Ruth flexed her shoulders, and bounced herself from

leaning against the wall, so she could walk a couple of quiet steps to stand square in front of him. She had a knife in her hand – one of his knives, pulled from the knife-block that sat on his kitchen counter downstairs. Johnny tried to project impassiveness, but he was scared. She held all the power, and he had precious little to barter with.

He looked at her again, fully this time. It was as if the woman he had met a few hours ago had been completely hollowed out, and replaced with something *other*. The features were the same, the build was the same, but everything was off-kilter. That Ruth was long-gone and she was replaced by something that terrified him.

"I'm going to show you some pictures now, and then I'm going to ask you some questions about them," she said. "We are going to go slowly, because I want everything you say..." She giggled at this, a handful of sharp sounds that fell like darts on his ears. "Excuse me. I meant to say every *response* to be the truth, without you trying to deceive me. Nod if you understand."

Johnny nodded. He felt hot, yet the sweat on his spine chilled him. The tiniest hint of a smile twitched at the corners of Ruth's mouth, then vanished, replaced again with death-mask inscrutability.

Ruth picked up a phone she had set down on the desk behind Johnny, reaching over him slowly and deliberately, as if she was daring him to try and break his bonds. Her body brushed against his, the tenderness of the touch felt as sharp as the knife she held in her other hand. She moved to stand behind him, holding the phone in her right hand, her arm reaching round him so the phone screen was in front of his face. Her other hand rested on his left shoulder, the cold of the knife blade pressed up against his neck, a steel reminder of what was promised. The screen lit up.

Johnny focussed on the phone. It was information, and information was the only way he was going to get out of this, giving or receiving. The screen displayed a picture of a group of people, mugging for the camera. He tried to concentrate, pulling names through his concussion. He knew them. Of course he knew them.

"I want to know if you recognise this person," Ruth said. Her fingernail tap-tapped on the screen, indicating a face.

That face was the face of a friend. Someone he had gone to war with, who had supported him, and trained with him, and laughed with him. Someone he loved, like family. Seeing that face brought a burst of emotion with it – a sorrow of loss and of memory. His eyes filled with tears, and his face creased.

"Concentrate," Ruth said. Each syllable was underscored by the blade tapped on his shoulder.

Johnny nodded, shakily. It felt like a betrayal, but every extra second she granted him was another second for him to try and find a way out.

"Okay. Listen carefully. I'm going to say a name now. I want you to tell me if that is the name of the person in the picture." Ruth paused after speaking, ensuring that Johnny had time to fully process what was being asked of him.

"Eleanor Grace," Ruth said.

Hearing the name spoken out loud detonated his foundations like explosives. His lip trembled, his fingers stretched and flexed, bound to the chair, and his eyes streamed. A bubble of snot flushed from his nose. He moaned, his mouth full of blood and pain but no words. He nodded, defeated. Maybe if he could pacify this woman – this devil – he could find a way to getting out of here, and warning Eleanor, somehow.

He closed his eyes. In the maelstrom of his mind, at the

eye of that storm, was the firm ground of his training. It brought with it a cold reasoning that he needed. He was a soldier. He had a duty to his comrades, more than anything else. He knew he was going to die tonight. Dying well was all he had left to strive for.

Ruth took the phone away from in front of him, and stood up behind him, hovering over him like Death itself. Each passing second was another second that he had to come to terms with his situation. He was grateful for it.

Ruth displayed the picture for Johnny again, resuming her position with one hand draped over him, holding the phone, and the other pressed against his throat. The taste of blood in his mouth was sharp, and he couldn't help his gag reflex causing him to cough some gobbets, some splashes landing on the screen.

"Dirty boy," Ruth said, wiping the phone on his chest to clear the blood from the screen. She pressed the button again, the screen lighting up, some of the faces now smeared, as if they were being erased by some godly force. Ruth wiped her thumb over the screen, revealing the faces once again.

"I'm going to point at each of these faces. I want you to tell me which one Eleanor Grace would call if she was in a spot of trouble. Do you understand?"

Johnny tried to find words, to tell this woman "no" but nothing would come. His mouth opened and closed, and all he heard was a sorrowful moan. It was his voice, somehow, as if he had already become a soulless wraith, cursed to haunt this sorry little room.

"Now, now," Ruth said, the knife held firmer now against his neck. "I know you can do this. Just tell me what I need to know, and it'll all be over."

All be over. He knew what that meant. Would it be a

painful end or a quick one? Is that all he could hope to gain now?

"Is it him? Or would she go to him?" Ruth said, each question underlined by a finger-tap on the glass phone screen. The knife she held in her other hand had shifted, a bloodthirsty dance around his neck until she had the tip pushed against his Adam's apple, ready to plunge in.

Johnny moaned again, the sound all he had to ward off her questions.

"Oh, now. I'm going to start cutting more things away. I know where all of these people are. You can't save them. All you can do is save yourself. Save yourself from some pain," Ruth said, in the same cold voice. The lack of emotion didn't scare him. It was when she had laughed before. That there was something maniacal hiding under this uniform exterior scared him more than anything he had ever known.

"I'm going to ask again. Very slowly. I want you to tell me which one of these people Eleanor Grace would go to for help," she said.

The knife remained poised, ready to impale him and bleed him out, or worse, move to somewhere less vital and start carving away. He tried to look away from the screen, stare at the wall, at the door, at anything. Find something to give him some respite, like a child hiding under the covers until the monsters left.

"Just show me who. Then it's done. Easy as that," Ruth said, dragging the photo across the screen with her fingertip.

Johnny said nothing.

Ruth sighed, and tapped and dragged on the phone until a new screen was displayed. Johnny looked sideways as her finger moved, trying to see what was coming next.

"Look," she said. The screen was now set to "camera".

She pressed an icon in the corner of the screen, and the view changed.

The phone screen now displayed a face, bruised and bloody, with one eye partially shut, and clotted blood smeared around the mouth. Some monster pulled up from some fierce hell. Behind that horrific face, he could see Ruth, a quiet smile on her face. The realisation was slow, but hit him like a gunshot. It was him. His face. Ruined, bloody and unrecognisable.

"That's where we are. That's how you look now. It is going to get an awful lot worse for you if you don't give me what I want. One little nod, and it's over." Ruth spoke quietly, into his ear, the voice coming from behind him, as the lips moved on the little screen in front of his eyes.

"I'm going to make it easy for you. I'm going to ask you the question one more time, and if you don't give me an answer, I'm going to take an eye." As she said this, Ruth reset the phone screen with one hand, back to the photograph of Eleanor, of him, and of the rest of their unit. At the same time, the knife moved from his neck, her grip shifting, until it was poised directly in front of his left eye. Ready to peck it out like a bird with some carrion. He tried to scream, and then he understood everything.

The mouth on the screen had opened, and a loud muffled moan filled the room. But no words would come. No words *could* come. His open mouth revealed why he couldn't speak. His tongue had been cut out.

"Who would Eleanor Grace go to? Just tell me, and we're done."

Johnny stared at the screen as the faces were shuttled across it, slowly. His breathing was heavy and slow, and all that he could hear, the music from downstairs having stopped as the vinyl record had reached the end of side.

Competing thoughts jostled for primacy, until he burned them away like chaff until all he had left was one. He could feel Ruth tense slightly, presumably readying herself to make good on her promise, his mouth proof enough of her conviction.

He knew what he had to do. He was a soldier. And his unit was his family. Betrayal was not an option. Everything else was irrelevant. He closed his eyes, made his cold, hard world immaterial, and made peace with what he had to do. He pulled his head back, fighting against Ruth's tensed arm around the back of his head. It was what he was banking on, though. That resistance. She was expecting him to pull away, and had braced hard for it. Suddenly, he pushed as hard as he could in the opposite direction, impaling himself on the knife.

# 18

Jackie Stark was nervous. She felt like she was being beset on all sides, with the worry that even just one more thing would be all that it would take for her to buckle, once and for all. She was being eased into a new life, deeper and deeper, not realising quite how far in she had been pulled until she was already too far in. She was still *Jackie.* The matriarch, her family relying on her for her strength and her spirit, as they always did. To them, Jim was always the comic relief, as far as they were concerned, with Jackie being the only one who was allowed to see the other side of him, ruthless and driven, and feared by those who needed to be scared.

But that position was vacant now, and she was the one who had to fill it. There were others who would happily and greedily take the throne. Jackie knew, though, that as tempting as it was for her to relinquish any claim to the organisation, or more particuarly, the assets of the organisation, letting go would likely lead to a more final outcome for her, and the family. It was the way of that world. To be the king, you had to kill the king. Or queen.

How had Jim done it? How did he balance a cosy home life of grandchildren and family meals with this constant pressure of watchfulness? Jackie was being asked to make decisions that would affect not just her, but potentially people she cared for. How did Jim manage not to be crippled by the anxiety of making a mistake that would bring it all down around him? Jackie drew deep on the cigarette she was smoking, exhaling doubt with the smoke. By being completely and utterly single-minded, she thought. That's what she needed to be.

She looked at Solomon, sat in the passenger seat of the car that his underling, Parker, was driving. He seemed like such an odd little man, mole-ish and meek-looking, but even in this short time in her life, Jackie could see he had a reptilian implacability that obviously served him well. He was one of those rare, and unsettling, people who never seemed to laugh. A smile, on occasion, but never with any warmth or humour. If she was honest with herself, he scared her. Far more than Parker, who dominated the front of the car, even though it was a large SUV. She had the feeling that Parker would kill you in seconds. Solomon would take his time over it, for no good reason other than he might squeeze something like enjoyment out of it, or have some new method of execution that he wanted to test. She was relieved, if that was the word, that they were working for her, and not against her.

She was being driven to a meeting, in one of the offices that Jim had run his taxi business from. His policy of hiding in plain sight was good enough for her, so she didn't feel it untoward to continue his practice of holding meetings for the real Stark organisation behind the gossamer thin veneer of respectability. And it was thin – Jim Stark was a name that inspired terror in the city. He would wield retribution decisively and remorselessly, vanishing enough names that he became an almost-mythical figure. But though it was thin, no-one had ever had the will or desire to tear through, and bring Jim and his backroom world out into the light, thanks to a combination of unmarked graves and greased palms.

This was to be her audition. She had called the meeting, at Solomon's gentle prompting, summoning the most senior members of the Stark business that hadn't been cut down by Tony and Eleanor Grace. Jackie wanted to have the whole world thrown at the Graces, and damn the consequences, but Solomon had given quiet counsel and firm assurances that their time would come, and that reminding people that there was still a Stark at the top of the tree was a requirement that couldn't be put off any longer. If she whistled in the dark long enough, maybe she could convince herself that she was capable of this, and then everyone else might just believe her as well.

The car pulled up on the busy street, parking itself over the road from the office, a few hundred yards back from being adjacent. This was good practice, and Jackie was used to it, rare though it was that she was brought anywhere where the distance between her life and Jim's work life would narrow. It was always best to take a breath, and take in the environment, as best you could. Jim hid behind a role – the jovial small businessman – but before he allowed himself to show that role to the world, he made sure he knew what he was walking into. He would always check for the unusual. A car that looked out of place, perhaps with two plainclothes policemen sitting in it, eager to curry favour from their bosses, despite Jim having most of them on his payroll in one form or another. Or worse, perhaps there might be someone ready to make a more fatal intervention, to claim turf, or avenge some wrong. Jim was able to make a cool assessment, drawing on years of navigating his world. Jackie tried to do the same.

The street was full of the usual people at this time of day. Single mothers wheeling twin prams, teenagers who saw school as an occasional distraction rather than any kind of obligation, the oblivious pensioners stiffly walking along the middle of the pavement. Jackie took them all in, as if she was looking at them for the first time. A thought blindsided her. Why hadn't Jim followed his own rules a few weeks ago? Why had he let hot blood overcome cool thoughts and allow him to put himself in the crosshairs? She was angry at him. Angry enough to swear that she would not make that same mistake.

"Now?" she asked, breaking the silence in the car.

"I believe so," Solomon said, having completed his own checks. He had Parker, who was formidable, but his habits were carved on stone tablets, and no temptation would ever see them changed.

Parker took the hint, and opened the driver's door, before moving around the car to open the door for Jackie. Once she was out, he side-stepped, and did the same for Solomon, waiting for his boss to get out of the car, before taking his place behind the pair of them. He stood above them, a mountain more than willing to break thunderheads on his back.

They moved through the foot traffic easily, the mere presence of Parker acting like an Arctic icebreaker, the pedestrians almost subconsciously moving aside as their group walked towards the office.

As they approached the front of the office, Solomon took a quick stride in order to open the door for Jackie, which he held open for Parker to enter after Jackie. There were two doors at the front of the building – a public entrance, and one for employees only. The public door led to a small lobby and a counter, in the event of any walk-ins from the street, and the other opened directly into an office space of desks and chairs. Solomon knew what he was doing by opening the door for Jackie and Parker. He understood first impressions, and it was important for whoever was inside, waiting for them, to understand that, firstly, Jackie had arrived, and secondly, that Parker was very definitely associated with her. Parker was the heavy artillery, drawing attention, and Solomon could then be the sniper, who would only demonstrate his less immediately obvious talents if the need arose.

It had the desired effect. Heads turned as soon as Jackie walked in, as expected. But then there was a very obvious widening of eyes, as those inside saw the man who walked in behind her. Solomon followed at the rear, and immediately began making assessments of the people inside, easier to read with their attention distracted.

Jackie knew most of the faces staring across the room at her. They had congregated in the middle of the taxi office, perched on the desks and leaning on a couple of filing cabinets, some with mugs of tea or coffee in their hands. Clearly they had all seen a benefit in being early, desperate for gossip, or eager to strategise, as they waited for Jackie. It would've been a poker game, everyone testing everyone else in order to best assess who might make a play first, or who remained loyal to anyone named Stark. Jackie took in the faces, all staring at her, smiling yet at the same time weighing up those in attendance. Looking for allies, or threats, or those who remained to be persuaded one way or the other.

"Nice and early, then," she said, as she walked in. Parker stood behind her, implacable as ever, until Solomon stepped around him, and indicated to one of the doors at the back of the room.

"Mrs Stark," Solomon said. "I wonder if there is anywhere where we can discuss with the gentlemen in a little more privacy? Perhaps through here?"

"Good idea, Mr Solomon," Jackie said. "There's a meeting room through here. I'm sure these lads have tidied it up for us?"

One of the men, a thin, grey man called Hastings broke away from the rest of them, and opened the door to the meeting room, eager to see if the room was in a presentable state. He ran this office, and the taxis that reported here, part of a de-facto fiefdom in this part of the city that Jim had carved up as he conquered district after district. Hastings always appeared nervous and on edge, and the distraction of gossip had meant he had not thought ahead to check on the state of the place before the meeting was convened.

Jackie enjoyed the effect she had on him, and hopefully some of the others as well. She wanted them nervous. Hastings audibly swore as he stepped into the meeting room, before hurriedly sweeping a few polystyrene takeaway containers and paper coffee cups from the tables in there into a waste paper bin he had grabbed from the corner of the room.

"How are we, Hast?" she said, "Good to go?"

"All good, Jackie," Hastings replied. "Just some messy bastards who really should know better."

There was sniggering from some of the other men, visibly delighting in Hastings' embarrassment. Even that was a tell – Jackie saw who was laughing and who wasn't. The ones who remained quiet were the ones to watch out for.

Solomon again indicated with his arm that Jackie should step ahead. She looked at him, and he pursed his lips and almost imperceptibly nodded. *All is as it should be*, his expression indicated. *This is under control.* She walked towards the room, determinedly.

She walked past the crowd of men with a confident smile on her face, but a fixed, determined look in her eyes. Solomon followed on behind her and Parker after him. The men all watched her walk past, before they gradually got themselves to their feet to follow on after.

The room was windowless, with a couple of desks pushed together to make something approaching a conference table. Hastings was still scurrying around, tidying papers and moving chairs, angry at himself that he had embarrassed himself like this in front of everyone. Solomon pulled a chair out at the top of the table, and Jackie sat down. Solomon sat next to her, and Parker stood behind them both, eyes on the door watching the men file in with cold eyes.

"Who are these, Jackie?" one of the men said. His name was Connor, a thirty-something man in a loose fitting, short-sleeve shirt, not loose enough to disguise the hefty stomach he hefted around in front of him. "Stark employees only, surely? I've left my fellas outside. It's only polite, no?"

"They stay, Connor," Jackie said. Here it comes. The testing. Gently at first, but she'd seen this before, even with Jim. She resolved to respond as he would've done – firmly and decisively. "Now, are we all in? Shut that door will you, Hastings, love?"

Hastings snapped back to concentrating on the matter in

hand, and stopped his fussing and tidying. He did as he was bidden, and closed the door, and sat down in the last empty chair. There were seven men now sat down, plus Jackie and Solomon, all eyes trained on the woman at the head of the table.

"If I can just introduce Mr Solomon," Jackie said, the eyes of the room now turning to the odd, little man sat next to her. He smiled thinly, nodding in acknowledgement of his introduction. "Mr Solomon has been helping me manage things since Jim..." – Jackie faltered, briefly – "...since Jim left us."

Jackie dug her sharp nails into her leg, angry at letting emotion show itself, however briefly. She gathered herself, returning to the words she had rehearsed in her head in the car on the way over.

"Thank you all for coming today. I am grateful that you have all continued to show up for work, and that our business is still operating, given all the...upheaval of the last month."

Mr Solomon turned slowly to Parker, beckoning him to come close. He whispered something to Parker, who nodded, and then walked the length of the room, opened the door, and walked out, closing the door behind him.

"My apologies, Mrs Stark," Solomon said.

Jackie continued.

"I wanted to get you all together for us to discuss exactly who is going to do what, and how we are going to continue as an organisation. I don't need to tell you how difficult things have been for all of us lately, and amongst everything else, how difficult it has been to work through the changes that have been...forced on us, but we need to pull together and keep going."

Connor interrupted. It had to be him. Loud and boorish,

traits that served him well when barking orders in one of the other taxi offices that he ran, in a different part of the city, but grating and challenging here. He wasn't liked by anyone, and Jim had had to be talked down from making a more terminal decision regarding his prospects on more than one occasion, dissuaded only by the money that he brought to the table. He was going to be Jackie's biggest problem here, she knew.

"Jackie, it's all fucked. Jim's dead, we've lost all the heads, and no-one knows what's going on anymore. We haven't had any decent work for weeks, as no-one trusts us to pay our debts until we can prove that we're good for it. We've no money, Jackie. We're on our arses here."

There were a few supportive grumbles from the others, pleased that Connor had vocalised their grievances, but not brave enough to be the first to say it. He used the word "work" but he meant "product".

Stark had understood very quickly that the best way to control the black market somewhere was to control the transit of goods, and that's when he made the decision to tailor the taxi business into transporting more than just the late night piss-heads or the early morning commuters. From controlling the transport it was a straightforward enough evolution into supplying product as well, leveraging their monopoly on transport until the motley gaggle of local dealers had to choose between paying a tithe or being cut loose to wither on the vine. In time, Stark controlled the business from start to finish. His drugs, his drivers, his transport, his money.

But Stark was dead. His problem-solvers were dead along with him. It just left whoever was in this room to pick up the pieces, and all of them were looking at Jackie to see if she had anything like the answers they needed.

"Please, Connor, there is a way out of this. We didn't spend all these years building this for it to fall over now," Jackie said, trying to maintain a calm voice despite a building frustration within her.

"We? We? Sorry, Jackie, but what have you actually done here?" Connor was letting his mouth run now, so full of indignation he completely disregarded any need to be politic. "Far as I can see, it was Jim who ran the business, and you've come here to, what? Try and fill his chair?"

Jackie saw a slight movement in the corner of her eye, as Mr Solomon just shifted in his chair, slightly. A change of posture so he could better observe Connor, as if he had acknowledged that this is the person in the room that needed more of his attention. He said nothing. Maybe he was letting Connor follow the old adage – "say nothing and let people think you are an idiot, or say something and remove all doubt..."

One of the men sat next to Connor, an older man called Pete, could see which way this was going, and felt brave enough to say something, when the rest of the room were doing their best to stay well out of the to-and-fro until they felt confident they knew who held the upper-hand.

"Connor, perhaps best to just take it down a little bit," he said.

"Oh fuck off, Pete, lad," Connor said, hot blood shutting down any intervention. "Jim did alright for us, but even if he hadn't managed to get himself killed by a fucking *bouncer* and his bird, then maybe it was time for a change in any case."

Jackie felt the hairs on the back of her arms bristle. Insults and outright insubordination now. Jim would've had this man disappeared for speaking like this, and might have done something a little more overtly dramatic if he had dared say this to his wife with him around.

"Connor. Stop. That's enough. We've taken a blow. A real blow. More than that, we've lost..." Her voice quavered again, momentarily, but she pushed past that weakness this time. "You know what we've lost. But we have infrastructure. We have workers. And we have funds, right? No-ones taken that from us."

Connor was still red in the face, but he wasn't raising his voice anymore. He spoke with a quiet venom instead.

"We don't have any product, love," the last word thrown like an insult. Little lady, you're out of your depth, it said. "Well, tell you something. *You* don't. I just might have. Might have found new friends who can sort us out. All of us."

"I'm pleased to hear it, Connor," Jackie said. "I think we can all agree that new arrangements are going to be a huge help for us now, especially now that news has spread about our situation."

"You aren't getting it, Jackie. Way I see it is that you've no right to just sit at the top of the table just because of the ring you wear on your finger, and the way I see it is that you have done sweet fuck all in building this thing other than putting a plate on the table when your old man got home. Well, he's gone, love. And we haven't. So, here's what I'm going to do. I'm going to go and sort out some new gear for us, and then, I'm going to sit where you are sitting, and you can go and sit on a beach somewhere and leave this business to those who know what they're doing." Connor stood as he said all this, standing with such a jolt that his chair clattered against the back wall. He jabbed his finger to punctuate his words, then, once he had finished, flung his chair out of the way, and left, the door slammed behind him.

Then there was silence, as everyone in the room looked

at Jackie, then Solomon, then each other, as they each weighed up how to behave in the aftermath of the power-play they had just seen played out in front of them. Pete had the years, and enough goodwill in the bank, that he felt that he could speak first, without obvious risk of consequence. A calming voice.

"He's upset, Jackie. I'm sure he'll reflect on that," Pete said.

"We're all upset, Pete," Jackie said. "But I need to make one thing clear. The name of this firm is Stark. And that's how it's going to stay."

"Of course, of course," Pete said. "I'm sure you have the support of everyone else." Pete looked around at the rest of the men there, some wide-eyed, some grim-faced.

"Not yet," Jackie said. "Listen."

Jackie stood up, indicating that this was going to be her last word, for now.

"I'm going to say this for everyone to understand, and I want you to tell everyone who needs to hear it. I am in charge now. I am going to get everything we need in place so we can start earning again. I will not put up with any arguments. None. And if any of you speak to him – " she jabbed her finger at the door – "you better tell him that just because of the years he's worked for us, I'm going to let his little tantrum slide, but if he tries anything like that again..."

Jackie let the last sentence drift. The implication was clear.

"Ok, meeting over. I'll call us together when I have news. Earn with what you have, but take no risks," she said.

The men stood up, and went to leave. Hastings had scurried to open the door, to let everyone out, recoiling when he saw that Parker was stationed just outside. Hastings took a step back inside the room, unconsciously.

Another voice spoke. Solomon.

"Gentlemen, thank you for your attendance today. Please don't hesitate to contact me with any queries or grievances. I will then, of course, report them to Mrs Stark. Please do take one of my business cards from my colleague who is waiting just outside the room."

Jackie was again glad that Solomon was there. He was creating another shield around her, this time from her own employees. A barrier that would ensure that she had the time and space to maintain her poise, and buy some time to come up with the correct response, especially when her every word was going to be carefully scrutinised.

The men filed out, quietly. Parker had reached inside his jacket pocket, and opened a silver card holder, so he could hand out business cards to each man as they passed. Parker was a huge man, and knew it, and as each man passed him, he seemed to subtly look down over them, a white-text-on-black card in his hand for each person. Power. It was all about power. Every little gain was worth it. Jackie could see that. Maybe most of the men were too long in the tooth to be intimidated by something like this, but maybe one or two of them were, and that made it worthwhile. Solomon and Parker were new to them, and the unknown was where fears were sculpted. Be vague and mysterious and let them all talk. Gossip would reveal their intentions.

Once they had all filed out, Hastings nervously put his head around the door, briefly looking round at Parker, who stared at him with an implacable expression.

"Is there anything else, Mrs Stark?" he said, eager to be back to bullying those under him.

"We're done. I'm just going to have the room for five more minutes, thank you," she replied.

Hastings needed no further invitation, and scurried off,

out onto the street hoping that a nicotine fix would help him get a grip of himself. Jackie smiled as he went – one of the members of this committee wouldn't dare stand up to her, at least. Solomon nodded at Parker, and Parker quietly closed the door, leaving Solomon and Jackie alone in the room together.

"That went as expected, Mrs Stark," Solomon said. "Exactly as expected."

"You think?" Jackie said, vaguely unsure exactly what had just happened, and very much unsure whether it was good or bad.

"Quite so," Solomon said. "We have to let these men all find their feet in this brave, new world. They will have developed certain habits. We need to coax them towards developing new ones. Or we need to usher them quietly towards the exit door."

"The exit door...?" Jackie said. Was this a euphemism?

"We'll cross that bridge when we come to it, Mrs Stark. Try not to concern yourself. Our friend who became upset. He is going to be very useful to us. At times like this it is best not to let their little resentments and frustrations simmer. Much more useful for us if we know exactly what we have to deal with, and more precisely, exactly who we have to pay attention to. In my experience, there is always someone who voices their discomfort in a loud manner. What we very much need to be aware of are those who agree with that position, but do so in a much more circumspect fashion. And there will be some of those."

"Should I be worried? Will they try something?" Jackie could only think of her family, and how the Stark name might not be the insurance it once was.

"They may indeed, yes," Solomon said, matter-of-factly. "But this is the world we live in. This is what we have to prepare for. But Mr Stark spent his money well, I can assure you."

"Do I need to warn anyone? My family?"

"Mrs Stark," Solomon held her hand in his gloved hands, and looked her in the eye. "It will be us that will be doing the warning."

# 19

Jackie, Solomon and Parker sat in the car, Solomon keen to take advantage of the privacy in the event he needed to make more reassurances with Jackie. The car would be a safe place, away from the rank and file where Jackie could relax a little, and Solomon could offer guidance, before they made a decision on next steps.

Jackie had lit a cigarette almost as soon as Parker had closed her door, her hand nervous as the adrenaline raced around her body, any effort of control no longer needed behind closed doors. No words were said, Solomon letting Jackie have the time she needed to compose herself, to weigh up what had just happened, and come to her own conclusions about her situation.

A phone chirruped.

"Do please excuse me, Mrs Stark," Solomon said, before reaching into his inside pocket and retrieving his phone, checking the screen to see who was calling. He answered.

The conversation was clearly one-sided. Solomon simply listened, occasionally making noises to show understanding, before he eventually finished the call with one command - "Continue."

The phone was put back inside his jacket pocket, and he turned slightly to indicate that he was addressing Jackie.

"Mrs Stark. That was an acquaintance of ours, who I have tasked with carrying out enquiries into the location of those responsible for the death of your husband. Our colleague has reported that progress has been made, and that a line of investigation has opened up that may very well lead to those we seek."

The cigarette quietly crackled as Jackie took a long drag, looking out of the window at a different world that carried on outside. She took another drag, opened the car window with a button press, and flicked the cigarette butt into the street. She closed the window with a whirr.

"Good. I want them dead, Mr Solomon. Dead," she said in a quiet, steady voice. It was as if a new personality was pushing through the debris of the old one, taking its first few breaths of life. A harder, colder version of herself.

"This is our goal, Mrs Stark. Let me assure you that our associate is something of an expert at finding those who wish to remain hidden. And she is gifted in making those who may have some information share it with us."

"She?" Jackie said.

"Oh yes. A very gifted individual. Very gifted indeed."

Jackie nodded. She was getting accustomed to this world, the vague impressions that she had from Jim becoming more defined now she was swimming in these waters herself. She always knew what Jim did, and had a good idea what happened to people that were "disappeared" but now she was thinking about the methods in detail, cultivating a bloodlust of her own, all built on that bedrock of revenge.

"We have a very strong idea of who the Graces may turn to after their escape from the city," Solomon continued. "They do not appear to have a great many friends, given their tendency to move from one place to another. That is, of course, a disadvantage for them."

"What makes you think they'll go to someone, and not just start afresh somewhere?"

"A good point. But looking at their history, and the nature of their upheaval from Norfolk, when Mr Stark first ordered sanction against them, then I would contend that they do not have much in the way of ready resources, or, at least, organising any resources that they may be able to still access will prove difficult. Therefore, I think it is more than likely that they will need support somehow, until they are in a position to make more concrete arrangements."

Solomon adjusted his gloves, pulling them tighter onto his fingers. An idiosyncrasy as he prepared his words carefully.

"And, Mrs Stark, I'm afraid to say that Mr Stark did underestimate them. The nature of Mr Stark's demise does illustrate that the Graces, when properly challenged, are quite scrupulous with their planning and preparation. I think we should work under the assumption that they will continue to take all due care even after leaving the city having killed your husband."

Jackie felt like she was being scrutinised by Solomon as he spoke – him testing her for emotion, in order to best ascertain how she was dealing with this new position that life had thrust upon her. But she was finding her feet now. She didn't show a flicker of doubt.

"I don't care how long it takes. Just find them. And then, no waiting and no debating. Just get them somewhere where we kill them, as quickly as possible. If it hurts, then all the better," Jackie let some anger into her words. It felt good to release that pressure, even if just by a little.

"Quite so, Mrs Stark," Solomon said. "Quite so."

He turned to face forwards, signalling to Parker to move away.

"Shall we drop you at home, Mrs Stark? I think the excitement of the day has already occurred, and now we simply have to let the cards fall as they may."

"Home, yes. That'll be good," Jackie said. "Thank you, Mr Solomon."

"All part of the service, Mrs Stark. All part of the service."

He waved a finger forward, and Parker drove them away.

## 20

Cold Cut needed to think. There was an opportunity floating around him, like a plastic bag caught by an updraught, flirting close to his fingertips, but then caught by another gust and away, just out of reach again.

He was sat on one of the benches in the communal green space on the estate. A patch of green and brown and grey, where the local kids tried to find innovative new ways to torment each other until their tired, fierce mothers called them home. They called it "The Scrub", resolutely unromantic and realistic, all attempts at improving the space proving fruitless, soon falling back to rusted functionality and overgrown borders. As day turned to night, the kids were replaced by older, more threatening shapes – youths railing against the cards they had been dealt, learning quickly the jungle law of their district. In time, older men would appear around the periphery of this space, furtive and feral, making deals and swapping parcels, each one hoping that the next deal would be the one that delivered them the lifestyle they pawed over on their ever-updating social feeds.

Cold Cut was no different. He wanted nothing more than to escape this place. But not escape to somewhere else. Escape to be *someone* else. He had been forced to leave the city, fear and misunderstanding causing him to flee, convinced he had placed himself squarely in the crosshairs of the Stark crew. Eventually, he had found his way back to his city, given no choice to return if he had intention of continuing to draw breath.

As he looked around, Cold Cut felt that he did have one advantage over the rest of them in the small park space tonight. He had ambition, though that was not unique by any means. What he also had were the beginnings of a plan that might just get him to where he felt he deserved to be. But it required careful thought. His life seemed to become more perilous by the day, but if he could somehow steer his way through safely, there was a chance – a real chance – that he might just find his heart's desire. Status. To be better than the rest of this scum that he was trapped living amongst.

He pulled out another rolled cigarette and lit it. It was rolled tightly, every shred of tobacco put to use, and not a bit wasted, stretching out a whole pack for as long as he could. His fingers were long, thin and yellowed, with dirt under the nails. One day he would have beautiful women buffing his nails, gently pushing back cuticles, and looking up at him with demure, submissive eyes. He dragged hard on the cigarette, half of it burning up with one inhalation. He blew the smoke out, and that fantasy blew away as well, and he set his mind to the reality of his situation.

He had things which could be put to his advantage. He was known by those at the very top of the pyramid. Jackie Stark knew him, as did those newcomers that she had employed to guide her and look after her. Being known was always a double-edged sword for Cold Cut – his animal self-preservation advised him to keep his head down, and not be noticed, as being noticed was the first step in having expectations placed upon you. But he also knew that without being recognised, then he could never be respected, and without respect, he had no chance of ever succeeding.

And he had helped Stark and her men. Without him, they would not have found a way of tracking down the Graces. He had given them the end of the thread that wound through the maze, and he could only presume that they were inching along that thread, ready to plunge a blade into the Graces when they found them. That had to be good for him. He had proven himself useful.

Now he needed to prove himself useful again and again. That was clear. "How" was a different matter.

He sighed, stared at his feet, and inhaled the rest of the cigarette, before flicking the butt in the rough direction of the metal bin several metres away from him, it arcing through the air trailing flickering cinders behind it.

Could he help Stark and her men with the Graces somehow? What could he do? He wasn't a fighter. He was *most definitely* not a fighter. Should he offer his services to act as some kind of spotter? After all, he wasn't sure that there was anyone else in the city who had actually seen the Graces in the flesh. But he'd seen Eleanor Grace cut down the most brutal men in Liverpool as if she was shooting cans at a fairground shy. Being between the Starks and the Graces was not somewhere he ever wanted to find himself again.

Almost absent-mindedly, he noticed on the other side of the little park, two men, maybe in their early 20s, intimidating someone younger and smaller. The smaller youth had his hands up, a negotiation that had turned into pleading. The two older lads had bared their teeth, obligated to take action for some slight or disappointment, but ready to enjoy it nonetheless. Cold Cut watched, taking it as entertainment. The city in microcosm – deals and disappointments, respect and revenge. He knew which side of these situations he wanted to be on.

Could he offer Stark something? The organisation had had its head cut off, and with that, had lost its ability to earn. The need for revenge and retribution would be powerful, but beyond that visceral need, there was a universal truth that they would have to acknowledge – revenge doesn't pay the bills. And without the power to make money, they would lose everything else that came with it. The fear they wielded needed paying for, and with so many gaps in their operation, they had opened themselves up to the most hostile of takeovers, from without or from within. They needed to demonstrate that it was business as usual, or they would become the dust that someone else would build their empire on.

That was something else to consider. Should he do nothing? Let the cards fall, and then find a way to ingratiate himself with whoever came out on top? Maybe. But what he had with the Starks was a way-in. If he could find a way to exploit his situation, without nailing his colours to their mast wholly, then maybe he could find the best of both worlds.

Across the park, the youth had been beaten to the ground, with kicks delivered to his mid-section for good measure. The two men laughed, their own empathy long since beaten down as well, and proceeded to pick this piece of carrion clean. Pockets were emptied, and even the shoes pulled from the youth as he struggled to breath. This was an emasculation. On these streets, a Nike swoosh or Adidas stripes were badges of achievement, and to have even these taken from you was a piquant humiliation.

Cold Cut's phone buzzed in his pocket. He pulled it out, and accessed the screen, barely registering the hundreds of notifications that were accumulating on the patchwork quilt of app icons. A chat message had been delivered. It was Belly.

BELLY – "NEED TO TALK"

Cold Cut sighed. He fucking hated shit like this. Messages that just meant more messages. Why they couldn't just waste a bit of his time, rather than demand he waste a whole lot of it. He knew himself well enough to not reply immediately, distracting himself by probing at the boil that had become a lodger on his neck, throbbing and pulsing little darts of pain whenever he made the mistake of touching it. If he replied quickly, he might be off-hand or off-guard, and he was damn sure that he wasn't going to let Belly or any of his little group get the chance to get one over on him.

Eventually –

COLD CUT – "ABOUT?"

Instantly, the screen showed three dots, as Belly put together his reply. Cold Cut's eyes narrowed. This was good. Belly was showing *him* the weakness, and he was going to make the most of it. Little victories, and any chance to grab some higher ground.

BELLY – "THE OLYMPIC STUFF. NEED SOME."

Here we are then, thought Cold Cut. This is the nub of tonight's entertainment. Looks like Belly has his own ideas about making a play for promotion somehow.

The "Olympic stuff" was what they called the cocaine that appeared in the city in 2012, brought over by an ambitious Argentinian crew, looking to make a move into the local market. They rained it down like snow, and for a wonderful summer, there was grade-A stuff going around, turning the heads of the customer base away from Stark and towards the new player. Of course, Stark didn't take this in the good spirit of competition, and razed the ground of anyone who had even hinted that they might look to switch suppliers, and the Argentinians soon found themselves with no other choice but to shelve their insurgency. Cold Cut, somehow, had managed to keep hold of a brick of the stuff, and had squirrelled it away as something of a nest egg, to be used in extreme circumstances.

But he'd used it all up. When he had been forced to escape the city, chased away by his worries of Stark retribution, he had seen that nest egg slowly eroded as he used it to buy favours, putting a roof over his head and distance between him and the prospect of being found. He'd never told Belly, or Acer, or Cosmo, or any of that particular genus of plankton that it had all gone. He wasn't stupid enough to reveal a weakness like that.

So they believed he still had it. How could he use this to his advantage? Play the game a little longer, and don't reveal your hand, he thought.

Cold Cut – "CHANGED YOUR TUNE. THOUGHT YOU SAID YOU DIDN'T NEED IT NO MORE?"

Belly – "THINGS CHANGE. OPPORTUNITY. GOOD FOR ALL OF US."

Cold Cut – "I'M ON THE SCRUB. BETTER HURRY."

Cold Cut was happy to wait. How long he had to wait would tell him a lot about the position he held in the discussion to come. If the wait was short, then it would show that they were desperate and he would know that he could lean on them for advantages. If they were smart, they would circle the block a few times, get their plan straight between them, and attempt some kind of insouciance that would suggest that Cold Cut was not essential to their plans. But one thing Acer, Belly and Cosmo weren't was smart. Impulsive, with just a jungle-honed keenness in the place of real intelligence.

Cold Cut patted his pockets again, standing up to empty everything out onto the low, flat wall that the bench was adjacent to. Filters were dug out from various pockets, a half-empty packet of tobacco was fished out of another, and he laid everything out, along with the three or four papers that he also found. His nose wrinkled at the fairly feeble showing – not quite enough to get him through the rest of the night, but probably enough to make a couple of cigarettes whilst he waited. He set to work, his fingers nimble with the task, as his mind started rehearsing the potential conversations to come.

Finally, he completed his task, and flipped one of the cigarettes into his mouth, flick-flicking a lighter to ignite the end, before drawing deeply. He exhaled the smoke, taking his seat again, imagining that he was sat on a Monte Carlo lounger, fat cigar replacing the grubby, kinked roll-up he was smoking. The smoke dissipated, and there, loping lazily across the now-streetlit turf, were Belly, and the other heads of this sink estate Cerberus, Acer and Cosmo. Cold Cut didn't wave, he just looked at them coming, then looked away, projecting a carefree attitude as best he could with drag and puff, drag and puff.

They had come quickly, as he had hoped. Fifteen minutes or so from the last text sent, and that told him how important this conversation was going to be for them.

Perfect. He had always been the one doling out demands to these three, and he was smug that it looked like normal service was very much in order.

"Cutty, lad," Acer said. "Been a while."

"Yeah, been a while," parroted Cosmo.

Belly just nodded. This was his idea, and the conversation was going to be between Cold Cut and him, with the others just there as Greek chorus, even if they didn't realise how peripheral they were in all this, this time.

"Belly," Cold Cut said, cutting to the chase, "That was quick, man." Cold Cut couldn't resist pointing out the mistake he had made, and confident enough that Belly wasn't going to be smart enough or nimble enough to process that mistake and change tack.

"Yeah, well," Belly said, "this is important, and we haven't got time to hang around."

"Me neither, lad," Cold Cut said, "so shall we just get down to it. What do you want?"

"That gear, Cutty, the gear you had from the Argies. We need to get hold of more. Like a lot more. We would pay you like, like..." Belly drifted, second-guessing the number in his head, his own greed swamping any preparation he may have set. "Like 25 percent. Yeah, 25 percent."

"25 percent of sales, is it? No good." Cold Cut took another drag on his cigarette. Laughable if he was at a bigger, more prestigious negotiation, but oddly appropriate with a squabble of bottom-feeders like these. They wouldn't know cliché if it detonated between their eyes.

"35 percent?" Acer cut in. Belly shot him a fierce look, at daring to speak at his meet, but then turned back to Cold Cut.

"Yeah, 35, Cutty," Belly said. It was said now. He might as well make it look like it was all part of the plan.

"I'll think about it," Cold Cut said. He had no product to sell, but maybe he could glean some treasure of his own now. Information as reward. Panning for gold. "What's this all about? I couldn't give a fuck about all this, as I won't have trouble selling gear as good at that. Might do it myself, now you've given me the idea. If I can be bothered, like."

Belly looked at Acer, then Cosmo. They stared back, not daring to put voice to any concerns or warnings, both sides waiting for the other to break this impasse. All three heads turned back to Cold Cut. Cold Cut ground the end of his cigarette, now mostly smoked, on the armrest of the bench, slowly, then, only when he had wiped the ash lazily from the chipped metal, did he give Belly any kind of attention. He stared at Belly, daring him to speak.

"It's Stark, right? He's dead, now," Belly said.

"I know that, Belly. It's pretty fucking big news," Cold Cut said, not resisting slipping in another gut punch to let Bell know who held the power here.

"Yeah, ok, fuck," Belly said. "Right, just fucking listen, right? Stark is dead, and his best lads are dead, and all that's left is his missus, who seriously seems to think that she can just run the thing like nothing has changed. "

Here we go, though Cold Cut. This is the nub of it. Belly continued.

"Well, I know a guy who is one of the big names with Stark who didn't get involved in that fucking massacre. One of the earners. My uncle, right? He reckons the time is right for someone else to take over. Stark made mistakes, didn't he? Got himself killed because of it. So why should that stupid bitch of a wife of his get to just slide in like nothing's happened, right?"

Cold Cut nodded, his face implacable.

"Yeah, right. So, my uncle, he needs to persuade the rest

of them that he can take over without anyone losing money or losing what they have all put into the thing. And to do that he needs gear. Good gear. Gear like that stash you were shouting about before. If you could get hold of more of that. Like, a lot more, then we could all get something out of this."

Cold Cut leant back on the wall, his hands gripping the top of the waist-height brickwork, to let him recline, and puff out his cheeks.

"Lot of risk, this, you know," Cold Cut said. "Got to get hold of my hook-up, on the quiet, all whilst all these *politics* – " he spat the word out – "are bubbling away in the background. Can't be arsed with any grief, you know."

"Well, if you can't be fucking bothered," Belly said, showing his frustration, "we can just find someone who can be, and you can just get back to your corners and alleys."

Time to play your hand, Cold Cut thought, and see exactly what cards he was playing against.

"Don't fucking make me laugh, Belly," hissed Cold Cut. "You haven't got shit. You've never got shit. You might have an uncle, but that's just some fucking fluke of the right spunk happening to fly up the right bird. As always, you've done fuck all to earn anything. So, here's what's going to happen. I'm going to have a think about what I'm going to do about this little pearl of information you've seen fit to drop into my lap tonight. I'll make some calls, and maybe – just maybe – if everything works out, then I might just get in touch, and you can introduce me to this uncle of yours. Right?"

Silence. Cosmo gnawed at a fingernail. Acer had turned to watch yet another burgeoning beating on the other side of the scrub. Belly just stared back, his mouth opening and closing. Belly finally replied. He had folded his hand of cards, defeated.

"Yeah, ok, Cutty. Do that, mate. Do that. Quick, though, eh."

Cold Cut flashed a look back at Belly. Belly completely routed now.

"Please," Belly said, almost pitifully.

"Yeah, right," Cold Cut said, and walked away from them. He was halfway across the scrub before he broke into a smile. He could hear the three men behind him, now bickering between themselves. Cold Cut didn't get to experience victory that often. He was damn sure going to enjoy this one.

# 21

It was late afternoon by the time the train heaved into Stoke-on-Trent, darkening skies replacing the fitful sunshine of the day. The city radiated orange into the night, the streetlights creating a glow to fend off the night that threatened to swamp the huddle of towns that made up the city. The city was a curiosity –five towns that had decided to be treated as one, yet each of them with their own identity and parochial pride, confusing for the uninitiated as "Stoke-on-Trent" vanishes from road signs as soon as the city limits are crossed.

Tony and Eleanor had been here before. The station had barely changed since the last time they were here, old yet resilient, a Victorian stoic that had resisted any attempt at modernisation to retain a red brick resistance to change. They disembarked from the train, Tony acknowledging a couple who had stepped back as the doors opened to let Tony and Eleanor pass with a polite nod, before the Graces took the stairs to the underpass that led under the tracks above.

Tony laughed as they exited the station, pointing ahead.

"What?" Eleanor said, before she too smiled when she saw what Tony was pointing at.

Across the road, taxis queueing beneath his feet, stood the statue of Josiah Wedgwood, scrutinising a pot, as he had for decades. Or he would've done, had he not been remixed by whichever local wag had gotten to him most recently.

"Nothing changes, then," Eleanor said, looking up. There on the head of the statue was an orange traffic cone, a high visibility dunce's hat perched at a jaunty angle. In the right hand, the open hand was filled with a lager can.

"Do you think...?" Tony mused. "Do you think it's someone's actual job to take all that shit down every couple of days?"

"Like a Stokie Sissyphus," Eleanor giggled. They'd visited the town numerous times down the years, and the only thing that changed was the brand of lager can in Wedgwood's unmoving hand.

Cars crept along bumper-to-bumper on the narrow road opposite the station entrance, a combination of rush-hour navigation and the usual consistent flow of pick-ups from the station. Cars stopped sharply, whenever the traffic lights opposite the entrance flicked to red, taking the opportunity to either discharge their passengers, or open doors to let someone dive in, quickly, before the traffic moved forward again.

"Taxi?" Tony suggested.

"Can we walk, love?" Eleanor asked. "I know we've got these bags, but can we just stretch our legs for a bit?"

"Course we can," Tony said. "We can always grab a cab if we get fed up with it."

But Tony knew that wouldn't happen. They shared a stubbornness when they had agreed on a task – neither of them would back out until they had reached their goal, each encouraging the other to push on for just one more step. It was what made them so good for each other. Tony bounced on the balls of his feet, the heavy rucksack on his shoulders finding a more comfortable position. Eleanor adjusted the strap of her heavy bag on her shoulder, the black sports bag hiding the lethality of the rifle she had disassembled inside.

"It's up here first, isn't it?" Tony said, answering his own question by crossing the road and into the jumble of narrow streets that led off from the station road. Tony had a good memory for routes, provided that he didn't have to think laterally – as long as he could find waypoints along the way, stored away at the back of his mind from years hence, he could find his way. Ask him to improvise a short-cut, and he would almost certainly get lost, his wilful nature not letting him admit his mistake until it was absolutely unavoidable.

Steaky lived just outside Hanley, the de-facto city centre, in one of the estates that had been left to fall into such ruin that it was only ever discussed if it made the news in a story about urban degradation, or turned up on TV house auction shows. Steaky had lived there for years, trapped first by negative equity, and then by his own acceptance of his place in the world. He did his best to make the best of a bad situation, given it was unlikely that he would ever be able to move to somewhere where he could see trees or grass, and where every window had glass in it.

Of all of the names that the Graces could call on, Steaky was the most consistent – the odds in him not being in that house were negligible, for a variety of reasons, not least that lack of ambition as the roll of years washed the desire to escape his predicament away. They would carry him out of that house in a box.

It was that surety that made him their best option, especially given that they were determined to steer clear of communicating with anyone until they were certain that they were truly safe, however long that took. Steaky was the person they knew would definitely open the door to them, invite them in, and take any difficult news without query or pause.

As they walked, Tony and Eleanor kept quiet, both pondering their situation. Every so often, Tony or Eleanor would point out some subtle change to each other, as they noticed an old building cleared away for a newer one, or a remembered business now shuttered. Occasionally, they would share a quick anecdote about these markers with each other, of how "this was the place where Steaky got that kebab in a naan bread, so big it took him two days to eat it" or "wasn't this where that house club was where we all watched a DJ pretend to be Carl Cox when the real fella didn't show up?"

Then the conversation would ebb away again, and they returned to their mechanical procession through the city, up the bank to the city centre, to then descend down again as they headed to the bleak streets where Steaky lived. The city centre crowned the five towns, even if only geographically. The street lights had switched on, and the basin that contained the urban sprawl looked up at Tony and Eleanor, twinkling like a fallen firmament, the dark hiding a multitude of sins in this tired city.

Streets ran down from the city peak like streams from a watershed. Eleanor had, of course, been here recently, on a desperate dash to get armament from Steaky, but Tony didn't need any help in finding the right path. They had both been here on numerous occasions, in happier times, to check in with their old friend. For Tony it had been a few years, but he noted that the changes to the city were just subtractions – no shiny new buildings thrown up as a city bloomed. Instead, half-completed projects had stopped at merely raising to the ground old factories or warehouses, any optimism of blueprints and handshakes long since forgotten, and the rubble left to do nothing more than be overrun by the return of nature.

The effect was striking, even in the dark. Plague-yellow light glommed around the streetlamps as the night closed in, but what illumination could be thrown out still caused Tony to double-take.

"Wasn't there...?" he managed to say, Eleanor cutting in to finish his thought. She had had the same when she walked this road some days before.

"A big factory? Steaky told me it had been cleared, ready for some new development, but the money went. Now look at it. It's just bricks, and piles of soil, and only good for goats."

"It's sad. Look at the place. Why knock it all down, and then just leave it?" Tony pondered, but he knew the answer. He was happy for Eleanor to echo his internal conclusion, nonetheless, if only to hear a voice in a dark that was pressing in on him.

"It's always money, Tone. Big ideas, and then it all goes to shit, and they leave it like this, and scurry back to the board-room. Would've been better left as it was. At least it had four walls and roof then."

"It's everywhere isn't it? The north. The fucking north. Left to go to shit, and the great, gleaming metropolis in the south just builds and builds and builds."

London was verboten. Another city they had been forced to leave, never to return, the manner of their exit so painful that Tony just couldn't bring himself to say the word. A resentment had built from afar, as that forced distance had seen him assess his home city from a different perspective. And as well as that, bubbling away underneath was the very real fear that if he ever set foot on those streets, he would likely end up dead. It was what made their Liverpool experience so painful –it had happened again.

Eleanor knew where his mind was drifting to. She knew him too well. He was quiet. A stoic. But every so often, a smothered rage bubbled up and escaped, a valve releasing pressure. Afterwards came the silence, and that's when she could see he was letting himself drift away, musing on the "what could've beens" that would only bring him dark clouds.

"Tony," she said, as she stopped walking. She let her bags fall from her shoulders, and leant against the tall perimeter wall for a factory that didn't exist anymore.

"No, love. Fuck this. *Fuck* this. This stupid fucking country, where the money just slides south, and leaves a hundred towns just like this, like they're on life support. And then what happens? You get the Jim Starks of this world to pick over the bones. What the hell are we doing sucked into all this again? We were happy. Finally. In a sleepy little place, and a sleepy little life, and I liked it. Peace and quiet. That's all I ever wanted."

"Tony," she said again, and raised a hand to his cheek, waiting for him to stop his tirade long enough to look back at her. Saying his name gave him an anchor.

"It's just..." he said, his brow furrowed, a boyish helplessness on his face.

"We are going to get through this. We always do," Eleanor said. "We are clever, we have friends, and we have each other."

Tony was looking away now, gnawing on his bottom lip as he fought to box the emotion that had threatened to push its way out.

"Stick to the plan," Eleanor said, her voice soft and quiet. "We lay low for a few weeks here, and then we can start to poke our heads out to see how it's all looking. We made one mistake – a stupid photograph on a pub wall – and we got caught out. What are the odds that something like that could possibly happen again? Especially now we know we need to be even more careful."

Tony puffed his cheeks and exhaled. A reset.

"You're right," he said, finally. "I'm sorry, love. It's just been..." He didn't need to finish the sentence. His self-control was his anchor, and to find himself cast adrift in his emotions was weakness, even with Eleanor. He was angry at himself.

"Come on," Eleanor said, picking up her bags again. "Steaky is just round the corner, and we can find a safe haven for a bit. Maybe get one of those pizzas you like from the place round here."

"You think it's still going?" Tony said, perking up.

"Well, it was last time I was here. Mmm, spicy chicken deep pan..." Eleanor said, eyes sparkling, and they walked off with a fresh bounce in their step, so close to their goal.

## 22

It was only when Cold Cut had made it back to his flat that he realised that the victory he had revelled in was in real danger of being pyrrhic. He had left those three clowns bickering and beaten, but that sweet taste of that supremacy would soon turn sour if he couldn't turn his high-ground position into something tradeable or valuable. It was a promissory note, written in the sand, and a tide was heading in.

The Argentinian summer of 2012 was ancient history as far as the city was concerned. Long years had passed, and after these invaders had been repelled by the locals, things returned to whatever passed for normal on these streets. Those foolish enough to have had their heads turned by the pure product that these foreigners brought with them soon found themselves more concerned with keeping those heads on their shoulders. Stark and his gang underlined their capacity for brutality, a forest fire of retribution that scoured the tempted from the face of the earth. A handful ran from the city rather than stay and face certain death, with the story, never challenged, that Stark had deliberately allowed them to flee so as to spread the word of the consequences of betrayal.

Cold Cut didn't have friends. He just had names in his phone that he could try and negotiate with, trading gossip and deals for the similar scraps these names had available to barter. They were the tiny fish that fed on whatever fell from the mouths of whales. An eco-system of chancers and bandits hard-scrabbling to get a foothold.

He dug around the back of his stained and threadbare sofa, long fingers searching for one of the many cheap pens that would've rolled down there. A piece of junk mail would do as a notepad, and after a scribble to draw ink to the ballpoint, he started writing names down, as he shuttled through the long list of contacts on his phone.

A pop then a hiss as he opened a thin can that held some lurid caffeinated potion, angrily slurping a few gulps as he stared at the list. A few names were crossed through immediately, a few more were given question marks, and a couple more were underlined fiercely. Names that might just know enough to conjure a route to someone who could supply enough product to fill a city.

He scrabbled around the sofa cushions again, pulling out a buried roll-up cigarette that had fallen between the gaps who knows how many days previously. Cold Cut dusted it down gently, pulling lint from one end, before lighting it, as he picked the most promising name on the list to text first.

Just a few weeks ago, every name on this list would have ignored him. In fact, most of them still would. But Stark was dead, and the names he had dragged out of his phone, were the names of people who had left all those years ago, when Stark was tightening his grip on the town. To even respond to Cold Cut with Stark still alive, given Cold Cut was a man whose indiscretion and instinct for self-preservation were legendary, would have risked bringing trouble that these people could scarce afford. Even now, with Stark gone, there would be uncertainty – the king was dead, but surely another in that organisation would step up, and carry on as before?

But there was a reason why these people were bottom-feeders. They may have had a basic deviousness, good enough to make do at ground level, but never anything approaching the nuance to seriously climb the ladder. But temptation was a powerful lure, and the prospect of bartering their position to once again get a foothold on the next rung up might be hard to resist. This was what Cold Cut was depending on, and he only needed to be right once, out of all of these names.

This was a risk, Cold Cut realised. Just by sending these communications, he was putting himself in opposition to Jackie Stark. Jackie Stark who knew he was. Jackie Stark and her new hired help, those two differently terrifying men, Solomon and Parker – the stiletto and the cudgel. He would have to tread very carefully.

Each text was worded carefully. He couldn't afford to be vague, as he didn't have time to waste. He had whittled it down to eight names – some he sent texts as if they were old friends, others tentative teases to try and pique interest, but all of them designed as if he were baiting a hook. Too good to ignore. Money. Status. Power. *Opportunity.*

Just one. Cold Cut just needed one.

Texts sent, he shook the empty can of energy drink, just to double-check that the dayglo goop had been drained, before crunching the can and launching it across the room towards the door. Another can was on its side beneath what passed for a coffee table, buried as it was beneath the detritus that had built up since Cold Cut had returned. He opened it, looked sideways at his phone, as if daring it to stay quiet, and drained half of the can with loud slurps.

He set the can down on the floor by his feet, and slumped backwards, half-consumed by famished polyester. He rubbed his face with his cold hands, and puffed out his cheeks, absent-mindedly interlocking his fingers behind his neck. He instantly regretted it – a stab of pain radiated from the ever-more-angry boil that still squatted on his neck like a bad tenant. He hissed at the pain, and his forgetfulness, before he started to poke and prod at it with his dirty, nicotine-stained fingers. Oh, to have some relief! Some respite from this – just this one thing – yet again singing his song of "poor me" to an audience of himself.

The phone pinged.

Cold Cut leaned forward to read the notification that had lit up his screen. A new number, no name assigned, text simply reading "WHO IS THIS?"

Someone had clearly moved to a new phone, but kept their old one at hand, just in case. Even given his desperation to make progress, Cold Cut couldn't help but take the time to take offence that whoever it was had not saved his name and number from one phone to the next. Another minor grievance to add to the mountain of complaints and injustices if he ever got to face the Creator.

Cold Cut brought up the text message and started composing his reply. He typed, then deleted, his name. No, he thought, it's not quite the time for names until he was sure who this was he was replying to. There was too much at stake, not least his own skin, for him to be careless.

Cold Cut - "IF I KNOW YOU, YOU WILL KNOW ME. JUST LOOKING TO DO A BIT OF BUSINESS."

He pressed send, rubbed his chin, and typed again.

Cold Cut - "A BIG BIT OF BUSINESS"

The screen showed three pulsing dots below his sent text message – whoever this was was typing a response.

Message - "WHAT KIND OF BUSINESS?"

Cold Cut's list of names were all people, loathe as he was to admit it, just like him. City observers, who made it their business to know things, and know people, gauging the warp and weft of the relationships from one street corner dealer to another. He might not have seen these people in years, as they ran for cover from the Stark purges, but you didn't just stop that addiction to gossip, and the desire to use it to clamber over others towards the sun. They were greedy and desperate, and Cold Cut was no different.

Cold Cut - "I NEED AN INTRO. WE COULD ALL MAKE A LOT OF MONEY."

The three dots returned to the screen. Then vanished. Then appeared again. Whoever this was was making a decision on whether to proceed in real time, presumably oscillating from negative to positive and back again. Weighing up risks against benefit, and how desperate they were to dare believe the word of someone that was notable enough to have their number, but not notable enough to have seen the name worth saving. Cold Cut ground his teeth together as he stared at the screen.

Finally, another text arrived.

Message - "OK. WILL GIVE YOU A CHANCE. HERE'S WHAT YOU ARE GOING TO DO."

# 23

Jackie Stark had things to consider. She had taken herself to the huge private gym and leisure complex where she was a member, for the first time since Jim had been killed. It used to be one of her havens – a place where she would go to surround herself with vapid distraction and shallow tittle-tattle with other women of means, with exercise a second or third priority.

She used to go because she felt she couldn't afford to stop, as absence would lead to that void being filled with gossip about her. She had seen it happen to others who had made the mistake of not keeping up their attendance – snide asides about how so-and-so "really shouldn't give up as you know how she holds weight on her thighs". Even with the reputation that came with her name reaching even the rarified snobbery of a place like this, she just couldn't bear the thought that someone with a privilege that could only ever be inherited would turn their judgment towards her, her council-estate upbringing feeling like a stain that wouldn't fully rub off.

This time she went for a number of new reasons. This

place offered a comforting echo of a life before her husband had been murdered. Just by being here, maybe she could fool herself that Jim would still be waiting for her when she returned home, ready for a cup of tea and a to-and-fro about their day, with Jackie doing her best to make her day seem more exciting, and Jim doing his best to make his seem less so. Coming here also gave her an excuse to get out of a house that was now resembling a prison cell, the warm comforts of the place now cold and drained of colour with the shock of loss. And lastly, she wanted to use this place to make her body ache, her muscles burn and punish herself for letting herself grow as complacent and indulged as the others who spent hour after lazy hour in this place.

She had insisted that Solomon and Parker make themselves scarce, and not accompany her to the gym despite the risks, spelt out by Solomon, of powerplay and retribution. She was not going to hide behind them for the rest of her life. She had pulled herself out of her poor upbringing, and made herself into someone who demanded respect, and she simply would not jeopardise that by acting like a terrified hostage or a delicate china doll, irrespective of who might be circling. Jim would've done the same. "Don't let them see you scared," he would've said. Damn right, she thought.

This wasn't just a gym or a health spa – it was to be her crucible. The first hard mile on a long road to convincing the city, the world, and lastly herself, that she was going to win.

She blipped her card at the entrance, and the doors swished open, a strong aroma of chlorine instantly hitting her as she stepped inside. There was a constant hubbub – a steady flow of people stopping to chat by the water fountain, or a group of women heading off to a yoga class with a chorus of squeaks from their rubber soles on the always-clean tiled floor. The receptionist, wearing a fuchsia coloured polo shirt, was explaining the class timetable to a potential new member, but managed to look up and smile at Jackie as she walked past. Jackie was known here. She liked to think it was because she was popular and gregarious, in this environment she had conquered and made safe, but there was always the suspicion that it was her last name that commanded the respect, as it did with the rest of her life. How much weight would that name carry now?

The place was huge, and offered options. The memberships were expensive, and paid for the place to offer choice, irrespective of how many people were there to take advantage of it. Jackie didn't have to overly scrutinise any timetable – she knew that there was a cycle class every hour, on the hour, and if there were thirty people or just her, it would still run all the same.

She navigated her way around the sterile, open corridors, until she reached the door to the cycle studio, which already had a small group of women waiting for the instructor to open up the room. Jackie didn't know them per se, but was aware of them. These were the sort of people she would smile at simply due to the repetition of contact, who hadn't made the step to any kind of introduction. Perfect, she thought. If she could get through this without having to politely smile through a barrage of small-talk and platitudes, but still make it clear that she was very much in business, then she would consider that a resounding success.

The door was eventually opened, and the waiting women streamed in, desperate to secure the bikes that were set up in the best position to see the instructor, like try-hard pupils looking for the best desk in class. Jackie wasn't going to demean herself by looking needy, and walked in at her own pace, selecting a bike just away to the side, but still with good enough view of the instructor's bike, which was set out at the front of the room facing the two banks of bikes set up for the members.

Jackie adjusted the bike seat and handlebars, and then took out a small hand towel to drape over the handlebars, and her bottle of water that she slid into the holder on the frame. Once she had completed her set-up routine, only then did she sit on the bike, and start turning the pedals over, getting herself ready for the class ahead. As she cycled, she felt eyes on her. At first, she wondered if this was just paranoia – a misjudged fear that she would be the source of some gossip today, the test subject in the petri dish, set for scrutiny. But too many eyes were holding glances for longer than was usual. Normally loud voices were whispering to one another. She was being assessed, evaluated and judged.

Jackie knew what they would be saying – "look who it is," they would be whispering. "He's not even cold," they would say. "I didn't expect to see her here again," they would reply. "Doesn't she look sad?" they would judge. It didn't matter what Jackie did – they would say the same things, and then find some evidence to support their expectations.

Ignore them, she thought. Do the class, keep your dignity, and don't show a single weakness. The room was filled with loud music, and the instructor started her enthusiastic demands, and Jackie let herself focus only on her breathing, and the commands that she would do her best to follow. This needed to be her release.

It worked. For a long forty-five minutes, she threw herself into physical exertion. Her concentration bounced from watching the instructor, to focussing on the performance computer on the frame of the bike, and back again. Fast sprints to make the lungs burn, or leg-sapping climbs, and a clock that ticked down too slowly. The loud dance music ricocheting around the dark room from speaker banks masked her heavy breathing, and sweat dripped onto the hard floor.

"One more climb!" the instructor shouted, and Jackie knew she had only a few more minutes until she could take a drink, and find her feet again. One last push.

The lights came on, and the class ended. A queue formed for the paper towels and disinfectant to wipe down the machines, with Jackie holding back, happy to let others go first, mainly to avoid small talk she had no desire to entertain. She had done the hard part. She was visible. Not hiding. A call-back to a normality she hadn't realised was so tenuous, and a paper tiger for anyone watching and judging.

The class left the room in twos and threes, smiling and mopping their brows, sharing a post-exercise flush of relief and satisfaction. Jackie hung back, nodded and smiled to the instructor, and then made her way out, along the corridor, and then to the changing rooms, to splash water on her face and check her appearance.

The chattering stopped as soon as she walked into the changing rooms, and Jackie knew immediately that they were talking about her. Of course they were. The same whisperers from the cycle class, with their behind-hand mugging and raised eyebrows, had made their own way to the changing rooms. Jackie felt her cheeks redden, angry that she hadn't foreseen that she would walk into their judgments for a second time, and embarrassed that she was angry.

Jackie managed a smile, and walked past the three women, who had stopped rooting through their too-big exercise bags for make-up and combs and the like, silently watching Jackie as she walked past. The mirrors and sinks were on the other side of the room, lockers on the facing wall, and slatted benches in the middle. Jackie walked like she was on a high-wire, careful to just look straight ahead, now she had acknowledged the group, keen to get to the mirrors, do what she came in here for, and then get out.

"I'm surprised you've come in again," one of the women said, after Jackie had passed. Jackie turned to see who it was who had spoken – a woman she had seen before, one of so many who filled the car park with their massive black Chelsea tractors. No doubt the wife of some city trader or slick salesman, with nothing to fill her time but gossip and spite.

"Excuse me?" Jackie spluttered, aware that the comment required a response. The three women looked back at Jackie, and then two of them looked at the third, waiting.

"We heard, obviously," the woman said, the last word dripping in poison. She had clearly been waiting to make this point, whatever it was. "About the husband." *The* husband. Another little cruelty.

Jackie felt her eyes sting. The woman, bright spandex and tight ponytail, continued.

"So sad. But now he's gone, I suppose you're going to have to be a bit careful. You know, without money coming in. I suppose you'll have to..." she paused, the expression on her face like a torturer picking which knife would be the sharpest, "...get used to places a bit more in keeping with your...background." The woman had strangled the life out of any hint of an accent, making sure that every syllable was perfectly enunciated, adding another rung or two to the social ladder she was looking down from.

Jackie still couldn't speak. Her mouth had dried up, and lolled open, amazed that this woman, who once would have scurried away at the sight of Jackie, now had the chutzpah to dare speak to her like this. Is this what her life was going to be now? A peasant revolt to pull down her castle walls?

"It's not like you ever really fitted in here, is it?" The woman was still talking, clearly enjoying this. "Bit of a square peg, aren't you? New money. Bit too much of a sore thumb for a place like this. And now the husband has died, well, you'll probably have to get a job or something." She laughed at this, and her two accomplices joined in, happy to be led. The prospect of work was a punishment fit for only the very worst in society.

A flash cut of Jim's face appeared in the movie in Jackie's head. It was enough.

Jackie smiled. Her eyes cleared, and she felt a tingle run down her spine. Two steps towards the woman, then another, and another. The woman looked up at Jackie, the cruel smile still on her lips, but her eyes had widened a little now, Jackie not behaving as she had expected. This woman might not be the frightened rabbit she had expected her to be.

"You're right," Jackie said, in a steady tone. "I don't suppose I ever really fitted in here, with people like you. I've had to earn my place, love." Jackie's accent went in the opposite direction to the woman, leaning into the scouse, consonants that could shred steel.

"And I earned it...*we* earned it, my husband and me. And we worked so hard, and did so much, that all this – " Jackie spread her arms, indicating the room, the building, the city, "belongs to us."

Jackie struck quickly, her fist balled up, gold rings on her fingers becoming a knuckleduster, cracking the woman squarely on the nose, again and again, the woman flinging her arms about like she was trying to wave away a flock of birds. Three, four times Jackie hit her, the woman's face crumpling in, those delicate, bought-and-paid-for features nothing but mash underneath Jackie's knuckles.

Then silence. Jackie kept her fist cocked, as the woman slumped sidewards, blood gushing from her face into the lap of one of the other women, who was hyperventilating at the shock of the violence, and the crimson pooling in her lap.

Jackie had remembered who she was now. Left lost without Jim, she had found the part of herself that could lead her forwards. The name she was given was Jackie, but the name she had taken was Stark. She crouched down, so she was eye-level with the woman, who looked back at her, her one unswollen eye wide and scared.

"I want you to remember something. These..." Jackie indicated the two women to either side "...will tell people, I'm sure. But all I want you to do is remember. Perhaps when you look in the mirror, and see the state of your face. Just remember one thing. Remember my name. Remember what it means."

Jackie got up, slung her bag over her shoulder, and walked to the door. She opened it, and turned back. She knew who she was now. So did these women.

"My name is Stark."

# 24

The street was dark, with a few streetlights having failed, and being one of the parts of town that would never draw a quick response by the council, if at all. A terraced street, that banked up towards a huddle of anaemic looking trees leaning over a low-barred fence on what was laughably described as a communal play area. The houses were uniform in design, and fitfully decorated, some of the more optimistic owners having tried to break the monotony of the arrangement with now-faded paint jobs or washed-out cladding. Most of the inhabitants had left. Steel sheets had been screwed over many of the windows. Destitute housing trying to feebly dissuade squatters and junkies from moving in, either on a temporary basis until they found a better hideaway, or more permanently, moving friends and furniture in, to cling inside like limpets. Some of the steel sheets were graffitied, with warnings to the curious – "no electric" or "no water" – or as warnings and advertisement both – "whore house".

The street was an infection, a parasite that was draining the life out of the surrounding area. Now in the minority, occupied houses shone their internal lights brightly, warm and safe, as the bleak and relentless invasion of the derelict flanked them on all sides.

Steaky had lived on these streets for as long as they could both remember. He bought his house as soon as he had left the forces, taking advantage of a friendly housing market, and enough inheritance that he could avoid a mortgage that would become an albatross for him. He had never wanted to leave – a combination of stubbornness and a lack of ambition. So what if the street was going to hell? That sort of thing didn't bother him – in fact, he was more at ease around the crazed and the desperate than those pushing water uphill in the rat race. It was why he joined the forces in the first place – keen to get away from a road that was stretching out in front of him. Job, marriage, kids. This was his house, he would say. They can take me out of here in a box.

Tony had quickened his pace as they turned to walk into Steaky's street. Their bags were heavy, but he was keen to see Steaky. Tony liked him, with his honest, cheerful rejection of whatever a normal life was, and his always-entertaining anecdotes of the life he had built, just outside of that mainstream.

"Which one?" Tony asked, the street having changed since he was last here. A few more steel sheets, and a few more darkened windows.

"Next to the one with cladding," Eleanor said, pointing at a plain house, old brick and old curtains, flanked on both sides by empty houses.

"Ah yes, got it," Tony replied, renewing his pace, until he remembered his manners, and slowed down so Eleanor could knock on the door first. Tony liked Steaky, but he was her friend, after all, and things like politeness are still important to remember.

There were lights on inside the house. Above the front door was a frosted windowpane that revealed just the hint of light from further inside the house. An old shoe scraper was built into the wall by the foot of the door, a holdover from years ago, and another reminder of just how old these houses were.

Eleanor knocked, and then smiled. Tony saw her, and smiled as well. They both were excited to see their friend, and braced themselves for the inevitable greeting, as the door swung open.

"Fuck me!" Steaky said. "It's only the fucking Graces! Both of them, this time."

Steaky roared with laughter, the loudest noise for streets, no concession to neighbourly decorum, even if neighbours were in short supply.

"Look at you, mate," he said, launching himself at Tony and grabbing him in a hug that flirted with becoming an assault. The first time he had met Tony had been the same, but Tony was used to this now, and knew better than to do anything other than just go with it.

"What a fine figure of a man you've grown up to be," Steaky said, laughing. "And you again, Eleanor? So soon? Either you forgot a phone charger last time you were here, or you are both doubly fucked now. Anyway, get in, get in. I'll get a brew on."

"Thanks Steaky," said Eleanor, following them in, now that Steaky had released Tony from his bearhug hello.

The hallway was long and narrow, light coming from the other end, around a door that stood ajar. Another door opened off the hallway to the left, to a sitting room that was currently in darkness. The hallway was narrow, with the three having to walk in single file, Steaky leading the way. Despite the small space, an effort had been made to make this first impression notable, thanks to a decorative mosaic pattern inlaid into the floor. These houses were old, but built to last, and often, underneath the accretion of trends, the original workmanship still existed. Steaky was committed to making this house his home, and despite the disrepair the street had fallen into, was determined to make the best of what he had. Old carpets had been pulled up and thrown away, and original features cleaned, restored and proudly displayed. A lick of paint on that shoe scraper, skirting boards filled and sanded, the house number painted carefully onto the door.

Steaky pushed open the door at the end of the hallway, and walked into the living room.

"Take a seat, and I'll get the kettle on," he said. This was the north. There was no crisis too big that couldn't wait for a cup of tea.

A long table dominated one side of the living room, five chairs – two on either side, and one at the head – around it. An armchair was set in the corner for more informal relaxation, with the television, the stereo and the bookcase in the front room, the room they had passed in the hallway. Eleanor sat down first, after dropping her bags off at the foot of the table. Tony did the same and sat down next to her, as Steaky struck up conversation from the adjoining kitchen, shouting through as he rummaged around for mugs, teabags and milk.

"I've forgotten how you take it already, El," he said. "And what about you, Tone? Was it twenty sugars or twenty-one?"

"No sugar for either," Tony said, "Apparently, my sweet tooth is going to be the death of me." He looked at Eleanor as he called back, eyes glinting with the mischief of it.

"I did wonder," Steaky said, as the hiss of the boiling kettle got louder, "I thought to myself, 'Steaky, lad, that Grace fella is looking awfully svelte for his time of life. I wonder what his secret is.'"

Tony smiled.

"It's a constant treadmill of sacrifice, Steaky," he said. "Yes, I'll have a biscuit, if you've got one."

Eleanor snorted, and dug her elbow into Tony's ribs. She was relieved and comforted in equal measure – coming here was the perfect choice. Tony was shy by nature, at least at first, but Steaky was the one person she knew who didn't hold truck with any delicacy of feeling, and just steamrollered on through until you had no choice but to be charmed.

"Here you go," Steaky said, nudging the kitchen door open with his foot, as he carried a tray into the room with three mugs set on it, as well as a small plate of biscuits. There was something faintly ridiculous about Steaky, a big, broad, rough rockface of a man, tattooed and scarred, delicately placing a tray of tea and biscuits down on a table, before passing out coasters from a coaster set already on the table.

There was quiet for a few moments. Eleanor, now that Tony had cheekily made his demand for biscuits, was comfortable being his accomplice in taking advantage of Steaky's hospitality, and took one herself to nibble. Tony took a sip of tea, never one to let his tea cool by even the slightest amount before drinking, his hand grasping for a biscuit at the same time. Steaky waited patiently for his guests, then took a biscuit himself, smiling at his two old friends.

"So, what happened?" Steaky said.

Eleanor and Tony told their tale. Eleanor described how

she had made her way back to Liverpool, after she had picked up her rifle that Steaky had kept here for safe keeping. Tony interjected as best he could to fill in the gaps in the story, the pair of them doing their best to weave their two separate narratives together. They did their best to get their timelines straight, until their stories intersected with the shoot-out on the dockside. The reckoning with Stark and his cronies, after which they had no choice but to run. Run all the way to Stoke, to Steaky, and a safe harbour, or so they hoped.

Steaky listened intently, sipping his tea, and absent-mindedly reaching for biscuit after biscuit as they spun their tale. He said nothing other than the occasional incredulous curse, or loud exhalation of disbelief as Eleanor and Tony detailed how they had cut down the Stark crew. How Tony had faced down a gun to the head, how Eleanor had executed Stark once and for all, and how they had both made their escape from the city, unsure whether they had the hounds of hell on their heels or not.

"...and here we are," Tony said, reaching for another biscuit, before realising that Steaky had cleared the plate as he had listened. "Tired, worried and biscuitless."

Steaky coughed and spluttered as he laughed, and choked on his tea.

"I'll get the rest," he said, still coughing. He got up, went into the kitchen, open a cupboard or two, then returned, setting the opened and half-empty packet of biscuits back on the table.

"You think you're still in trouble?" Steaky said.

"We need to be sure we're clear. More than ever," Eleanor said.

"I think we were careless before, back in Norfolk. Yeah, I know that the odds were long on us being found, but we didn't help ourselves," Tony said, still angry at himself, blaming himself for this whole sequence of events. His own harshest critic.

The odds *were* long, but if they had stuck to their strict code, then maybe, just maybe, they could've avoided all this. A candid photograph of them that ended up on a pub wall, spotted by some Scouse exile, eager to cash in that knowledge to Stark for kudos and good favour. They had left Liverpool the first time under suspicion from Stark of a scam gone wrong. Now, the impetus was sharper – they had killed bad people. Bad people had bad friends.

"Maybe we've cut the head off the snake, and there's no-one left who cares about us," Tony said. "But I let us think that before. And if there *is* any of that crew left, then they will be looking for us. We need to disappear for a while, until we are completely sure that it's safe to move on again."

"They're a big firm, Steaky," Eleanor said. "They control the city, so God knows what kind of resources they've still got. Even if we've seen off their best, then they might have the funds to replace them with even better."

"I think we need to be paranoid, and second-guess everything," Tony said, emphasising the point with a munch of biscuit. He took one last sip of cooled tea, and look at Steaky. "Look, Steak. This could be nothing, but it could be something. Are you ok with us being here? Just dropping on you like this? Because if we are right to be worried, then some really bad people are looking for us."

Steaky smiled. Broad and warm.

"Family, aren't you?" he said, "That means forever."

# 25

Cold Cut didn't like trains. A car was his. A metal box he could move around in, that kept the outside world outside, and him in the security of his own space. He could lock the doors in his car, or take a turn off to get some fast food or caffeine in a tin whenever he felt like it.

A train was a trap. Trapped with other people, who he uniformly resented, and no way to escape. Members of the general public could sit next to him, for fuck's sake, or worse yet, try and talk to him. Even with him projecting the most toxic anti-social aura, there was always some old biddy who wanted to chat about the weather or the queue at the shops.

He slumped back in the seat, before immediately recoiling when he realised he had aggravated the deep boil that continued to torment him.

He swore, loudly. The heads of other passengers spun around to see what the noise was about, a tut coming from one of those old biddies he was so resentful of.

"What?" he spat back, looking daggers, before looking

out of the window, hiding his embarrassment behind misanthropy.

The train from Liverpool to Manchester was not one of the more scenic routes in the country. Sweeping green hills and verdant embankments were not evident. Instead, he took in a panorama of cracked brick and grey concrete. Graffiti and fly-tipping. This was the city revealed, any chromed and clean façade facing the roads, and the train tracks seeing the worst of it. Everything looked like it was close to failing – the buildings that had clustered together like an infection, different sizes, shapes and colours, filling in every space, built on the ruins of the previous generation. The train itself was a wheezing relic. Cold Cut distracted himself from the journey by trying to make sense of the scribbled etchings on the back of the seats he was facing. Who loves who, who hates who, and which football team was either the best team that ever played, or a plague to be swept from the land. Not in so many words.

He was nervous. This was not unusual in and of itself. Cold Cut was usually nervous, his own honest appraisal of his limitations and his place in the world undeniable facts that fuelled his own angry self-loathing, but this situation was a step into the unknown, which added a new layer to it all.

He had been given specific instructions, and made clear that these instructions were not for negotiation. Get on the train, the text had said. At this time, at this station, and do nothing until you get to Manchester. Self-preservation ensured that he daren't consider even the slightest deviation from this.

The person who had sent the text was an old face from years ago. One of the few who had struck up a relationship, even if small, with the Argentinians, when they were keen to flood the city with the best gear it had ever seen, to push Stark and his crew out, market forces doing the job before guns and knives were needed. He had left the city once Stark had started his purges, left to tell the tale that Liverpool was off-limits to anyone who had ambitions to do business there. Cold Cut hoped that that relationship with the Argentinians was still alive somehow, and maybe he could be the one to re-open the city gates for the invaders, and take the reward for doing it. He had no loyalty to Stark, the dead one or his wife, or to anyone else for that matter. Just the insatiable drive to be given the reward and power he believed he so richly deserved. That sense of injustice was the only motivator powerful enough to supersede his innate cowardice.

The train journey was relatively short – thirty minutes or so, but he wished it would last days, nervous about what he was walking into. It stopped at station after station, every few minutes, with one or two people getting off, replaced by fresh passengers. Cold Cut, once they had left the city limits, stopped scrutinising the new faces, as the chance of him knowing them reduced with distance.

"Long time, youth," a voice said from the seat behind Cold Cut.

Cold Cut tensed, once it became apparent that he was the one being addressed. He did his best to fight that feeling, and project, at least, the impression of insouciance. He turned his head slowly, and looked up at the face peering down at him from above the headrests.

His name was Truth. He was clearly the same species as Cold Cut, whatever that was, in similar sports gear and absent concern for grooming routines. Wire-thin, rodent-features and perpetual movement, fidgeting and twitching like a corn kernel in a hot pan.

Truth was not his given name, but another one of those names that was bestowed onto someone thanks to some sepia-tinged incident from the past, or, more likely, given to themselves to create some kind of mystique. There was no need to wait too long for an explanation, because the reason Truth was Truth, is because he came as a pair.

As soon as Cold Cut saw Truth, he was looking over his shoulder to see if he could find the other part of the double act. And there he was, sat a few rows back, looking back at Cold Cut with a shark grin and cold, wild eyes. He was the same height as Truth, but more solid, as if he was more real, every movement slow and considered, but really, as Cold Cut knew, just a coiling of springs ready to explode as soon as the word was given. This was Truth's literal partner-in-crime, Consequences.

It was a bad joke, and one that never drew laughter, especially not from those who knew these two. Truth had personality for two, chattering about everything and anything, somehow managing to still be standing, breathing and in full possession of all of his limbs, despite being notoriously indiscreet. The reason for that was probably Consequences, who, due to some obligation of shared parenthood, was more than happy to look out for his step-brother, not least because just being around Truth gave him more than enough opportunity to indulge in his first and only real passion – fucking people up.

Cold Cut, stomach knotting despite knowing full well what he was walking into, looked back at Truth, who was still looming over Cold Cut from the row behind.

"Well, it's been a while, Cutty, old lad," Truth said. "Was a surprise to see that you were still up and around, truth be told." Oh god, thought Cold Cut, the catchphrase already.

"Yeah, well, needs must. Bit of business, and who better than you, Truth?" Cold Cut said.

Truth leaned closer, lowering his voice.

"Now, luckily I'm not the sort of person who has feelings to hurt, but see, I know you've asked a few people, and reckon I'm probably the only person who got back to you. That right, Cutty?"

"Yeah, well. Even so. I've got a way-in that could work out very well for everyone who wants to be involved, so let's cut all the shit, and you tell me whether you can hold up your end of the bargain, and get me sat down with the Argies." Cold Cut surprised himself that he was so blunt, but he felt backed into a corner, and knew he had to at least appear to stand up for himself.

Truth grinned, looked back at Consequences, raising an eyebrow, and walked around the end of the row of seats so he could sidle in, and sat down next to Cold Cut.

"Straight to business, is it, Cutty? Time was you'd just love to shoot the shit about who was doing what to who, and which street corner was the best place to sling, but here you are, all grown up. So, Mr Business Man, why don't you tell me this plan of yours, who you know, and why me and Conny here should introduce you to our friends in Manchester?"

"I'm not doing that. The names can wait, until I meet your contacts. I'm not stupid enough to give you something like that just like that. Remember – I know you, mate, and I know that mouth of yours," Cold Cut said, picking at a bit of hard skin around his thumb nail.

"Oh, Cutty," Truth said, milking it, "you might just hurt my feelings. Okay, how about you tell me what you think might be enough to persuade my friends to sit down with you, then? They don't just arrange meetings with just any streak of piss who can manage to buy a train ticket. Sell it."

Cold Cut was expecting this. Dealing with Truth was like dealing with any other one of the names who haunt the back streets and dock roads of his city, even if Truth had been run out of town for years now. It was all about "respect", whatever that meant, or more accurately, "influence". Truth wanted to appear important to these Argentinians that he knew – a channel of communication he had presumably kept open since 2012, and their first attempt at taking a slice of the Liverpool business. Whether he had managed to keep on their good side despite them being forced out of town, or was just looking to curry new favour with them, either way, he just wanted to appear useful. Everyone had angles they were trying to play.

"Here's what I'm saying. Jim Stark is dead - " Cold Cut started.

"Heard that, yeah," Truth interrupted. Cold Cut sighed at the interjection.

"Jim Stark is dead," Cold Cut repeated, "and nearly all of his top men died with him. Shot in a fucking car park, right?"

"Who killed them?" Truth said. He hadn't got the hint, or had decided to just ignore it, and interrupt as often as the thought occurred to him.

"Husband and wife. Couple of old fuckers that Stark had a real hard-on for. Ex-Army or something, I heard. And before you ask, they aren't connected. This isn't some kind of move."

"So what did they kill them for?" Truth said.

"Stark thought they were to do with some robbery, and chased and chased them all over the fucking place. Wouldn't let it go, even when it didn't even look like they knew about any robbery. You know what he's like. *Was* like. Didn't know they had training or could handle a gun and the next thing they've had their brains blown out, and the two who did it just got out of town."

"How do you know these two weren't connected to anyone serious? My...friends won't make the mistake of a turf war again. Not now they are doing well for themselves in Manchester."

"I know them. Well, kinda. I found them, right? And I saw the whole shoot-out, and I saw them go. Just some stupid couple who Stark didn't do his homework with, and look where that left him," Cold Cut said. The train grumbled as it pulled away from another station, heaving and wheezing as it moved on.

"Fuck me. Jim Stark taken down by some nobodies," Truth grinned, delighted at the misfortune of others, as always.

"So, here's the thing, right?" Cold Cut said, getting to the hard sell of his sales pitch. "There's a big fucking vacancy in the city. The Stark business is still trading, just about, but Stark's missus, of all people, is the one trying to make a play for it. Some of the old heads – the ones still alive, that is – don't like the thought of that, so they are looking at taking it for themselves. And the only way they can do that..."

Cold Cut let the thought hang in the air between them, not stupid enough to spell out exactly what he was proposing, even if the train didn't seem the ideal place for some complicated police sting. He'd been candid enough. Let Truth do some thinking now.

"Okay, okay – I get it," Truth said. "You know one of these names in there, and need a little help getting the right...product into the right hands so they can make their move, with the best gear anyone has seen in that city for years."

Cold Cut rolled his eyes, Truth unable to resist spelling out the obvious and damn the ears of whoever might be listening.

"And what do you get out of this, Cutty?" Truth said.

"Maybe it's time I got a bit of recognition, mate. I'll be the one to make the introductions, and maybe I'll be the one who gets a little something for myself for doing it."

Truth leaned closer, an arm wrapping around Cold Cut's shoulders.

"And why shouldn't I just cut you out, and go and talk to the interested parties myself," he whispered.

"Because, Truth," Cold Cut said, unable to resist wriggling under Truth's arm, "there might still be a few people who would like to carry on conversations with you that were started back in 2012. Probably best if I handle them."

A bluff, but a good one. Cold Cut didn't know anyone who might possibly care about a near-decade old grudge. The only person who had any ill intent towards Truth and whoever he ran with was dead – shot in the head by Eleanor Grace a few weeks ago. But damned if he was going to ease Truth from his worries.

Truth wrenched on Cold Cut's neck in a way that could possibly be viewed as playful, if from a distance. He smiled at Cold Cut as he did it, but his eyes were burning. Cold Cut had a point, a fact he wasn't pleased to acknowledge.

Sharp pain jabbed into Cold Cut, his back fizzing like it had had electrodes jammed inbetween vertebrae. That fucking boil! The plague sore that sat like a squatter on his neck! He wriggled and spat, like a feral cat in a cage, much to Truth's delight.

"Easy, Cutty. I've washed my hands, mate," Truth laughed.

A mechanical whoosh broke the tension, as the train doors opened at another station.

"That's us," Truth said, patting the back of Cold Cut's neck, before getting to his feet. Cold Cut grimaced, doing his best to swaddle his pain as he followed Truth's lead, standing up. Cold Cut noticed Consequences getting up from his position behind them, happy to take the rear, making Cold Cut feel like a man being led to the gallows with his guards fore and aft, preventing escape.

They had disembarked at a station a few stops from the city centre. Here there were no shiny high-rises of chrome and glass. Modernity hadn't rippled this far out yet, and instead, the buildings were red brick and old, waiting for the new tides of investment and gentrification to wash out to them. This was old Manchester, at odds with the new one a mile or so further in.

Cold Cut was Liverpudlian to his core. He felt like he had been parachuted behind enemy lines, careful not to speak in case his razor-wire Scouse accent would draw attention he could do without. Truth was the opposite, fortified by his brutal accomplice a yard or two behind him, no doubt, speaking loudly and brashly without a care.

Truth steered Cold Cut away from the main road outside the station, into the maze of old streets that branched off like capillaries. It wasn't long before Cold Cut felt irretrievably lost, a cold tension in his knotted stomach at having to rely on Truth to lead him out again. Lefts and rights were taken, past grimy shopfronts with peeling paint, and cookie-cutter terracing. Eventually, they stopped in front of a terrace house that looked no different to any of the others – curtains tightly pulled, and a yard now lost to the weeds that had pushed their way through the gaps in the concrete.

Truth knocked on the door, twice. Cold Cut, rather than just stare at the door, took the opportunity to turn around to take a look up and down the street before he went inside, perhaps searching for someone who would remember him if he turned up on a "missing" poster. Consequences stood at the end of the short yard path, where the gate might once have stood. He looked at Cold Cut like a cat looks at a mouse, confident that at the very least, he was not going to be the one under the microscope.

The door opened, the dark inside at odds with the last shinings of the crisp winter afternoon outside. Cold Cut couldn't see who opened the door. Truth didn't wait, walking inside, Cold Cut given no choice but to follow on. He passed a dark figure who had opened the door, and had stood aside to let the newcomers enter. Truth had turned right off the hallway, into the front room. Cold Cut looked behind him, one last look at the open air before Consequences came inside, and the door closed, trapping him inside.

Cold Cut followed Truth into the front room. Another man stood just inside the room, shaven-headed and huge, olive-skinned, plain even in the muted darkness of the room. The room itself was bare, stripped of whatever ornaments and comforts Cold Cut might have expected to find in a house like this. Instead there were two plastic chairs, the sort you might find in a school hall or back-street café, facing each other in the centre of the room. One was empty, and clearly left for Cold Cut, Truth standing behind it, holding the back of it by way of invitation. The other chair was not empty.

Sat in the chair was a man in his 50s, clearly of latin

origin, judging by his dark eyes and darker hair. He had a thick beard on his face, and was wearing designer glasses. His legs were crossed, almost primly, and his hands rested on one knee. He indicated to Cold Cut to sit, saying nothing.

Cold Cut did as he was bid. The man looked back at him, unblinking. Cold Cut said nothing, smart enough to realise to speak when he was spoken to, letting the man make his assessment of him without giving him any reason for prejudice.

Finally, the man spoke with perfect diction, only a trace of an accent at the edges of the vowels and consonants, that gave a hint of his true origin.

“Thank you for coming,” the man said. “I understand from our colleague here that you might be in a position to present us with an opportunity.”

## 26

Jackie felt different. She felt that she had burnt away some old part of herself in the same flames as her husband – the warmth, the kindness, the hope. All that was left, like a diamond in the coal, was a yearning for revenge, and a steely determination to hold onto what her husband had built.

She was sat at her breakfast bar in her dressing gown, curtains still pulled despite the sun having come up an hour ago. She was staring at the black coffee in front of her, allowing herself to focus on the battles that she expected to face in the coming days, Tony and Eleanor Grace most prominent in her mind's eye.

She heard a key in the door, and then it open, a voice calling through from the front of the house.

"Mum? It's only me."

Jackie didn't answer at first. She heard Carol, her daughter, diligently wipe her feet on the mat just inside the doorway, then closing the door behind her. It was a routine that Carol had gone through hundreds of times in the past, and one that Jackie knew well. She treated it like she was listening to a hypnotist counting backwards - a count that pulled her away from the distractions she had found in the black of the coffee, and back to the here and now of her kitchen.

"I'm in here, love," Jackie eventually said, quietly, but still loud enough to carry through.

Carol announced herself by popping her head around the door, a warm smile on her face, but still the faintest trace of tiredness around her eyes. It had been tough for her too, of course, Jackie realised. Carol had lost her father, but also her kids had lost their grandfather, and she was the first breakwater against the waves of their grief.

"Hiya, mum," Carol said. "Are you ok? In the dark here?"

"Just waking up slowly, love," Jackie said. "Did you want one? I think there's some coffee left in the pot..." Her voice trailed off as she turned her head to check.

"I'll do it, mum," Carol said, comfortable in a house that was once her own home, washing out a dirty mug in the sink, and going about the mechanics of making a new pot of coffee.

"I've been worried," Carol eventually said, happy to have something to distract her instead of having to raise this with her mum face-to-face. She didn't want to see Jackie's face, as seeing her mother upset was something she couldn't bear, especially given how Jackie was typically the one who was the anchor point that the family would tether itself to in times of stress.

"About...?" Jackie said, though she knew the answer. She was uncomfortable with the conversation that was blooming, and any delay before reaching the heart of it was welcome, however brief.

"You, mum," Carol said. A kettle was now on the hob, boiling water for a fresh batch of grounds.

"I know, love. I know," Jackie hoped that that would be enough, and she could steer the conversation away from her.

Carol didn't respond, and instead focussed on the task at hand. Jackie knew something was on her mind – a conversation she didn't want to have, but knew it needed to be dealt with now before it had time to build into something more.

The kettle had boiled, the water poured over the grounds, and the brown, rich coffee blip-blipped through the filter into the glass pot. Carol absent-mindedly tapped her manicured nails on the counter top, waiting. Nothing was said as they both waited for the coffee to be ready.

Finally, the coffee was poured, and Carol took the mug across the room, to sit opposite Jackie on the breakfast bar. She took a sip, savoured the strong taste, then looked across at her mum.

"What's going on, mum?" she said. "It's been...weird since Dad, you know..."

Carol gnawed at the inside of her lip, and looked away, briefly, before taking another sip of coffee.

"Of course it has," Jackie said. "It's been a shock. A massive shock for all of us."

"I know that. But since then, I'm just...I've just been worried about you. I mean, what's going on with you, and dad's business, and I don't..." Carol floundered. She wasn't used to talking to her mum like this, bordering on the accusatory. There was an elephant in the room, and she didn't want to face it.

"Dad's business. Yes. Okay. Now, your dad worked very hard to give us the life that we've got, and now he's...gone, then someone has got to work as hard as him to make sure that people don't take it away from us. There's no-one else, Carol. It's got to be me that does it."

"But, dad's work was..." Carol trailed off.

"Dangerous," Jackie said.

"Dangerous," Carol echoed.

Jackie had a mouthful of cool coffee at the bottom of her mug. She put the mug to her mouth and drank it all down. The bitter taste was the shock that she needed to spur her to speak truths.

"Carol. Love. Your dad was a gangster. He loved us more than life itself, but you need to hear this. He was a crook, who did whatever it took to stay at the top of the tree round here, and woe betide anyone who got in his way. You *do* know that, don't you?"

Carol opened her mouth to reply, then closed it, looked down at her mug, and nodded.

"I know you know this. You live in this town. You'll have heard all the stories about your dad, and I know he used to laugh and joke and wave all that stuff away, but I'm telling you, most of it was true. Maybe all of it was true. He wouldn't even tell me the half of it, in the end."

Carol kept quiet. She knew all this already, but that reality was always just something she kept inside her head. Jackie was making it real, putting flesh on the bones, leaving no space for any deniability between them.

"So, whatever happens, it's going to be bumpy in the next few weeks. Maybe longer. Because your dad is dead, and everyone knows that, and there are going to be people who look at that and just see an opportunity. All those people that your dad used to deal with, however he had to, are going to try their luck again. They want what we have. What he gave us."

"Is that what those two men are here for? The men I've seen you with?"

"Your dad loved us. And he was clever with it. So, those two men – Mr Solomon and Mr Parker – were a little security service that your dad arranged just in case anything like this happened. Because he knew what would happen if something happened to him. They are going to help me, and help us, get through this."

"What do you mean? What are you doing? Mum, I'm scared."

"I'm sorry, Carol. I'm sorry you're scared. But I want you to listen to me very carefully now."

Jackie reached her hand across the bar, and rested it on Carol's hand. Carol grasped at her mother's hand, squeezing it, years seeming to fall off her until she looked at Jackie like she was like a child again. Two weeks ago – a day ago, even – Jackie might have softened her tone, and dealt in euphemism, seeing her daughter look at her as a little girl would again. But Jackie had changed. She had to. There was too much at stake for anything else now.

"There are people who are going to want to come after what your dad built. They will do whatever it takes to get it. That means that we are all going to have be careful. But I want you to know something. I want you to hear this from me, from my lips, as God listens.

"There is no-one on this earth who is going to take what we have from us. I am going to do everything to keep it. To protect us. Anyone who even thinks about making a move, I'm going to deal with them. Do you hear me, Carol? You need to understand this.

"I'm going to deal with them. I'm going to fucking kill them, Carol. If they want what we have, I'm going to kill them."

Carol's hand pulled away from Jackie's grasp as she heard this. Carol's eyes widened.

"Mum, I'm scared. I'm scared of all this," Carol said, her voice quavering. Her eyes had reddened and cheeks flushed. "I'm scared of you."

Carol stood up.

"Mum, I don't know who my dad was," she said, walking backwards away from the breakfast bar, towards the door.

"I don't know who you are," Carol said. "Not like this."

"You know who your father was, Carol. You knew what he did. You might have tried to avoid thinking about it, but you knew all those stories couldn't all be lies."

"Just let them have it, mum. Whoever wants it, let them have it. I don't want people to look at us – look at *my kids* – and think they can hurt us because of dad"

"No!" Jackie stood up now, hands slapping on the marble surface of the bar. "No. Your dad didn't end up with a bullet in his fucking head for us to just let it all slip away at the first problem. No. That is not going to happen. Business as usual. Our business."

Her raised voice had scared Carol. She was at the doorway of the kitchen now, ready to escape whoever this person was that had replaced her mother. Or was she fooling herself? Deep-down, did she always know that this was always inside her mother, ready to come out and scrap and scrape, tooth and claw, for what she saw as hers?

"You need to trust me, Carol," Jackie continued. "I'll make it safe. For you and the kids. Until this is all over. And it will be over. Things won't need to change."

"But you have, mum," Carol responded. "You have."

Those words cooled the heat of the conversation. But it was too late. Carol had left, walking through the house, opening the front door to escape this. Back to the self-delusion of her safe, mundane life, hoping to bury any truths about her family back where they usually lay.

Jackie called through.

"We need to face this. As a family. I'll deal with it, Carol. We're going to be okay. Nothing is going to change."

The front door slammed. She knew she was fooling herself. She had changed. Everything had.

# 27

Cold Cut wasn't stupid. He may not have academic smarts, or way with words, but he had a feral intelligence that had enabled him to make it through his life to this point without much harm, though not without stress. A survival instinct that knew when he needed to fight against his personality and be quiet and do as he was told. Though, it would take a special kind of idiot who would attempt anything more forceful in a situation like this.

He was in a room in a house in a city that wasn't his. In this room were two men he knew – Truth and Consequences – and two he didn't – the two foreign men. He had no reason to believe that any of them would veer towards the sympathetic should he make any kind of mistake. They held the power, and he knew it all too well.

He felt like he was being scrutinised. The man sat across from him understood the power of silence. He had a faint smile on his face, and unblinking eyes, taking the measure of Cold Cut, who was fidgeting in his seat across from him. Cold Cut did his best not to look back, instead looking around the room, fully aware that he was trapped here, and would only leave with the blessing of others.

The room struck Cold Cut as bizarre. There was no furniture in the room, other than the two chairs he and the man were sat on, but the walls still had traces of whoever once lived here – a garish feature-wall dominated by a black-painted fireplace, and an empty picture frame on one of the walls, shaped as the word “LOVE”. A memorial to a family home, now hollowed out, home only to more sinister undertakings.

The man finally spoke, and Cold Cut had the sense to give him his full attention.

“Our mutual associates,” the man indicated the two who had brought Cold Cut here, “have told us a little of you, and what you are proposing, but I think it might be prudent for you to tell us this suggestion of yours, so as not to risk confusing your purpose.”

Cold Cut nodded, and tried to speak in the affirmative, but was betrayed by his voice, which had deserted him. A cough, then he regrouped, and started to speak.

“Yes, okay. Yes. So, right, the thing is, right...”

The man held his hand up.

“Take your time. I understand that you might be feeling intimidated. Please. It is important that you are clear and do not feel any pressure that might cause you to miss something vital,” the man said, smiling warmly, which only served to chill Cold Cut further.

Cold Cut took a deep breath, and started again, speaking slowly so his words did not run away from him.

“Sorry. Sorry. So, the thing is, I know people in Liverpool. I know you haven’t tried anything there for years, not since you were run off...”

Cold Cut regretted that. The man shifted his position,

uncrossing and then recrossing his legs. Cold Cut needed to be careful, as he was in danger of letting this situation turn into something sharper and more unpleasant. He tried again.

"...since you tried before. But I don't know if you know, but Mr Stark, who you had problems with before, has died..."

The man interrupted, with that soft voice that Cold Cut found so unsettling.

"We are aware of the incident that led to Mr Stark becoming deceased."

"Right, so, now Stark has died, as well as all of his main men, there's an opportunity, right? Most of the business is still in place, but there's going to be a scrap over who runs the thing. See, Stark's missus is thinking she can just take over, and some of the lads aren't happy about that at all. One of them reckons he can take over, and all he needs is some product to get it all earning again. So, that's where I thought you might come in."

The man interlinked his fingers on his knees, and leaned forward slightly, but saying nothing, letting Cold Cut have the space to continue talking. Plenty of room to hang a noose over his own neck.

"See, I can be the link between you and your business here, and inside the Stark business, and help you arrange to get your gear in the right hands. You can have all the benefits of running Liverpool without anyone knowing, or even having to get your hands dirty."

"This is an interesting proposal to us," said the man. "We were inconvenienced some years ago due to the disagreement between ourselves and Mr Stark. It would be a positive for us to pick up where we left off without the need for any wastefulness or rashness."

"Well, see, that's what I thought," Cold Cut said. "I mean, there was never any doubt about your gear, like. Really top stuff."

"I feel it would be remiss of me not to raise a few challenges to your proposal, though," the man said. "A few points I would be interested to hear your feedback on."

Cold Cut gulped, then rubbed the back of his neck, irritating that angry growth on his neck. It throbbed down his spine and to his temples as if his nerves were burning. The man continued.

"Why do we need to deal with you at all? What is to stop us just carrying on from where we were interrupted those years ago? You said yourself that the Stark hierarchy has been decimated."

"That's just it. Bad for business, isn't it? Yeah, a lot of them are dead, but not all of them, and there would still be bad feeling that some foreign lads – no offence – were trying to muscle in on their business. Why risk it? Why not just get in early, without any bother, and get your gear moving. Once you're all set up as the supplier, you can come along later and start to run things directly, right?"

The man looked at Cold Cut, absent-mindedly rubbing his beard as he did so.

"I am intrigued by your proposal. It has...merit," the man said. "And what would be your role in this arrangement?"

Here it is, thought Cold Cut. The important part.

"Look, I'm a useful lad to have around, right?" Cold Cut said. "I thought I would be the one to arrange the meetings so your gear gets to the right people, and you would pay me like an administrative fee for handling it?"

"I see," the man said. "Go on."

"Right, so I know which of the Stark crew are still loyal

to his wife, and which are not. I'd be the one to make sure that the right people are set up ready for you to do business, and to sort it all out before there's any chance of it getting messy."

"Messy," the man said. It wasn't a question. More of a mental note to himself.

"Yeah. I know you are the sort of firm – "

"Enterprise," the man corrected.

"Enterprise, right," Cold Cut echoed. "The sort of *enterprise* that didn't want to waste time and effort on drama. I would make sure you avoided all of that."

"I see," the man said. "And what would you want for doing this management for us?"

"I was thinking, like, ten percent of what the Liverpool lads pay you for the gear. A finder's fee, sort of thing."

"Ten percent," the man said, the act of saying it out loud, back to Cold Cut, making it seem as implausible as Cold Cut turning lead into gold. "That is a little rich for our tastes, I'm afraid."

"Sure, sure, ok. Five percent. How about five percent?" Cold Cut stammered, floundering. He was so far out of his depth he couldn't feel the bottom or see the top.

"Two percent of the first drop, and one percent of the second, and then we will review your ongoing usefulness," the man said.

"Deal, deal, yes, like it," Cold Cut blurted, jumping out of his seat, hand thrust forward as if the preposterousness of his success could actually be secured with a handshake.

The man smiled, got to his feet slowly, indicating to his underling to ease back. Cold Cut hadn't noticed that the huge man, who had stood guard on the door, had taken two steps towards him when he had stood up, ready to wring Cold Cut's neck for the audacity of moving too quickly in front of his boss. Cold Cut looked around at the bodyguard, smiling nervously, palms up.

"Sorry, sorry," Cold Cut said, before turning back to the man's superior.

"My colleagues here – " he nodded to Truth and Consequences – "will supervise the first transaction you make. It will be your responsibility to ensure that any deal is undertaken with no drama, as you say. I sincerely hope you appreciate the position of trust that we are placing in you."

"Of course," Cold Cut said. "I understand. Completely."

"I'm sure you do," the man said, "but I wish to show you something before you leave us today."

The man walked past Cold Cut, past the bodyguard, and past Truth and Consequences.

"Please follow me," he said.

Cold Cut followed behind, out of the room, the bodyguard trailing behind, blocking any escape, should one be needed. They walked into the hallway, and then through the ground floor of the house, into the kitchen, and then through the kitchen to the bathroom at the back of the house. The man in front pushed open the white painted door of the bathroom, and indicated for Cold Cut to step inside.

Cold Cut recoiled as soon as he put a foot on the tiled floor of the bathroom. It was a fairly small room, with a sink and toilet on one side of the room, and the other dominated by a bath and shower screen. He had never seen anything as terrifying as what he saw in the bath.

Hanging from the ceiling, on a strong rope and hook, was a body, feet and hands tied together behind the back. The hook was looped through the bindings, so the body swung like a carcass in an abattoir. And this was what this room had become – an abattoir. Cold Cut thought the body was male, but beyond that he couldn't be completely sure, as it had been so brutally tortured it was hard to be definitive. Gaping wounds across the body, and the remnants of clothing soaked through with dark blood. Wire cut into the skin at the hands and the ankles, so any struggle would just cause more injury. The mouth was gagged, on a face that had been the focus of most of the torment, any individuality scoured away by whatever evil had been delivered to it.

The man in charge spoke from behind Cold Cut, the sound of it causing Cold Cut to flinch, further stimulus to process in his already-fraying mind.

"I hope you appreciate the need to focus. The need to deliver your promises," the man said.

Cold Cut tried to speak, but again, found his voice missing. As his mouth flapped, impotently, he felt the man rest his hand on his shoulder. It was almost friendly, and completely chilling.

"Do not fail us," the man said.

As he said this, the body hanging over the bath flicked open its eyelids, wild-eyes desperate for help. Or desperate for an end to the pain. The eyes stared at Cold Cut urging him to do something. Anything.

"I promise," Cold Cut sputtered. "I promise."

He turned away, the man permitting him to leave, his point made. He scurried through the house, to the front door, which he opened and closed quickly behind him. His breathing was fast and shallow, the shock of that vile sight difficult to push down. Instinctively, he reached inside his coat for a cigarette, which he held in his shaking fingers as he struggled to ignite his lighter. Truth and Consequences opened the front door, and joined him in the street, Consequences smiling manically, enjoying the freak show in the same way as a kid enjoys pulling the legs from insects.

"Hold on, Cutty," Truth said, squeezing every drop of enjoyment out of Cold Cut's terror. "Hold your hand out."

Cold Cut did as he was told, as if in a trance. Truth put a small plastic bag into his palm.

"A sample," Truth said. "For them to try before they buy."

Cold Cut couldn't stop his hands from shaking, so just stuffed both fists into his pockets, the bag of coke tightly clutched in one of them.

The body in the bath was a warning. It scared Cold Cut like nothing he had ever seen before. This was a gangster fairy-tale made flesh. A whispered story told in kebab-shop doorways to keep slingers straight. But he'd seen it, with his own two eyes. These things really did happen. There were people in this world – his world – that really did do stuff like this. And they had felt so comfortable with it, with their position, that they shared it with him like they were showing him a holiday photo. And more than that.

Cold Cut was scared because he knew what he had done. He had opened a Pandora's Box, and there was no closing it now. He knew if he didn't deliver, then it would be him hanging upside down in a place like that, watching his life flow from him down a drain in some forgotten house somewhere.

# 28

Tony and Eleanor had put the best part of three weeks between them and the carnage they had caused in Liverpool. Drifting on their whims around Yorkshire until they had been forced to return to the real world and come to Stoke, to Steaky. They'd spent a couple of days with him, not leaving the house, grateful for a new voice to ask their old questions to, in the hope that he might have an answer for them that neither of them had considered until now.

Steaky was one of those people who offered a new perspective. A brain that had been wired a little differently to others, leading to a sense of humour that bordered on the atomic, and a way with logic that defied debate. If he was omnipotent, he would be the kind of Creator that moulds the platypus out of the holy clay. It was never dull with Steaky.

Paranoia was the mindset that would see them through this. Steaky needed no excuse to not indulge in that, given that it was his design for life on any given day. He loved spinning stories about moon landings and phone signals and shadowy government secret societies, all with a verve and a joy that left his audience never entirely sure how much of it he actually believed. There was no conspiracy theory too outré for him, and he had built his life carefully, so he could be best placed if ever the scales fell and the shadowy cabal that ran the world was unmasked.

His life was a patchwork quilt of pseudonym and smoke-screen, where, to all intents and purposes, his name – his real name – simply stopped mattering years ago, once he had left the service. He wasn't on any electoral roll, and a life of cash purchases had seen him vanish from the databases that organise the rest of the population. Only a select few knew who he was, and it served him well to keep it that way, making the occasions where he needed to earn easier, given the type of work that he found himself drawn to.

He had a contact – someone he had known for years – who had given him a burner phone. If the phone rang, Steaky wouldn't answer, but knew that he needed to make the long walk to the nearest working phone box and ring a different number. There he would be given a place to meet, different every time, and only then would he be given his task. It was all shadow-work – tracking someone for a day or two, and preparing a file on their movements and their associates, in exchange for payment in cash. He lived frugally, and the work was easy and well-rewarded, and he found he had more than enough. More than enough to continue living his life in shadows and smoke.

That's why Tony and Eleanor had chosen to look to Steaky for sanctuary. Eleanor's old comrades – the "Family" – would've all put themselves in the way of the Graces and whoever was coming for them, but of all of them, Steaky was the one who was best placed to help them hide. To find themselves sheltered by someone who made it his life's work to live on the periphery, with no mortgage, no bank account, and as light an impression on the world as possible. There was also a kind of selfishness about their decision to look to Steaky for safety – of all of the names that they could've called on, Steaky was the one with no dependents to be put at risk. Minimal collateral damage, using the language of the missions the Family were sent on, all those years ago.

But whatever guilt they felt for putting their friend at risk was soon assuaged by the fierce brio of the man himself.

"Fuck that!" Steaky exclaimed when Tony quietly mentioned that they didn't want to overstay their welcome because of the risks.

"You stay for as long as you have to," Steaky said, "and if anyone wants to come at you, then those motherfuckers are going to see how sharp I can be."

Eleanor was cooking in the tight kitchen, happy to throw herself into something creative, and happy to let the "boys" blather on in the front room, knowing how Steaky had a way of barrelling through the usual wall of reserve that Tony erected, more so than almost anyone else she knew. Tony was shy, and needed coaxing into any conversation, but Steaky was the sort of person who ran headlong into traffic for shits and giggles, and that attitude was infectious, even with Tony.

Tony and Steaky were sipping at cups of tea, an almost constant replenishment of hot drinks since their imposed house lockdown. The flatscreen TV was on, with the sound down, a spaghetti of wires snaking from the back of the unit into all manner of hooky receivers, as Steaky took the same relaxed attitude to TV subscriptions as he did to the rest of his life. On the screen was the kaleidoscope clash of pro-wrestling, with teak-tough men, chiselled and fierce, beating merry hell out of each other, or rather, doing their best to make it look like that. Every so often, Steaky would puff out an exclamation as a wicked blow was struck. Both men stayed glued to the screen, even as the conversation developed.

"I love this shit, Tone," Steaky said, with a schoolboy grin. "It's a real art to be as big as that, and not actually smash the shit out of the other fella."

"I guess," Tony said, humouring his host. "But that one has got blood all over his face. Did he screw up somewhere?"

"Nah. They do this thing called 'blading', right? Tiny little razor blade hidden in that tape around their wrists. When the camera is off, they slip it out, and cut away at their forehead a little bit. Forehead bleeds like a bastard. All part of the theatre."

"Oh," Tony said, and they both returned to watching some gigantic brute fling another out of the wrestling ring and into a balsa table, to oohs and ahhs from the watching crowd. Eventually, Tony spoke again.

"Steaky, mate, we really appreciate it, but we don't want to be a burden. Not only that, but this could get really flaky, if they do actually get their shit together and come looking."

"Burden? Don't be soft," Steaky said, taking a sip of tea, "It's so good to see you. And this is Family, right? Come for one, come for all. You know I loves yer." With that, Steaky broke from gazing at the screen, and flashed a toothy grin at Tony, which Tony could not help but smile at.

"I know El doesn't like to ask, but I know when my friends need help, and what good am I if I'm not there for them. What's the point otherwise?" Steaky said, more quietly. He wasn't used to talking to people so openly. He wasn't used to talking to people at all.

"Well, we're open to ideas, Steak," Tony replied. "We don't know what to expect. How long we need to stay here to stay safe. Whether anyone is coming for us – for you, too – or not."

"So, what do they know? You two did for the top men in that crew, right? They know it was you, and they know that you will have left town, right? What will they have done next...?"

Steaky eased back into his chair, crossing his legs, finally moving the TV entertainment to a background distraction so he could work through this conundrum.

"They would've gone to your house out East, and just made sure you weren't stupid enough to go back there. Give that a few days, to make sure the lights stay off. Okay. Then what?"

"Family and friends," Tony replied.

"Family and friends. Exactly," Steaky echoed. "Have you checked your family?"

"Mum is in sheltered accommodation. We haven't called, and there's no way we would risk going to visit. We're just going to have to gamble that they won't be so stupid as to think they *we* would be so stupid as to go there."

"Makes sense. They know that you would go somewhere for help, not to put someone else in the firing line," Steaky said. He paused, then roared with laughter. "Well, only a twat like me, right?"

"No, no!" Tony laughed back, "It's not like that."

Tony took a beat.

"Okay, it's exactly like that," he said, and both men fell about laughing all over again.

"What is it?" came the voice from the kitchen, "What are you two bell-ends cackling about?"

"Nothing, dear," Tony called back through, miming an

"uh-oh" expression to Steaky as he said it. There was a moment of silence, as the conversation reset, and then Tony continued working through the problem with Steaky.

"I think that mum is okay. It makes sense. Look, I know they could just get to her for the hell of it, but if we are off the radar, and they know we are not stupid enough to risk getting in touch with her, then them hurting her doesn't seem like a good move. How would we find out?"

"Seems right. You need help. Someone who can put a roof over your head, and maybe even go a bit further. They would know that you might not risk hitting your bank account, not right now, as that might flag something up. The logical step is that you would come to one of us – one of the Family. Do they know about us? Eleanor's history?"

"I don't know. The top guy knew about it, but he's dead. Would he have told anyone? I don't know. The only way they would find out is..." Tony's voice trailed off, as the conclusion loomed into view.

"What?" Steaky said, impatient.

"We left some stuff in a flat. We had to leave in a hurry, and never went back for it. There was some of Eleanor's service memorabilia there. They'd have to have found it. Fuck, it's the first place I would've gone if I was them."

"So they will know about us by now."

"I think we have to assume so," Tony said. He swilled the tea around in his mug, as if he was hoping to divine some truths in the liquid, like an old carny fortune-teller.

"So let's work to that assumption. We need to warn the boys. Warn them that someone might come knocking for them."

~

"Do we need to do anything? Take more precautions?" Eleanor asked, as she scooped a spoonful of rice up for another bite.

"We can't be too careful," Steaky said.

There was a brief pause, before Tony and Eleanor both snorted, then stopped trying to smother the giggles that had bubbled up.

"What?" Steaky said, smiling.

It was something of a catchphrase. A bit of homespun wisdom that might as well have been chiselled into every brick of his house, and tattooed on every bare bit of his skin. An entire philosophy of life distilled into five words. As soon as he said it, and saw the reaction in Tony and Eleanor he knew what he had done.

"If I could ask the good lady and the good gentleman to perhaps focus on the task at hand, I would be most appreciative," Steaky said, in as broad an approximation of english gentry as he could get away with. It was to impersonation as an articulated lorry is to roadkill.

Eleanor looked at Tony, and allowed herself a moment of relaxation, despite the atmosphere of pursuit that they shouldered. She loved Tony, and if this curious lummox of a friend could distract Tony from the whetted blade of their situation if only for a brief moment, then she was going to be grateful for it. Steaky was the kind of person who would comment on the evening's meal choices as grenades exploded around him. Even Tony with all his reserve and his introspection was incapable of resisting the relentless good nature of Steaky.

"I'm sorry, Steak. Sorry," Tony said, hands up in surrender, before mopping up the last traces of the sauce at the side of his plate with a piece of bread. "Do go on."

"We were talking about precautions," Steaky said, trying to get the conversation back on track.

"We can make sure we stay in for a bit longer?" Tony said.

"It's a bit of a rat run around here, but the good news is that most of these houses are empty," Eleanor said. "Or at least, *mostly* empty."

"I think that's a safe bet," Steaky said. "If anyone is in any of these houses they are going to be far too strung out to give a shit about the likes of youse. But I agree. Stay in for now. You need to keep your heads down, and I'll look at the matter in hand."

"Like what?" Eleanor said.

"Well, we need to check in with the lads, to see if they are okay, and to give them a bit of heads up that there might be some shit heading their way as well. We owe them that."

"How do we do that?" Tony said. "We can't phone them. Fuck, mate, you don't even *have* a phone."

"Let me worry about that. First, I need to show you something," Steaky said.

He stood up, gathered up the finished plates, and walked into the kitchen to put them in the sink to be washed up. Eleanor and Tony got to their feet as well, Eleanor grabbing the glasses, and Tony the condiments, before they too went into the kitchen.

The kitchen window looked out onto a small yard, with whitewashed brick walls, six feet high, forming the border between that yard and the next. Seperate from the main construction of the house was a separate outhouse, also made from brick and painted white, with a black wooden door locked with a padlock. It was an old coal store, which Tony and Eleanor had presumed had just been repurposed into a shed for whatever ephemera Steaky wanted to keep, but not inside the house. A rocket launcher or alcohol still, most likely.

"Okay, just a second. Wait there," Steaky said, and opened the back door. He walked outside, as casually as he could, idly scanning left and right just in case there was some villain in the shadows observing them. Satisfied, he turned back, and beckoned them outside.

Tony and Eleanor followed on, quietly waiting as Steaky fished in his pockets for a set of keys, which he produced with a triumphant jangle. He selected a key, and unlocked the padlock of the coal store, before opening the door. Tony and Eleanor looked at each other, raising an eyebrow to each other, then back to watch the main show.

Steaky plinked the light on, and beckoned them inside.

"Here," Steaky said. "Look."

In the middle of the small coal store was a trapdoor, drawbolted shut. Steaky had unlocked the padlock that had secured the trapdoor, and swung it open.

"Holy shit, Steak," Tony said.

With the trapdoor open, Tony and Eleanor could see what it had covered - a ladder that led down into blackness.

"Come on down," Steaky said with a smile, and disappeared down the hole. Tony and Eleanor again looked at each other, with Eleanor offering an "after you" gesture with a smile.

Steaky was waiting for them at the bottom of the hole, which he had illuminated by switching on another light at the bottom. Tony and Eleanor were used to his eccentricities but even this was a surprise to them.

"Of course you have," Eleanor said. "Of course."

Beneath the coal store was what was left of an old cellar that would've served the house. The store was built on top of the entrance at a later date, ostensibly to tidy up the yard, and hide the cellar trapdoor from the outside elements, or the nefarious who might've had their own intentions if they could access it. Steaky had turned the cellar into his own private bunker.

"So, here we are," Steaky said, proudly. "My own private hideaway."

The cellar, like everything Steaky put his hand to, was fit for purpose, even if that purpose appeared to be organised in such a chaotic manner that no sense could be made of it. The cellar was large enough for the three of them to be accommodated without any discomfort, even with the heavy wooden desk and swivel chair that dominated one side of the room. On the opposite wall were a couple of bookcases, one full of all manner of electronic equipment, some flashing lights to show they were operational, whilst others were carefully stacked, the purposes of all of them mysterious. The other bookcase was full of books, all looking like they had been read in the manner of an assault, with creased spines and bent edges, covering all manner of subjects, but all subjects that they knew Steaky had a passion for – warfare, communications, politics, history.

One of the walls, underneath the border between Steaky's yard and one of the neighbouring ones, had a curtain pulled across part of it.

"It gets better," Steaky said.

"I dread to think," Eleanor replied, quietly.

Steaky swept the curtain aside, and revealed a rough opening, where the brickwork had been removed, opening out into another room, the contents hidden by the heavy darkness within. He reached through the opening, and around onto the reverse of the wall, clunking a heavy switch that he had screwed to the wall on the other side. A row of temporary lights blinked on, hung from the ceiling of the room on hooks.

"I don't know what to say," Tony said. "What is all this?"

Steaky stepped through the opening, into the new room, then turned back, and hands on either side of the opening, swung back and forth like a naughty child, proud and embarrassed in equal measure.

"It's my den," he said.

Tony and Eleanor both laughed. Laughter was never far away when they were around Steaky, him always cooking up some scheme or other in his plot to either erase a bit more of himself from the wider world, or some new way of establishing a change to the world order. He knew how ridiculous many of his plans were, but he was never deterred or dissuaded. All manner of things could be achieved by someone happy to embrace the unusual.

"So, these houses all had a serving cellar, some bigger than others, but only a wall or two keeping them from all being directly connected. So, as I've had a go at seeing how many of them I can open up."

"But don't people mind you bashing around underneath their houses?" Tony said.

"That's the thing, though. There's no-one in any of these houses, and I've secured all of them from above. The smackheads can barely find the strength to kick the front door in, let alone start smashing their way through trapdoors. And that's if they even get in in the first place," Steaky replied.

"And what if, I don't know, someone actually moves into these houses?" Eleanor asked. "Aren't these the ones that are in that cheap purchase scheme?"

"That load of shit," Steaky countered. "Public relations exercise. Well, disaster, more like. They only managed to sell a couple of them in the next street, and they moved out sharpish when they saw what a shithole they were living in. There's no-one moving into these houses anytime soon."

Tony opened his mouth to ask another question. Steaky was ready for it.

"And no-one is rebuilding anything round here. Have you seen the place? They only had enough money to knock shit down, and then they run out. It's why the old factories are now just piles of bricks. They aren't knocking these houses down before they fall down."

"Well, I'm impressed," Eleanor said. "And, par for the course, a little bit scared as well, Steak. What are you showing us all this for, though?"

"Yeah, good point, sorry. I get excited. So, provided you're careful getting to the trapdoor, you can get into the cellar pretty much unseen. If the worst happens, and someone comes looking for you, then you can get out, and down, and away before they know what's happening. There's another way out at the far end, through all the cellars. It comes out in a coal store like this, in the house on the end of the row."

"Steak, mate. It's perfect," Tony said. "No-one would have any idea, looking at the house from the outside."

"It might not have all the mod-cons, but it's rigged for an electric fire, and we can get some bedding in here. It'll do until we can be sure that the coast is clear," Steaky said.

He moved back into the first room, and across to his desk.

"I've got something else to show you," he said.

He reached up to the bookcase, and pulled down an old laptop, the casing covered in stickers and marker-pen graffiti. He plugged a few leads into the back, and opened it up.

It powered up, and the screen glowed indistinctly, before settling down into recognisable shapes. The display showed a grid of images, three by three.

"CCTV?" Eleanor asked, incredulously.

"CCTV," Steaky confirmed. "I've got a few cameras front and back. Just in case."

"In case of what, you lunatic?" Eleanor said. "What were you planning on using all this space for?"

"Well, I was thinking, once I've insulated the rooms a bit more, and got the power properly siphoned from some of the meters in these houses, well, I might just have myself the perfect little underground farm."

"I might've known," Eleanor said, hands on hips. It was a charade, though. She liked playing the older sister role for Steaky, and for the rest of the unit, but they both knew that any attempt at putting Steaky on the straight and narrow was a battle that had long ago been lost.

"Man's gotta earn," Steaky replied, with a playful shrug.

"Amen, brother," Tony said.

"Don't you fucking start," Eleanor said. "You're meant to be a respectable retiree, old man."

"Not that old, love," Tony said. "Not yet. Not all that respectable either, truth be told."

"Look, here's what we do," Steaky said. "I'll start calling the lads, careful like, just to give them the heads up to be careful. Code words and all that, and you two just keep your heads down here until we know for certain the Family are all in the clear. Maybe we can find a way to check around Liverpool to take the temperature there as well."

Steaky put his arms around Tony and Eleanor, pulling them into him with a tight squeeze.

"You just leave it to old Steak, okay?"

## 29

Jackie was surprised how quickly any old nervousness on her part had been swallowed whole by this new version of her that she was constructing. Jim was far more comfortable with the nature of his criminal life, and had become so confident in his position that he made precious few concessions to appearances. Jim always argued that all you needed was confidence – a projection of belief that you were meant to be somewhere, or be someone, and human nature would trust that the world was working how it was meant to work. He would say "never look up in a big city, because you'll just look like a tourist" whenever anyone pointed out the risk of operating in plain sight.

It was ludicrous. How could this seemingly average man, with his polyester jacket and high street shoes seriously be the same man that ran the rackets across the city, from tenement to new build estate. But it worked, maybe just through force of will.

Jackie had always tried not to analyse this confidence trick too closely. All she knew was that she felt no less safe from one day to the next, and Jim had a way of waving away even the prospect of storm clouds with fierce and relentless surety.

And even though Jim was gone, she had found that this lesson he had taught her was one that she adopted with ease, any trace of doubt or worry burnt away by the white heat of her anger.

This was why she felt no concern walking around the docks with Solomon and Parker, and if anyone was watching them with curious eyes, then damn them. Her single-mindedness made her feel invulnerable. "If you look up, at all the skyscrapers," Jim would say, "you'll miss the hand that has your wallet out of your back pocket. Always believe that you belong somewhere, and no-one will be able to challenge you." So let them look, whoever they might be.

It was a bright, crisply cold morning. She had her hands in the pockets of her thick coat, walking at a slow meander, with Solomon at her shoulder, and Parker steadily pacing behind both of them.

"The matter I mainly wish to discuss with you today, Mrs Stark, is the matter of our ongoing search for the Graces," Solomon said. They were an odd threesome, with Parker in tow, but this was Liverpool, and there was always the occasion for strangeness, irrespective of time and place. They drew no stares.

"I feel it would be pertinent to speak to our colleague who is undertaking this search for us, and for them to appraise all of us together," he continued. "I feel it would be useful for you to be involved in this discussion, not least as the person with the most vested interest in finding those we seek. Of course, you will have your own questions as well, and this will be an opportunity for you to raise them."

"I'd like that, Mr Solomon," Jackie said, half-looking at a

window of apartment listings for the gentrified docks. "I appreciate the thought."

"Perhaps we should move to a more private location for such a discussion?" Solomon asked in his usual syrupy tone. "To the car, perhaps?"

"Oh, I don't think so, Mr Solomon. It's a bright day, and I'm really not in the mood for skulking about in the shadows again. Look. There's a bench over there, by the water side. That looks perfect."

"Mrs Stark," Solomon began, "I think, given the likely subject matter, that it really might be best to find a more secure place for this conversation."

"Please, Mr Solomon. Let's do it there. I'm not going to hide away."

Solomon shared the briefest of looks with Parker, before nodding and indicating for Jackie to lead, deferential as ever.

Jackie walked to the steel bench, taking a seat on the black painted slats, and setting her handbag down next to her. Solomon took a seat next to her, with Parker remaining standing next to them. It was quieter, away from the main route for foot traffic, but occasionally people still ambled past – a mum with a push-chair, an old couple linked arm in arm, a jogger leaving a tinny echo of music as he padded past.

"I'll make the call," Solomon said, removing his immaculate black phone from his inside pocket. He pressed the screen a few times, then held it to his ear, as it rang through. The call was answered.

"Good morning. This is Mr Solomon. I am with the client, and we are keen to discuss your current progress. I must add that you will shortly be on speaker with myself and the client, and that our location is not secure."

Solomon waited for an acknowledgement, before looking at Jackie as he held the phone flat in his hand, pressing the screen to change the call setting. Jackie nodded.

"You are now on speaker with myself and the client," Solomon said. "Please begin your update."

"I've been having fun," the voice said. It was a woman's voice, which surprised Jackie, especially as it was soft and girlish. She had made assumptions, fed by television cliché, that she was going to hear from a gravel-voiced Cockney or have to decipher some Caribbean patois. This was unexpected.

"Ahem," Solomon coughed. He was the consummate professional, and this was no time for levity.

"Okay, okay. I'll get to it," the voice said. "I'm getting closer. I've...visited three of her unit so far, and have made best efforts at getting answers from them. Unfortunately, there hasn't been anything definitive as of yet."

"But you have made progress?" Solomon asked.

"Oh yes. Process of elimination. Literally." The voice giggled. Jackie had met a lot of people, even if only peripherally via Jim, that would unnerve an average person, and was used to their callousness and their sociopathies, but even so, that high-pitched laugh unsettled her.

"Carry on..." Solomon urged.

"None of the ones I've spoken to know anything. Or if they do, they haven't talked, despite my best efforts. And I think you know about my best efforts. But, the thing is, from what I can see, even with me shaking trees, it's not prompted any kind of reaction or communication. Not yet anyway."

"This doesn't sound much like progress. I fear we may run the risk of scaring our quarry further underground," Solomon said.

Jackie reached over and pulled Solomon's hand closer to her, moving the phone nearer to her mouth.

"Have you got anywhere or not?" Jackie said. She was unable to observe silently for any longer.

"Is this the client?" the voice on the other end of the line asked. The voice sounded surprised, as if Jackie had made some faux pas, most clients used to receiving information with several degrees of separation, by way of plausible deniability.

"This is the client," confirmed Solomon. "Hold please..."

A couple of besuited men were ambling along the promenade, deep in conversation, arms waving and brows furrowing. One of them was taking the opportunity to smoke a cigarette, now they were both outside of the office that they had clearly escaped from. They were heading towards the bench where Solomon and Jackie were sitting. One of the men was so lost in the sound of his own voice that he hadn't noticed Parker take a small step from his sentry position, to reveal himself as an intimidating obstacle for anyone daring to come too close. The quieter man had noticed Parker move before the other, and had pulled back, but it wasn't until the louder man was almost within touching distance of Parker that he realised how close he was to making a mistake.

Almost imperceptibly, Parker made another movement towards the man, who was now looking upwards to take in the size of this massive human being. Parker glared white-hot at the man, who shrank, fumbled his cigarette to the floor, and took two quick steps backwards.

"Sorry, sorry..." the man stammered, and retreated as quickly as he could without breaking into a run, back to his more-aware colleague. Parker, satisfied, retook his previous position.

Solomon smiled. "Continue please," he said.

"Well, it's like this," the woman said. "There's one of the unit who seems to drop out of life when he left the service. I only know a few things about him, and even those are vague, despite my best efforts at persuading the others to spill their guts."

The voice giggled again, pleased at her apparent word-play. The old Jackie would have baulked at the implicit violence of the world she was now in, but that Jackie felt like a different person to her now.

"I think I know what city he is probably in, or at least where I'm going to start looking," the voice said, "and there might be a few ways of picking up the trail once I get there."

"How sure are you that they have even gone back to these friends of theres?" Jackie said.

"Well, I'm not," the woman said. "But logically it makes the most sense. They are going to need help, and they don't have many people that they can rely on for that. Certainly not many who would be prepared to help in a situation like this. And from what I can tell, they are the sort of people who won't want to risk any civilians getting dragged into this. That's what makes me think that this guy – this drop-out – is the perfect candidate."

"Where do you think they are?" Solomon interjected.

"Stoke-on-Trent," the woman said.

"Hmm," Solomon said. He turned to Jackie. "It's plausible. If our colleague's assumptions are correct it does also fit into possible behaviour before the incident with your husband. We know that the wife left the city for a short time, and Stoke is certainly close enough that she may have made the trip before returning in the window of time we know she had when she left the city prior to the incident with Mr Stark. If this gentleman is supporting the Graces currently, then he may have supported them previously as well. That makes him reliable. Reliable is predictable."

No-one spoke for a moment, processing this theory. Finally, Solomon spoke again, addressing Jackie.

"Do you have any further questions?"

Jackie shook her head. Solomon moved the phone closer to his mouth, intending to give a last instruction to his operative, before Jackie grabbed his hand again, and pulled the phone back towards her.

"Find them," Jackie said. "Find them, and keep them there. Then I want to be there."

"Yes, ma'am," the voice said, still disconcertingly playful.

Jackie spoke in a soft, sure voice.

"I want to be there when they die."

# 30

Cold Cut felt sick. The low-level nausea that had been with him for what seemed like weeks was now threatening to bring him to his knees. He felt buffeted, threatened on all sides by powerful and ruthless forces, at real risk of being atomised in a cross-fire. But, he also knew that this could be his crucible. He just had to navigate these fierce waters for a little longer, and then, only then, might he emerge from all of this in a better place, his life transformed with money, power, and most importantly, status.

And then there was that throbbing, pulsing boil on the back of his neck, a mainline that shot electricity down his spine when he dared forget about it for a second, like someone was warming up the electric chair for him.

He had made a deal with the Argentinians. They would supply so much cocaine that this city would think it was snowing. Cold Cut would get this gear into the hands of those who were angling to wrench the Stark business from out of the manicured hands of Jim Stark's wife, and then both sides would reward him for his initiative. He tried to weigh up all the angles – even if this new regime wasn't all it was cracked up to be, then if he maintained a professional distance, maybe he could persuade Jackie Stark to take the gear from the Argentinians herself. They need never know, at least until they saw how much money it brought in, and Cold Cut would still get his just rewards. He was a way to the Argentinians, which was the only way to get a quick supply, and both sides needed supply more than anything else. Supply meant sales, and sales meant money. And with money? Anything was possible.

There were risks. Of course there were risks. What if Jackie Stark found out about this little rebellion? There would have to be an example made. A brutal one. And if the Argentinians came out of this arrangement feeling disappointment of any kind, then Cold Cut could hope for no better than a slow end in an empty house, surrounded by knives and wires and blowtorches.

No. He had put himself in this position, and this was going to be his time to finally pull himself up to the level that he deserved. It was all going to change, starting now.

He tapped out the text to Belly, and waited for the reply. It came almost instantly, as if the recipient had the phone in his hand, waiting. It just said one word -

"WHERE?"

This was interesting. Usually, it was Cold Cut who was the one traipsing across town, at the beck and call of whoever had deigned to notice him that time. A little power is still power.

Cold Cut tapped out another message. Let them come to him, and his streets, and his corners. Let people see that he was the one having the meetings with powerful people, that finish with handshakes and respect. Let them see who his peers were now.

There was a supermarket that had elbowed its way between the high terraces of the main street in his part of the city – a crouching building that broke up the relentless uniformity of the off-licences, betting shops and hair salons. Some ancient building would have been bulldozed to make room for it, and the car park that it sat on, like a frog on a lily-pad. It would be visible enough for all to see, especially those tired and listless sorts who spilled in and out of the chain pub on the opposite side of the road, who Cold Cut could trust would be free enough with their gossip that his meeting would not go unnoticed. But the space of the car park would also allow there to be some discretion – seen but not heard – which was exactly how he wanted it. And, old habits dying hard, a spiderweb of alleys and backstreets led from the car park, just in case, somehow, things took a turn for the worst.

It was agreed. Belly would bring his uncle in an hour, and Cold Cut would lay out exactly what he was offering, and his price for doing it. He wasn't an idiot. The Argentinians had agreed a rate for him, but they had not said anything about him discussing his own "introduction" terms with the buyers. Get paid, and if you're smart, get paid twice.

An hour was long enough for him to get ready. He threw a ready meal in the microwave to warm up, as he pulled off his tracksuit, and got changed into his best gear. The trousers from his "court suit" and his only shirt, just about passing a sniff test under the arms. He was going to make an effort – this was a new beginning for him, after all, and he had wallowed in enough envy-scrolling on Instagram to know that the perception of success was the first step to achieving it. He wiped a mud stain from the toe of his best Nikes with the arm of his discarded tracksuit, and then stood up to look at his reflection in his living room window.

This was it.

Cold Cut waited just out of sight on a street corner that led off from the main drag of this satellite centre of the city. He wanted to be a minute or two late, and didn't want to make the mistake of getting there too soon, before the others had arrived. It gave him the opportunity to have a steadying cigarette or two, and run through the conversations he might expect to have in his head.

"Nervous, is it?"

Cold Cut started as he heard the voice behind him. He turned around, surprised, and deflated when he saw who it was. Acer and Cosmo, playfully barrelling into one another as they walked up the street behind Cold Cut, laughing and elbowing each other.

"Love's young dream come to mix it with the grown ups, is it?" was the best Cold Cut could fire back, caught on the hop like he was.

"Can you see a grown up, Cosmo? I can just see this streak of piss hanging round street corners again," Acer replied. The three of them – Acer, Belly and Cosmo – had made their own small move up the ladder before, and they would aggressively defend the progress, however meagre, they had made.

Cold Cut felt himself snarl. Angry and embarrassed to be caught out, and then made into a figure of fun for those he knew deserved to be beneath him. This was his moment, and there was no fucking way he was going to pass it up. He pushed his chips in, and called their bluff.

"Fine. You tell Belly and his uncle that I'm going to go. I didn't ask for you clowns to be here, and, to be honest, I don't really feel like this whole thing is worth my time. It's not like this is the only show in town, is it?"

It worked. He could see it in Cosmo's face most obviously, who looked at his mate with real worry, that shattered any pretence that Acer had of maintaining the ball-busting. Acer's eyebrows headed north. Cold Cut walked away from them, ostensibly in the direction of the supermarket car park, but on the other side of the road, so he could maintain this bluff that he was ready to walk away.

Cosmo scurried after him, Acer following behind. It was Cosmo who started the pleading.

"Look, Cutty, lad. We was just messing, like. Don't be like that, eh?"

"Nah, fuck that. Don't need the hassle. You tell Belly I said hi," Cold Cut said, as he walked on.

"Cutty, please. Tell him, Acer. Tell him we were only messing," Cosmo said, pathetically.

"Yeah, just messing. We'll go. Don't say nothing, Cutty. Look. They're here now," Acer said, putting an arm on Cutty's shoulder in as gentle and non-threatening a way as possible. Cold Cut turned back, to look at these two fools, allowing himself a moment's satisfaction at the expressions on their faces. It had worked. Belly's uncle must be important – important enough to frighten these clowns, if he found out that they had risked jeopardising the meeting, before it had even started. Good, thought Cold Cut. He only wanted to talk to important men, not bottom-feeders like Acer, Belly and Cosmo. Not anymore.

Cold Cut looked over the road, following Acer's eyeline, to see who he was referring to. He could see Belly, sat on the knee-high wall that separated the car park from the pavement traffic, facing towards the supermarket building. An older man, late-thirties, was walking towards Belly, with a small cigar in his mouth.

He was broad, which was for the best, given the weight that his frame had to carry. A red, round face sunk into those broad shoulders, looking like a scowl drawn on a thumb. He was in a loose fitting shirt, short sleeved revealing heavy, powerful arms. As he moved towards Belly, Cold Cut could see the man's face break into a broad grin, though the eyes narrowed – there was no warmth there. A loud, high-pitched laugh escaped from his red face, before he leant down to Belly, patted him on the shoulder, and said something to Belly that saw the younger man recoil.

Cold Cut had known people like this all his life – yet another variation of the predators that prowled this inner-city habitat. Angry, spiteful men, railing at whatever perceived slight had been meted down to them from whoever *they* were this week. These people laughed long and often, but only when there was someone for them to laugh down at. Their whole life a competition, and one they never felt they had a chance of winning. And Cold Cut wanted to be like them. No, he thought. That wasn't right. He wanted to be above them. And he'd climb on whoever he had to to get there.

Cold Cut crossed the road, and entered the car park, walking to the end of the wall where Belly and the man had met, Belly now standing as they waited for him. As he got closer to the pair, Cold Cut could see what the man had been laughing about.

Belly's face was swollen on one side, his right eye was almost closed, ringed with an angry, purplish colour that would surely only get darker. His nose was red, and one side of his mouth looked like it had cotton wool stuffed inside it. The surprise of seeing Belly's face jettisoned any pretence

Cold Cut had of introducing himself as the reserved, capable businessman he was planning on portraying. His own cruelty was too hard to control, and he found himself laughing as well.

"Fucking hell, Belly. Playing with the kids again?" Cold Cut sniggered. The other man found this funny as well, and started laughing again, in the same fierce, high-pitched way as before. This was how it was – laugh at the weaker, and if this was done in numbers, all the better.

"Yeah, well, fuck off," Belly mumbled, with a mixture of pain and embarrassment.

"Oh, now, don't be like that, lad. Next time you try and get some kid's pocket money, make sure you go with bigger boys, eh?" Cold Cut said, twisting the knife.

"Now, don't let him get soft, mate," the man said to Cold Cut, enjoying the double-team. "He needs to stand on his own two feet. You fight your own battles, Belly lad, and if that's really too much for you, I'll get my three year old to follow you around."

More laughter at Belly's expense. His already-red face reddened further, and he looked at his shoes, waiting for his turn in sharp focus to be over. He tried to move things along, and away from him.

"Are you both finished?" Belly said, finally, as the laughter died down slightly. "Thank fuck. Look, I'm only here to do both of you a favour, so why don't you two crack on, and I'll just leave you to it, eh?"

"Whatever you like, Belly," the man said. "Do your job first, though, eh?"

Belly sighed.

"Okay," Belly said, turning to Cold Cut. "This is my uncle, Connor. He is one of the top men in the taxi game round here."

Cold Cut knew what that meant. There was only one crew who could be described that way, but old habits died hard, so the name "Stark" was meant, even if it was not said. Belly turned to Cold Cut now.

"And this is Cold Cut. He's the one I told you about. The one who can help you with that business arrangement you are looking to put together." As Belly introduced Cold Cut, he put his arm around him, patting him on the shoulder. Cold Cut recoiled, and flashed a glare at Belly – what the hell was he doing touching him?

Connor held out his heavy hand for a handshake. Cold Cut shook his hand, immediately registering the subtle squeezing from the bigger man. Posturing and point-scoring. Keep calm, he thought. A means to an end. Climb, and keep climbing.

"Nice to meet you, Cold Cut," Connor said. "What's the name all about then?"

"Long story. It's not important for now," Cold Cut deflected. The origin of his name was deliberately vague, and he wanted to keep it that way, happy to think that it hid some dark story of sharp knives and retribution, and trying to ignore the received wisdom that it was just because he seemed to subsist on a diet of pre-packed sandwich fillings.

"Busy man, okay. Fair enough," Connor said. The attempt at a welcoming tone evaporated, and his expression changed back to the angry scowl that was his default. "So, what can you do for me, mate? He's told me a little, but let's just stop fucking around and start from the beginning."

Belly dared a look when Connor mentioned him, but almost immediately turned his eyes away. He wanted desperately to curry favour with his uncle, but was completely terrified of him.

"Should I...?" Belly mumbled, indicating to leave, to

maybe cross the street over to Acer and Cosmo, who were wise enough to watch this scene from a safe distance.

"You stay right there, boy," Connor growled, the last word a clear reminder of Belly's position here. "This is your meeting. You wait there and keep quiet."

Connor turned back to Cold Cut, irritated that he had been interrupted.

"Go on, Cold Cut, tell me what you've got."

Cold Cut found that his mouth had gone dry. This was his moment. This might be his only chance to drag himself out of his shitty little flat, and out of these shitty little streets and up towards something better. He did his best to hide a gulp.

"It's like this. I can arrange for you to get your hands on the best product this city has ever seen. Well, seen for the best part of a decade, that is."

"The Argie stuff?" Connor said. "That product? Not seen that stuff since..."

"Since Stark chased them out of town," Cold Cut said. "Well, they haven't gone far, and if they can find the right partners, well, they are keen to come back."

"This is...interesting," Connor said, rubbing his fat chin, scratching stubble he was too lazy to shave. "It was good gear. Really good."

"Still is," Cold Cut said. "Didn't you ever wonder why you never clawed back the sales from what you lost when they tried to move in last time? They didn't move all that far away, and some of your smarter customers just hopped on a train."

"Yeah, we never did get back to where we were before they came in," Connor said. "Stark never bothered doing too much digging into it. Stupid twat."

"So, here's where we are, then. And correct me if I'm

wrong with any of this," Cold Cut said. "But Stark is out of the picture, as are most of his inner circle. So, seems to me like there's a vacancy at the top, not to mention a lack of decent product anywhere in the city. That's what I heard, anyway."

"That's what you've heard, right?" Connor said, irritated. He might hate Jim Stark, but he had nailed his colours to that mast for years now, and couldn't shake the feeling that there was a criticism implicit in what Cold Cut was laying out to him.

"Am I wrong? Look. I'm not having a dig," Cold Cut said. "Wasn't you who pushed them Argies away, was it? Just think there's a second chance here, and a way for you to buy yourself to the top table. And that's where I come in."

"Go on," Connor said.

"I know these fellas, right," Cold Cut said. "I've met them. Introduced myself, like. I'm the one they trust to help them get this deal done. Belly here tells me that you're the man most likely, so just seems daft to not work together. Could be good for both of us, no?"

"Okay, I'm listening. Good for me, I can see. Good for you how?"

"Well, a little introduction fee, and a supply rate, and maybe a way in to *your* new organisation," Cold Cut said. Here we go.

Connor smiled, dug into his back pocket, and pulled out a square tin case. He popped it open, took out the thin cigar that was inside, which he lit with the gas lighter he had fished out of one of his pockets. He puffed a few times, ensuring the cigar was fully lit, but before dragging low and hard on it, holding the smoke in his cheeks. Then he huffed out the smoke, a thick cloud that wafted over the wall and hovered over the pavement, just as a woman walked past, pushing a pushchair with a child wriggling in the seat.

"Fuck's sake, twat," the woman said, without stopping.

"Fuck off," Connor shot back, immediately, not even deigning to turn his head. He was looking at Cold Cut intently.

"Presume you've got a sample?" Connor said.

Cold Cut couldn't help himself from glancing left and right, doing more to draw attention to himself by checking to see if anyone was watching, than if he retained his composure. As soon as he did it, he realised how he had revealed his naivety, and hated himself for it. He dug into his trouser pocket, wrapped his spidery fingers around the baggie that he had been given by Truth, and pulled it out, palming it to Connor as quickly and quietly as he could. Belly looked up at the exchange with wide-eyes.

Connor knew what was going on. Some chancer had lucked his way into a deal. Plankton trying to negotiate with a whale, as if they were peers. He couldn't resist turning the temperature up on this pale, desperate creature in front of him, more suited to lurking in alleys behind takeaways or on corners underneath flickering street lamps. He opened his palm to look at the baggie that Cold Cut had handed to him, and held it up by the ziplock seal to scrutinise it like it was a dodgy banknote.

"Careful..." hissed Cold Cut, again flicking his eyes left and right. Belly shuffled uneasily in his seat, wary enough of his proximity to the two men that he might be somehow implicated.

"Easy, boy. It's such a little thing to worry about. But I guess you're used to that," Connor laughed. Everything was what he wanted it to be – a weak chancer, rolling the dice on his only chance at mixing it with the grown-ups, who could be disposed of, one way or the other, when the supply lines opened up. Connor knew that Cold Cut would give him what he wanted, in the end. This was no longer a negotiation.

"Here's what happens now, lad," Connor continued. "I'm going to stick this gear up a few people's noses, and if they like it, I'm going to get this little twat - " he pointed at Belly - "to sort out a proper order with you. If you try and find me directly, then you're not going to like what happens. This is my show, and you do as you're told, or you and your Argie mates, whoever they are, can go fuck themselves. Right?"

"Wait," Cold Cut stammered. He regrouped, and tried again. "Wait. This is the best gear. You'll see. Go and try it out, sure. But then I want paying. I want what I'm due."

"Do you now?" Connor was amused by this little pipsqueak. The real negotiation was to come, as and when he met the Argentinians, but he liked the novelty of this little man gasping for air.

"Well, yeah. Without me, there is no deal, so it's only right I get something. A fair percentage." Cold Cut's voice tremored as he spoke.

Connor put the baggie in one pocket, and then dug around in another. He pulled out a wad of notes, secured with a rubber band. He snapped the band off the notes, and around his fingers, and pulled off one of the twenties. In a smooth motion, he rerolled the notes, wrapped the band back around them, and stuffed it back into his pocket.

"This -" Connor reached across, slipping the twenty pound note into Cold Cut's shirt pocket - "is your fair percentage." Connor patted Cold Cut's pocket, firmly. "And if you've got a problem with that, then take it up with the Argies."

The meeting was over. Connor turned and strode off,

leaving Cold Cut stood with his mouth open, struggling to process exactly what had just happened. His cheeks had flushed, and his eyes stung, and the fierce boil on the back of his neck was throbbing. A laughing stock. Again.

Belly sniggered, a noise that shocked Cold Cut back to the here and now. Cold Cut was seething.

"Fuck you, and fuck him," Cold Cut said. "He wants to be careful, that fucking uncle of yours. He's not the only show in town."

"He is for you," Belly said. "See, he knows you now, and if you were to take that gear to anyone else – Stark, for instance – then who do you think is going to be the first one he calls on?"

Cold Cut stared Belly in the face, long and hard, his mouth opening and closing as he struggled to organise all the curses that were fizzing around his mind into some kind of order. All he saw was Belly, grinning as best as he could given his swollen face. Belly was right.

"He should be careful," Cold Cut said. "I'm not to be fucked with. Not anymore."

"I'll be sure to tell him," Belly said, getting to his feet with a wince, waving to his two accomplices over the road, and walking off towards them.

"I am not to be fucked with," Cold Cut said again. But it was too late. He was utterly defeated, and left with nothing but a crumped twenty in his top pocket, and rage at his place in the world, the sharp point of his indignation filed to a diamond-hard tip.

## 31

Cold Cut chain-smoked as he sloped home. He wanted nothing more than to get in and shut the door, and keep the world at bay so he could regroup, but somehow, his legs betrayed him, and he just found himself wandering. His mind was a stuck record, replaying the meeting with Connor over and over in his head - stop-and-rewind, stop-and-rewind – weighing each word for dual purpose, and looking for cracks that he could somehow exploit. But there were none. He had been given a lesson on his place in the world, and no parsing of what had been said would reveal a different conclusion.

The city carried on obliviously. The night descended, and the grey streets lit up in a sickly orange from the street-lights. Neon signs flickered into life, and the night trade took over from the transactions of the day – takeaways and off-licences, instead of coffee and groceries. The people on the streets seemed to shrink from the dark, huddling over as the colder night air and the deep black of the night sky loomed over them. Conversations were quieter, other than from the occasional loud explosion of noise from an argument or a joke, from those too drunk to fear the night.

It was muscle memory that navigated Cold Cut to the front door of his flat. A chipped paint door that opened to stairs that led up to his flat, perched above a storefront that currently sold electronic cigarettes, but would no doubt be replaced with another faddish trade in due course. Cold Cut liked that his flat was above ground level. He would sometimes sit by his window and watch the streets below, in the hope that some drama or excitement would happen by, and he could make himself feel better by enjoying someone else feeling worse.

The world found sharp focus again, stood at his front door on the pavement, like a crash zoom pulling tight, and he fumbled in his pocket for his key. He turned it *just so* in order to bypass the temperamental lock tumbler, and pushed the door hard, knowing full well that the pile of takeaway menus and free newspapers behind the door would only have been added to. He'd tidy them up tomorrow. Always tomorrow.

He climbed the stairs, leaving the door to shut itself with the closer fitted to the frame above the door. It was only as he opened the door to his flat, at the top of the stairs, that a part of his brain registered that the front door hadn't slammed shut as it usually did. Too late.

Cold Cut was slammed through his front door so quickly and forcefully, that all the air was knocked from his lungs. He was ragdolled through the air, something powerful lifting him from his feet and carrying him with frightening ease, before crashing him down, and onto his sofa, face-down. Something – *someone* – pushed a heavy hand onto the back of his skull, and a heavier knee onto the small of his back, pinning him completely.

"One sound, and it'll hurt. Understand?" a voice said.

Cold Cut nodded, frantically. He understood.

"Christ, mate," the voice said. "What the fuck is that growing out of your neck? A second head?"

Cold Cut felt the grip shift from the back of his head, moving to grab him by the wrist, and twist and pull until his arm was grapevined with the strong arm of whoever it was that had hold of him. The voice spoke again.

"I'm not touching that neck of yours. Looks like it might explode at the slightest touch. No, no. Anyway, see, this is called a 'chickenwing' and if you struggle too much, you'll just make your arm hurt so much you'll be begging me to twist it all the way off. I don't plan on leaving you with injuries, but, to be quite honest, I don't really care either way. Nod again if you're still listening."

Cold Cut nodded, his panicked breath hot against the sofa he was pressed facedown into.

"So, you are probably wondering how it could be that you are in this awkward position. Well, I'm an open book. No secrets between friends. And we're friends aren't we? Course we are." It was the jocularity that terrified Cold Cut. He was used to people shouting at him, or cursing him out. This was...different.

"I'm a friend of some people you will have heard of," the voice continued. "Will have met. And I'm doing them a favour, seeing as they didn't think it all that clever for them to come to town themselves."

The man shifted his weight slightly, now he was convinced that Cold Cut was suitably aware of his predicament. Cold Cut wasn't stupid enough to test boundaries.

"It's good having friends. I feel for you, mate. You see, one of yours gave you up to me. Let me know who you were."

Belly. Cold Cut knew straight away. The showy display during the introduction with Connor. At the time it seemed odd, and now it all made sense with an icy clarity.

"Oh, don't be too hard on the lad. You'll have noticed the state of his face, I'm sure."

The man laughed, sounding like all he was doing was telling a funny story in the pub.

"So I know who you are, and I know you know my friends, and I know you know Jim Stark. Or rather you did."

Cold Cut finally spoke.

"No, no. I didn't know him. I didn't know him at all."

"That's not what I've been told. You were part of his crew, weren't you? Got yourself all the way to Norfolk with them, looking for my friends."

The Graces. Cold Cut had his suspicions, but this confirmed it. This man was associated with Tony and Eleanor Grace. The same Tony and Eleanor Grace who had wiped out the best of the Stark crew as if they were culling livestock. If this man knew them, and they had trusted him to come to Liverpool to dig around on their behalf, then Cold Cut knew, if he didn't already, he was most definitely not to be messed with.

"Not really. I just got dragged along. Come on, man. Do I look like one of the inner circle?"

The man puffed out a sigh.

"Well, that's true. Maybe you were more like a pet? But, no, I tend to believe people who know that if they don't tell me the truth, I'm going to give them another clout. And your friend couldn't help mention how you were still doing little errands for them."

Fucking Belly, thought Cold Cut, again. If he got out of this mess...

"No, no, it's nothing like that. They just wanted to know if I knew..."

"If you knew what?" the man said.

"If I knew how to find your...friends," Cold Cut said.

"And?"

"And..?" Cold Cut stammered.

"Did you? Know how to find them?"

Cold Cut said nothing. Frantic equations were whirring in his head, but he couldn't shake the conclusion that risk to his health tomorrow was worse than the risk to his health right now. As if to underline the point, the man applied a fraction of pressure to the hold he had Cold Cut in, sending a jolt of pain up his arm. Cold Cut yelped.

"They found something," Cold Cut said. "They found their stuff in a lock-up, and knew who to go looking for. The army stuff."

"Okay, that's worth knowing. And they're looking, are they?"

"I'm sure they are. There are some new people helping her. Stark's wife. A couple of people from down south. Scary fuckers. They're doing the searching. They want your friends. Want them dead."

The pressure on his arm eased, as the man shifted his weight again. It felt like a reward, as well as a relief.

"See how good honesty feels," the man said. "Now I want you to tell me everything you know about these 'scary fuckers' who have come to play."

Cold Cut did as he was told. He described Solomon and Parker in as much detail as he could. How they looked, how they talked, who was in command and who did the heavy work. Cold Cut told him about the beating Parker had dished out in the lock-up. Every whisper and suspicion that he had heard, or observed, he passed on. He just wanted this man gone, and the only loyalty Cold Cut ever observed was loyalty to himself. Anything to satisfy this man, and then he could assess how the sands had shifted.

"Well, I can't sit here all night," the man said, when the well of words from Cold Cut had run dry. "So I'm going to tell you a few things, which you might expect me to say, but, you know, never leave room for guesswork, as my old mum used to say."

The man moved his head closer to Cold Cut's, the subtle shift of pressure just firing up his nerve endings again, ensuring what was said came with a painful emphasis.

"I know who you are and I know where you live. I can find you in all manner of ways. And if I find out that you have done anything – *anything* – that might make this situation worse for my friends, I am going to come back and kill you. Do you believe me?"

Cold Cut nodded, frantically.

"Good. I believe you. I'm going to go now – I've got a train to catch - but I'm afraid I can't have you trying to follow me or anything like that. So, I want you to relax. This won't take long."

Cold Cut immediately started struggling, unsure quite what was meant, but certain it was nothing good. It didn't matter. The man unwrapped his grip from the hold he had Cold Cut in, and snaked his massive arms around Cold Cut's head and neck, locking it in tightly.

"This is called a sleeper hold. You get the picture."

The man squeezed, and Cold Cut struggled as he fought for air. But he didn't struggle for long, and within seconds, everything faded to black.

# 32

"We need to get our shit together," Tony said to Eleanor.

Steaky had left earlier that morning, having won the argument that it should be him that made the trip to Liverpool, given he had the advantage of anonymity that Tony and Eleanor would not have had. Despite his numerous peccadilloes, they both had every confidence in Steaky's capabilities, as well as his uncanny knack for coming through the toughest of situations with a smile and without a scratch. But despite that, their fondness for him led them to worry, and they both knew they needed to occupy themselves to take their minds off things, until their friend returned safely.

Eleanor, as always, had noticed the dangers of brooding and had decided to do her best to keep bleak thoughts at bay by being proactive. At the first hint that a break in conversation would turn into a long silence, she slapped her thighs, pushed herself to her feet, and started tidying up the plates and cups from the morning breakfast.

Not a word was said, but Tony wasn't going to let Eleanor fall into chores as he sat in silence on his own, so he stood up and walked through to the kitchen, where Eleanor was piling plates next to the sink.

"We've got a few hours until he gets back," Tony said to Eleanor. "So, I think we should get ourselves game-ready. Just in case."

"You think?" Eleanor said. "Do you wonder if we're just driving ourselves nuts with all this? Paranoid?"

"I think either one of us could've said that back in Norfolk, and look how that turned out," Tony said. There was a pause as they both dwelt on the implausibility of how they were tracked down to their seaside village, all the way from Liverpool. A photo of them, stuck amongst a wall of others in their local pub, which had been spotted by the same piece of pondlife that Steaky had gone to Liverpool to monster.

"You've got a point," Eleanor said, finally. "Fuck."

"What?" Tony said, as Eleanor looked away from him. He put a hand on her shoulder, gently, and she turned back to him, biting her bottom lip as she fought to control her emotions which were bubbling up, unbidden. "Oh, love..."

"I'm sick of it, Tone," she said, quietly. "Sick of it. We didn't ask for any of this, and here we are, living out of bags, not sure if someone is going to kick that fucking door in and put a bullet in our head. Can't they just leave us alone?"

"I know, I know," Tony said, rubbing her back as tenderly as he could. She was his lighthouse, and despite his stoic exterior, he needed her positivity and strength more than she could ever know. To see her falter was difficult to take. "Love. Listen."

She was attacking a dirty plate with a scouring pad, her frustration needing to go somewhere.

"Eleanor," Tony said. They didn't use each other's names often, and only ever when it was important.

Eleanor dropped the plate and the pad into the bowl of hot water, looked out of the kitchen window at nothing, and then, reconstituted, looked at her husband.

"We need to keep going," he said. "I need you to keep going. To keep me going. We can do anything when we put our minds to it. Let's just push on, one more time, and get ourselves ready for the worst. The absolute worst. Just in case."

Eleanor sighed, letting the stored tension out of her in one long breath, then put a soap-covered hand to Tony's cheek, and kissed him tenderly on the lips.

"Thanks, my love," she said.

TONY LEFT Eleanor in the house, letting her have her own space, as she concentrated on not only tidying up their morning mess, but knowing her, also making "improvements" to the chaos that Steaky lived amongst. It was the pulled thread of a sweater, and as she straightened one pile of books, she found she two more that needed the same treatment. Tony left her to it, knowing her well enough to know when she could do with her own company. The inevitable bickering when Steaky returned and found his house aggressively tidied was also something to look forward to.

Tony had made his way to the cellar, still fascinated by the novelty of the set-up that Steaky had carved out of the ground beneath his feet. The quiet darkness was reassuring, like he was under the surface of another planet, light-years away from the problems that loomed over them. It gave him clarity, and no opportunity for distraction, as he laid out everything they had brought with them, both to see what he had, and what he felt they still needed, to best prepare themselves for what might be coming.

He left Eleanor's rifle to one side. That was hers and hers alone, and he knew better than to interfere with it. She knew every curve of it, and had finessed it so it was almost a physical extension of herself. There was no way he would dare presume to second-guess her management of it – it was just too personal to her.

He emptied out their bags, and laid out everything on the camp beds that Steaky had set up for them down here. This subterranean bolthole was more comfortable than some of the places they had found themselves over the years, and Tony was grateful that Steaky had that oddly unique mind that never felt there was something so trivial that it might not come in useful in the future. The cellar was full of plastic storage crates full of all manner of things that "might just come in handy" and now was certainly the time to test the breadth of that hypothesis.

There were camping provisions, a portable stove, and some pots and pans designed for those who take their enjoyment by being rained on halfway up a mountain. Tony separated out enough to see them through a day or two, just in case they were forced to evacuate this bolthole at short notice. Once done, he then looked at equipment. Defence *and* offence.

Steaky had handed Tony a pistol, presented to him wrapped in a cloth to keep it dry in the dampness of these cellars, with sombre seriousness that soon melted to hilarity when Eleanor pointed out how ridiculous Steaky was being. It was a practical weapon – old but well-maintained, and good enough for Tony, especially given how awkward he was around guns. Tony open the cloth to look at the gun, checked the bullets in the magazine, and then rewrapped it and placed it carefully back on the camp bed.

Steaky had also handed over two knives, one for Tony and one for Eleanor, both big enough to be do terminal damage, but small enough to be easily hidden. They were sheathed, but Tony knew they would be terrifyingly sharp – Steaky had a reputation for knives. His nickname was well-earned – *Steak Knife*, or so he had been told. Steaky was the sort of person who slept with a knife under his pillow, and most likely gave it a woman's name.

One gun each, and one knife each. Now what? Tony closed his eyes, and put his hands on his hips, and tried to think. Think of the worst possible outcomes that might happen if they were really were being hunted. Aggression and violence was one thing, but after that, there was the prospect of capture.

He unzipped Eleanor's washbag, and, as he hoped, found some hairpins at the bottom of the bag, amongst the toothpaste and the tweezers. He had taken a pair of pliers from Steaky's tools, and used the cable cutter part to snip the rounded ends from the end of four of the hairpins. Once finished, he sat down on the edge of the camp bed, and slipped off his trainers. As carefully as he could, using a craft knife, again grabbed from the tool stash, he cut a small incision in the heel padding on each trainer, and then inserted a hairpin into each hole, then slipped the shoes back on. The other two hairpins he pocketed, until he could give them to Eleanor.

One last thing to do, Tony thought. This might be nonsense, but an idea had occurred to him, and he was going to try it out. It's only paranoia until you need it. The craft knife was thin and long, with dividing marks along the length of the blade, so as the blade dulled, a new edge could be made by easily snapping it off, section by section. Tony did exactly that – snapping off a section, then another, then another, until he had three small pieces of the blade, all about the size of a postage stamp.

He wrapped one of the blade sections in insulation tape, folding the tape over the blade so the sharp edge was hidden. So far, so good. Now to find somewhere to hide them. He looked at his clothes, wondering whether he could fit the blade into a hemline or a lining somehow. A tiny, sharp last resort that he could reach if all else had failed.

He tried inside the waistband of his underwear, figuring that this would be the last thing even the most hardnosed of villains would look at. A tiny cut with the knife opened it up, and he slipped one of the wrapped blades inside. He patted the blade through the cloth, looking to see if it would dig into him, and satisfied, he twisted and lunged, contorting his body to see if this ridiculousness actually had some worth.

Eleanor would laugh at him. He'd show her later, and see if she would even consider the other blades he had prepared. At the very least, if it raised a smile, then this scheme was good for something.

He spent a final few minutes packing and repacking the bags, nothing left out, just in case they needed to grab and run. Everything had a place, and he could put his hand on it without looking. He felt ready. The ritual of preparation had worked on his mind at the same time as everything else, with each item squared away feeling like it was another doubt or internal argument laid to rest. As he zipped up the final bag, he felt calmer, more assured, and more determined than ever to come through this whole and intact. Then, finally, he could find somewhere to live quietly with his wife, and let this life of guns, and knives, and the relentless tick of the clock wash away like so much driftwood after a storm.

## 33

Jackie Stark was finding the hard edges of her anger eroded by the persistent lapping of regret and sadness. Solomon and Parker were always close, but Jackie had found herself pushing back a little, the new responsibilities and demands of this new life smothering her, making her old routine seem more appealing by comparison. They were her employees, she reasoned, and their counsel was to be heeded, but not necessarily followed.

So it was that she had decided to go to her grandchildren's school. She hadn't heard from Carol in a few days, their last encounter still raw. They would talk every day, one way or the other, but since Carol left there had been no contact between them, and each passing minute felt like it was creating more distance between them. Carol would come round, Jackie thought. She would have to. Carol can't have been so naïve that she didn't appreciate exactly how Jim had made his living, and she must have a vague idea where those envelopes of cash he would give to her to solve problems or "treat yourself" had come from. But saying it out loud put flesh on the bones, and made it real, and undeniable. Jackie knew that that could be a terrifying prospect. She had had a similar experience the first time she came to the conclusion that Jim had blood on his hands. But it soon passed. The mind can perform acrobatics when it has to.

Carol needed time. But Jackie was not prepared to abdicate her role as grandmother as Carol did so. Maybe one day those two kids would have a reckoning of their own when they learnt of the power of the Stark name. But until then, she was Nannie Jacks to them, and Carol or no, she wasn't going to miss out on being there for them.

The school was red brick and old, barely changing for a hundred years. Black-painted railings circled the buildings, and the schoolyard, the paint chipped and rust blooming on the bare metal underneath. Some shrubs had been planted in a few borders, to break up the concrete monotony, but these seemed incongruous. The soft greens of nature fighting a rearguard action against the grey and reds of the school, the yard, and the surrounding buildings.

The light was failing, and the winter air was sharp – a splash of water that stings the eyes, and reddens the cheeks. A few parents were milling around the school gates mostly in small groups, passing the time until the bell rang with small-talk and gossip. Jackie had walked to the school, enjoying the solitude of the forty-five minute walk that tuned out the static in her head. As she turned the corner bringing the school into view, she quickened her pace, excited to see her beloved grandchildren, and looking forward to the purity of their affection.

Some of the parents smiled and waved at Jackie as she approached. She was a common fixture at the school-gates, and was not afraid to strike up small-talk of her own to pass the time until the hometime bell was sounded. Jackie waved back, and mouthed a "hello" to one of the women already part of a conversation, who acknowledged her in return. Then Jackie noticed something different. Something hard to identify at first, but then unavoidable. She was being talked about.

She had noticed the warm greetings, but for every one of those she now noticed the next person turning away, or turning to their neighbour to whisper, furtive glances shot back in her direction. She thought this was just paranoia – some guilt at her new life and her new choices made manifest, but no, this wasn't a trick of the mind. They were scared of her.

Jackie dug her hands into her pocket, as she stood alone. Almost imperceptibly, the other parents had inched away from her, even those sympathetic to her not brave enough to challenge the unspoken judgement of the others. Was this how it was going to be? Was the Stark name a weapon to be feared as well as a shield? She frowned, hunched her shoulders against the winter air that now felt a degree or two colder, and waited.

The bell rang, and she was shook from her brooding. A distant rumble and a faraway shriek got closer, until the double doors of the school were thrown open, and the children flooded out to a soundtrack of screams and laughter. Jackie watched the parents watching the children, as they scanned the faces for their offspring, a wave indicating that they had found each other, the children more excited than the parents.

"Nannie Jacks!"

Megan had spotted Jackie, shrieking her name with the impromptu surprise of recognition. She ran over, arms wide in her slightly-too-big coat, hair smushed down by the woolly hat she had pulled down onto her head. Jackie crouched down so she could be at the same height as Megan, and smiled. They hugged, and Jackie felt the salve of that pure love, a sweet relief from this new world she lived in.

"Oh, my love," Jackie said, "Nannie has missed you!"

Jackie stood up, and playfully pulled Megan's hat down, over her eyes.

"Nannie, no!" Megan squealed, enjoying the slapstick of it.

"Hi, Nannie," Toby said, a few years older, and a few years cooler than his sister, wandering up at his own pace, ensuring that he didn't give his peers any ammunition on the off-chance that they were watching.

"Hi, Tobes," Jackie said. She slipped an arm around him, which he tolerated.

"So, I just thought I'd come and surprise you, and see if we could all go for a drink or something, when mummy arrives," Jackie said. "What do you think?"

"Uh-huh," Megan said, always happy to go somewhere where she could try and cutely extort a sweet treat from Jackie.

"What's this, mum?"

Carol was approaching, walking with a sure stride, and a not-happy expression on her face.

"I just thought it would be..." Jackie said.

"You can't just show up, mum. You can't just..." The words fell out of Carol in a hurry, then trailed off as her confidence petered out. She turned her head away from Jackie as her eyes filled, knowing that looking at her mum might set her sobbing, in front of her children and the other parents, insatiable for topics for future gossip.

"I'm not looking for an argument, Carol," Jackie said. "I just wanted to see the kids. That's allowed, isn't it?"

Megan was looking up at the two adults, not understanding the conversation, and confused by the tone of it. Toby was looking away, struggling to maintain the veneer of indifference, as some of his friends walked by.

"Mum, no. I'm not ready to see you," Carol lowered her voice, which just made the two children keener to hear what was being said. "There's just too...too much to think about. I'm worried it's not safe." The last word was a whisper.

"Of course you're safe." Jackie didn't whisper. Her irritation at the implication refused to let her be diplomatic like that. How dare her daughter suggest that she was putting them in jeopardy. How could she think that she would be so thoughtless?

"You don't know that, mum," Carol said. Her eyes widened at something on the other side of the road. "If you did, you wouldn't need *him*, would you?"

Carol pointed at whatever was on the other side of the road. Jackie turned, and there, a monolith in a black coat, was Parker. Jackie's mouth opened, furious that this man would dare follow her like this, knowing full well how important her family was to her, his very presence proof positive that Carol was right. Jackie stared at Parker, incredulous. As she stared, Carol had corralled the children, grabbing one with each hand, even Toby, despite his initial protestations. Jackie span round, but it was too late. Carol was already dragging the children away, hoping that being near the remaining parents, still hanging around finishing conversations or greeting children, would dissuade Jackie from continuing the conversation.

"Carol..." Jackie said, but it was in vain. Carol was walking away, and there was no stopping her. Megan managed a plaintive look back at her grandmother, a look of bafflement on her face, all prospect of treats and indulgence banished now, until they all turned a corner at the end of the railings, and were gone.

Jackie stood alone. The schoolyard and the street were deserted now, the children and parents headed home, and any teachers that had looked to supervise the end of the day now safely inside the school, to share war stories about the day's experiences. Only Parker was left on the street, quiet, patient and permanent.

Jackie dug into her handbag, and pulled out a cigarette, which she lit as she crossed the road towards Parker. The nicotine hit did not soothe her irritation.

"What are you doing here?" she said.

"I apologise, Mrs Stark," he said, in his London accent that sounded like gears grinding without oil. "Mr Solomon asked that I find you, as there is a development that he is certain you need to be aware of. A development of some urgency, he said."

"I just wanted five minutes – five *fucking* minutes – to myself and...oh never mind," she trailed off. It was like arguing with an earthmover. She sighed, defeated. "Okay, Mr Parker. Where do I need to be?"

"Mr Solomon is in a car, just around the corner. Please follow me."

Parker walked off, Jackie following behind. In one of the side streets was their car, Solomon sat in the rear passenger seat, waiting patiently, his Easter Island face impassive and unmoving. As Jackie approached, he wound down the window.

"I am incredibly sorry to have to disturb you, Mrs Stark," he said, in honeyed tones as usual. "There has been a development of great import, and I'm afraid time is really of the essence."

"What kind of development?" Jackie said, still flushed from the pile-up of indignities she felt she had experienced.

"In this instance, I think it might be better to show you. Mr Parker has something you should see, but please"- he beckoned her to come closer, so he could lower his voice and still be heard – "you may well be surprised. Please prepare yourself."

She stared, dumbfounded at Solomon, then up at Parker, then back to Solomon again. He wound his window back up, closing the conversation as well, leaving Jackie with no choice but to follow Parker to the rear of the car.

The street was quiet – a collective deep breath in, as the parents and children had gone home, before the long, sad breath out when the drinkers and the schemers fell out of their houses to go and find distraction. Jackie looked at the huge man, indicating for her to come around to the back of the car and felt suddenly so alone, but with no way back to the life she once had. She had no choice but to continue on, wherever that might take her, and however she might change along the way.

"I'm going to open this now. Are you ready?" Parker said.

Jackie nodded. The boot opened. She wasn't surprised, but still her stomach flipped.

Parker held the boot open for no more than five seconds. Jackie looked inside. Gagged and bound, with a blindfold over his eyes was Connor, his bloated frame unmistakeable despite the coverings. His huge chest still moved, but Jackie was unsure whether him being still alive was a good thing or a bad thing – did it just mean that murder was something that she was going to be party to? Or would it have been better if that deed had already been done, and Connor was just meat – something to be dealt with in the abstract.

And then she noticed something else. Connor was a big

man. Broad and overweight, filling the trunk of the car. But behind that huge frame was something else. *Someone* else. Parker had one hand on the boot lid, a de facto shield against prying eyes, unlikely though that was on this quiet street. Jackie came closer, and saw another face, half-smothered behind Connor's shoulder, and then suddenly, recognition.

It was that horrible little man who Jim had brought into her house, before he died. Who had appeared at the funeral of her husband. The street corner rodent who had been there when her Jim had been killed. Unlike Connor, he was conscious, wise enough to be quiet, but his eyes were wide and scared. Parker shut the boot, and walked around the car, to open the passenger door for Jackie to get in. She did as she was bid, and then Parker walked around to the driver's side, and got in himself.

"There have been developments, Mrs Stark," said Solomon. "As you have seen."

Jackie needed to do something. She dug around in her handbag for another cigarette.

"Yes," was all she managed to say. Any more words than that would have been a challenge. Solomon spoke, which was a relief.

"We felt it prudent to keep Connor under observation. We have been in similar situations, Mrs Stark, and we had the impression that he would be the most likely to attempt some challenge to your new position. We were not incorrect in this assumption."

"He was trying something on?" Jackie said. The indignation helped her. She had always hated Connor, him being the most vocal of those who dared criticise Jim.

"Quite so. We observed him meeting our other guest. Once that meeting had concluded, Mr Parker persuaded

Connor to brief us on exactly what was discussed. I must say, I was somewhat surprised to hear what was said."

"Surprised? How?" Jackie said.

"Well, it appears that this Cold Cut gentleman has somehow managed to make acquaintance with an Argentinian business who you may or may not be aware of. A large operation who have desires to add this city to their portfolio. Connor was to be the customer, with the Argentinian supply being his leverage to take over your business. I certainly would not expect someone of this Cold Cut's standing to have the...wherewithal to attempt something like this."

"Once we learned this, we felt it pertinent to discuss the matter with Cold Cut directly," Solomon continued. "We found him in his apartment, in a state of unconsciousness. Mr Parker had to be quite forceful in order to bring him around. And we discovered something most fortuitous. It seems Cold Cut had been visited by an acquaintance of our quarry. The Graces. A visit to see whether there was anyone looking for them."

"The Graces..." Jackie said, under her breath. Everything else was secondary. They were what drove her now.

"On the one hand, we weren't able to identify this acquaintance, but he did say something that might help us. You see, we know of this man – we believe he is an old comrade of the woman, and we know he lives in Stoke-on-Trent, but not exactly where in the city. But thanks to the gentleman currently in our boot, because he was wise enough to remember an offhand comment, we believe this associate decided to travel home by train. We have someone in the city who is going to observe the station, and then, if all goes well, follow this acquaintance back to the two people we are all so desperately keen to find."

"When will we know?" Jackie said, after puffing out a cloud of cigarette smoke. She wound the window down slightly, to let the smoke escape.

Solomon held a finger up, then reached inside his coat pocket, to pull out his phone. A thin smile spread on his face.

"Ah," Solomon said. "I believe our luck is in."

## 34

Tony had prepared for the worst. But he was wrong. The worst came to them quickly and violently.

Steaky had arrived back from Liverpool, a broad grin across his face, pleased that his task had both gone well, and given him yet another anecdote for his collection. He had walked the couple of miles back from the station, up the shallow incline to the centre of the city, which sat above the rest of the towns that made up Stoke-on-Trent. So buoyed by his adventure, he had stopped off at an off-licence en route, and announced his return by the clink of bottles inside a plastic bag, as he walked to his front door.

It was bad news he was delivering, but at least it was definitive. The little rodent man in Liverpool hadn't lied to him. He knew that. And knowing that there were people actively looking for Tony and Eleanor meant that now they could prepare for it, and maybe even push back.

"You're enjoying this, aren't you?" Eleanor said to Steaky, after he breathlessly recounted what had happened in

Liverpool earlier. It was late now, pushing close to midnight, and the empty bottles were piling up. One last blow-out before they all got down to the hard work of addressing this situation.

"I shouldn't, I know," Steaky said, as he gulped back another swig of beer, wiping his lips with the back of his hand. "But I'm sorry. I don't get excitement round here anymore. It's not like I've even got any neighbours to piss off."

"You do know they are trying to kill us, right?" Tony said, unable to be as serious as he hoped when he started to speak. Steaky was the sort of person who could fall into a lake and not get wet. It was hard to take any threat seriously with him around.

"You're right. They don't know we checked in on them, so we've got all the time we want to plan what we are going to do," Steaky said, chastened, like a naughty schoolboy. "We can dig around in the bunker. And the surgeon here – " he thumbed at Eleanor – "has always got that rifle of hers, just like last time, right?"

"We were lucky last time. If you can call it that," Eleanor said. "They were stupid. Didn't know about me. They won't be so stupid this time. We need to think this through."

"I don't think we can just try to vanish," Tony said. "They're not going to stop, are they?"

"Looks that way," Steaky said. "That lad said they were definitely looking. And this outside help, from down south, well, they're not going to give up easily."

"There are two ways this ends," Eleanor said. "We take them out, and cut the head off properly this time, or we do enough damage that it's just not economic for them to keep on with this."

"Well, there is a third," Tony said.

"Let's not think about that," Eleanor said. Steaky looked at them, puzzled, until the cogs clicked into place, and his eyebrows raised, the conundrum solved.

"Oh...!" he said, finally. "If we all get killed!"

Eleanor put her face in her hands, this ridiculous friend of theirs shaping even the most desperate of situations into something approaching a farce. Thank god that there were enough stories about how he had single-handedly turned the tide when they had been in tight spots before – that same optimism he lived by, able to be redirected into a fearlessness that defied danger. They were lucky he was with them on this.

"Well, thank you for saying that out loud, you dickhead," Eleanor said. She popped the cap on another bottle of beer, rolled her eyes at Steaky, and took a swig.

They stayed up for an hour or so, the beers not doing more than give them a buzz. The adrenaline was too overpowering for the alcohol to have any serious effect on them. Plans were made, discussed and thrown out, sometimes in less than a minute, the three of them taking turns in raising a suggestion, before the other two pointed out a flaw. Did they wait for them to find them? Too open-ended. Did they lure them into a trap? Too dangerous. Did they take the battle to them? Too reckless.

Around and around they went, until, eventually, the beers were gone, and the time had stopped being "late night" and started to think about being "early morning". Eleanor stood up.

"I'll clear up in the morning, Steak, but we should get our heads down," she said. "Fresh start tomorrow. Coffee and a clear head."

"Okay, El. I'm just going to have a smoke first, and then

I'll do the same," Steaky said, delighted to have found a half-smoked spliff down the side of the chair he was sitting in.

"In the cellar?" Tony said, getting to his feet as well. "We should, shouldn't we?"

"I think so," Eleanor said. "Take no chances. That okay, Steak?"

"Yep, yep," he said, rummaging down the other side of the chair for a lighter this time.

"Okay, mate," Tony said. "Bright and early tomorrow, eh?"

"Something like that," Steaky said. "Something like that."

TONY WOKE IN COMPLETE DARKNESS. It took him a few moments for him to orient himself, forgetting for a few seconds the chaos of the last few weeks, until it dawned on him that he wasn't in his comfortable bed in his comfortable house on the Norfolk coast anymore. It felt like an old wound had reopened again.

The black of the cellar was total, as was the quiet. He could have been hundreds of feet underground, falling and falling down a hole that had no bottom. Lost forever, and unable to even touch the sides as he went.

His hand spidered away from the camp bed, to feel around on the floor for his phone. Basic though it was, it still lit up with a press of one of the buttons, the screen illuminated with the time. 4am – a halfway house between days. A limbo to get lost in.

Tony knew he wouldn't be able to just fall back to sleep again. He was better if he just stretched his legs, maybe dragged himself up to the back yard, and take some solace from the stars turning and the bite of the cold air.

He swung his legs up so he was sitting on the edge of the low camp bed, the cold brick floor underneath his bare feet. He pressed the button on the phone again, the screen lighting up again so he could take another mental snapshot of the room he was in. Eleanor was asleep on a camp bed a few feet away from him. At least one of them was getting some sleep. He rubbed his face with his hand, then, by pushing with his hands on his legs, stood up with a few rough creaks in his knees. There were always aches and pains.

Steaky had left them thick blankets and a three-bar fire, but even so, it was still too cold to attempt to sleep without being fully clothed. Tony slipped his feet into his boots, tied the laces to avoid the very real risk of tripping or clattering into something, and, using bursts of screen light to illuminate his path, walked through to the cellar directly below Steaky's yard, and started to quietly climb the ladder to ground level.

The night sky was bright and clear, amplified by how Tony's eyes had adjusted in the cellar black. A full moon shone silver, and stars were out dancing, crashing against the yellow shore of the streetlamp glow on the opposite side of his vision. It was quiet and still. The city centre was a mile away, and any noise that there might be, even at this hour, was insulated by distance and the emptiness of the houses that haunted these streets.

Behind him, Steaky's house showed some signs of life. A radio in the kitchen glowed blue from its digital display, and further into the house, a kaleidoscope of coloured patterns danced on the hallway wall, from the television in the living room. Tony smiled to himself. Steaky had probably fell asleep on the couch, never a slave to the anxieties that normal human beings seemed to suffer from.

It was easy to forget about the sinister forces that he now knew were still hell-bent on finding them, surrounded by this quiet. It was as if those that meant them harm might as well be orbiting around one of those distant stars that hung in the sky above him.

He walked the five or so metres past the coal shed to the end of the yard, leaning on the waist high wall that separated the yard from the communal alley that ran along the bottom of the houses. The cold was sharp, and he rubbed his hands together, getting some warmth back in fingers that were turning white from the fingertips down. He wouldn't stay out here for long. Just long enough to clear his head, and try again at sleep.

He leant over the wall, so he could see along the alley. A cat was silhouetted at the bottom of the alley, where it opened out onto the road that ran at ninety degrees to the street Steaky's house was on. Tony stared at it, still and quiet, watching this other night refugee making its way. It cheered him to see it.

As the thick arm wrapped around his neck, he thought it odd that the first thing he considered was how he hadn't heard anyone coming. The arm was huge, and had quickly wrapped itself around its twin, a heavy hand wrenched onto the top of his skull as his airway was constricted. As he flailed, unable to make a sound from his choked throat, he could feel the power from whoever it was throttling him. A big man, solid and muscular, and able to lift Tony from his feet as he was ragdolled, the violence of it adding disorientation to the light head as he fought to stay conscious.

It was futile. He found his rage and fear too late to be useful. His friend and his wife were near, and he had knew he had failed them. His last thought before he gave into the rising dark, his flailing arms pawing ever more weakly at the assailant, was just a last wish that somehow Eleanor would be able to get away from whoever this was. Let her be safe, even if he would never see her again. Just her.

## 35

Tony came round in more darkness. At first, he wondered if he had dreamt the encounter outside, and had woken up back in the cellar, next to his wife. But this darkness had space, a cumulation of almost imperceptible impressions that left him feeling small in a black that was hungry for whatever morsel was thrown to it.

He couldn't see, and slowly, as he came to his senses, did he realise it was because there was something covering his eyes.

His other senses strained to compensate. The smell of a dust and old water. A cold breeze that fluttered past his cheeks, and his bare shoulders. A rhythmic dripping seemingly miles away, a counterpoint to his own steady breathing. The near and the far, only underlining the space of the room he was in.

He felt cold. He tried to move, to see if he could find a way of finding warmth, but he just felt a sharp pain at his wrists instead. They were bound behind him tightly with something – not rope or cord, something more unforgiving.

Cable ties, tight enough to cut into his skin. He struggled for a minute or two, muscles bunching as he pulled and twisted, but he made no progress, and remained bound. Tied to a wooden chair in a darkness he couldn't see the edges of. Trapped. Lost.

The breeze whipped past again, raising gooseflesh on his skin. He realised that he was naked, a realisation that had him snort a mirthless laugh, as he thought of how even his ridiculous scheme with the knife blade had turned out to be a fruitless defence. Wrong again. Yet another underestimation.

"Oh, awake, are we?"

As soon as the words were spoken, Tony's senses sharpened to a point. He wasn't alone. He made estimations instantly, trying to sift through whatever stimulus he was given, as if he was panning for gold – some tiny sliver of value that he could trade for a little more life, or maybe, if he could ever dare to hope again, a way out of this somehow.

It was a woman's voice, girlish and light, completely at odds with whatever expectations Tony had of whoever had brought him here. Again, he snorted to himself. Don't make assumptions, Tony. Jim Stark made an assumption about Tony and Eleanor, and he ended up with a hole in the front of his head.

"You sound like a stuck pig," the voice said. "Which is fitting, I guess. Piggy piggy."

There was a giggle, high and light. Tony wondered if it was the scariest thing he had ever heard.

"Who are you?" he said.

"Does it matter?" the voice said. "As far as you are concerned, I am the Lord, your God,"

There was that giggle again. Tony felt colder.

"I know how this is going to go," Tony said. "I'm honest enough to realise that. So how about just taking this blindfold off. Let me at least die with my eyes open."

"Die?" the woman said. "All in good time. You just sit there, sweating. Tenderising the meat. You won't have long to wait."

Tony wasn't going to give whoever this was the pleasure of seeing him struggle. It was just so much wasted energy, and would be nothing but noise. Noise that might just lead to him missing something he might be able to use. Something that might give him some idea of where his wife was. Or his friend.

"That'll do, thank you. Now, what was it…? You are using Ruth this time, I think?"

Another voice. The voice was rich, certain and honeyed, finding its way around the consonants and vowels precisely. An older man, refined and confident. The boss?

"Is that all of them?" the woman said.

"Shortly," the man said.

Tony could hear the footsteps of the man as he walked across whatever room they were in. The footsteps echoed, heeled soles on a hard floor. Another sound followed afterwards – heavier steps, slower and more deliberate, and then a dragging noise. Something heavy being heaved across the room by a third person. A henchman or similar?

Whoever this person was, he dropped whatever he was dragging within a few metres of Tony, with the unmistakeable flat slap of bare flesh on concrete. He didn't need to see what was happening to know what it was – a body, dragged and dropped, ready for whatever was in store for it. It was a heavy sound. Too heavy to be Eleanor, Tony thought. Steaky?

"Bring the woman, please," the older man said.

The heavy footsteps moved away from Tony and out of the room, before returning, this time dragging something louder and harder across the concrete floor.

"Now," the older man said, once the noise had stopped, and suddenly Tony squinted as the light attacked his eyes, his blindfold removed. It took him a few seconds to focus, the blacks and the bright whites taking time to settle into discernable shapes as his eyes adjusted.

He took in as much as he could. Every detail mattered. If this was going to be the room that he died in, then, at the very least, he was going to absorb as much of it as he could. Information is power, and with the precious little power he had available to him, he couldn't afford to ignore anything.

He was in a warehouse. No, not a warehouse. This was an old factory, stripped bare of machines and anything of value, and left to rust and rot, the bustle of industry now good for nothing more than a rat-run for the bored, the disaffected and the addicted. Too ruined to be worth the cost of improvement, but still too expensive to level.

The ceiling was high and dark, but still some moonlight managed to find its way in through gaps in the slates. The long room had windows running along the length of one side, but every pane was broken, used as target practice during bored moments by whoever had found their way in to enjoy some consequence-free destruction. The paint was chipped on the frames, birdshit had piled up underneath ceiling beams, the old life of the factory increasingly hidden by time and disinterest.

There were three people in the room with Tony. Three people *standing*.

The woman was sitting on an ancient wooden desk, swinging her feet as she idly chipped away at the wood with a knife, next to a black binliner bag, full of something. She was slight in frame, but flashed a look at Tony with a fierceness that burned into him. The smile beneath those caustic eyes was incongruous and terrifying.

Stood close to her was the older man. He was short, with a tendency towards a paunch, wire-rimmed glasses perched owlishly on a large nose on his round, jowly face. The hair was thinning, and slicked back. His shoes gleamed.

Tony turned his head to look for the third person. The heavy footsteps belonged to a giant. Well over six feet tall, and nearly that wide, hair buzzcut-short, and a face that looked like it was carved from rock. Almost ludicrously, tiny ears clung to the side of his head, like God had run out of flesh making this monster. And there, bound to the chair that had been dragged the length of the room by this brute, was Eleanor.

She looked bad. Her face was bloodied, the dark red of the dried blood harsh against the pinks and purples of her bruised face. But she was conscious, looking at her husband with a look that shared rage, indignation, determination and a little fear. There was relief there too, for both of them. The situation was desperate, and likely terminal, but they were still alive, and alive meant that hope had not been completely extinguished.

Tony was glad that she had not been stripped, as he had. The injury to her was hard enough to take, but humiliation would've been too much. Eleanor was a survivor, and no delicate porcelain figure to be treated with gentle care, but he still felt an obligation to protect her. He couldn't help but feel like his failure was total.

Eleanor was dragged a couple of metres from Tony, in the middle of the room. In front of them both, was the unconscious body of another man, hands bound behind his back – the first person that was brought into the room by the brute who dominated the space, enormous though it was. The unconscious man was big in a different way – broad too, but shorter, his wide shoulders just a frame to hang his huge belly from. This was someone Tony had never seen before. Why was he here? Who was he?

"It is safe for you to enter," the older man said, extending an arm to beckon another player onto the stage.

The empty room echoed with footsteps as heeled shoes walked across the wooden floor. Tony squinted, trying to focus on whoever this was. A woman, walking steadily, but in a manner that suggested she was having to concentrate, so as not to reveal more about herself than she would like. It was a tightrope, and it was a challenge for her, but Tony didn't know what she was trying to push down – fear? Or anger?

His eyes cleared enough for him to recognise her, as the woman walked into the light thrown up from the street-lights below, and through the windows, or what was left of them. He had met her before. At the top of the rollercoaster they had been clinging onto for what seemed like an eternity and an instant, all at the same time. This was Jackie Stark. The wife of the man who had wanted them dead. The wife of the man they had killed. She was the one holding the leashes of the dogs sent to hunt them down. And she was presumably, the one who would see them killed, finally.

Tony kept quiet. Eleanor did the same. Both of them lockstep in understanding that it is better to wait, to assess, in the hope, however vain, that some information might be revealed that they could exploit. Conversation would lead to escalation, and escalation was something that would just see them dead quicker. Let the enemy show their hand, however strong it might be.

Jackie Stark hadn't looked at anyone other than the older man as she walked across the room. Only once she had reached him did she look at Tony and Eleanor. Her eyes were wide and wet, and her cheeks flushed, the emotion she was feeling starting to find ways to show itself, despite her best efforts to keep it in check. It was anger. Anger at them, but perhaps anger at bringing her to this place – this Golgotha, this reckoning – and anger at how she had had to change herself to be here herself.

The older man brought her back to herself, simply by resting a gloved hand on her upper arm. He had been in places like this many, many times, and was steering Jackie Stark through this, step-by-step.

"Mrs Stark," he said. "We need to make our enquiries with the gentleman at our feet. We have found a smaller room that is probably more suited to our needs. Will you accompany me there?"

Jackie nodded, and the older man indicated for her to walk on, with him out of the huge room through a door at the opposite end to the one she entered through.

"Mr Parker?" the man said, turning back to point at the unconscious man on the floor.

Parker was like a golem – impassive and still until given a task, becoming steady and unstoppable movement. He reached down, grabbing a leg of the large man, and pulling him along, with the ease of someone pulling a bin to the kerbside.

Tony and Eleanor were left in the room with the woman, who had said nothing for some minutes now, idly picking at her nails with a knife. Every so often, she looked up at them, and grinned, before going back to her knife play.

Tony was scanning the room for anything that might help him. An escape route, as unlikely as escape seemed now, or some way of cutting through the cable ties. Eleanor was groggy, clearly, her head lolling as a concussion had its way with her. He couldn't rely on her to be able to help much, even with this psychopath in the room with them. He wasn't sure how long he had, but however long it was it wasn't going to be long enough.

The huge man returned to the room. Tony braced himself for *something* but the man ignored them, and walked the length of the room, and went out through the door at the bottom. Some minutes passed, and then he returned to the room, this time with someone else. Another face that Tony recognised.

It was the thin, rodent-like man that had been part of the Stark crew that found them in Norfolk. The same man who had given up his phone to Tony. The same man who had been there, on the water front, when Eleanor had cut down the Stark gang like it was a duck shoot. The one that Steaky had found in Liverpool to interrogate. But clearly, things had not gone well for him since. His hands were bound behind him too, though he was able to walk, nudged forward by firm prods in the small of the back by this Parker, walking slowly behind him. The thin man was furtive and scared, a feral creature surrounded by predators, and unable to find a way of escaping that wouldn't see him dead.

The man's nervous eyes widened when he saw Tony and Eleanor. Recognition battled against surprise, the dawning of understanding perplexing him as he saw who else was in this building, with their hands tied. A heavy paw jabbed him onwards from behind, and the thin man stumbled forwards.

Parker and the man walked across the room, to the

doorway that Jackie Stark and the older man had walked through. Parker turned back, and spoke to the woman.

"Go through his stuff, then do the same for her," he said, then he left the room, pushing the other man ahead of him.

Tony and Eleanor were left alone with the woman. She looked up at them, a huge grin on her face.

"Isn't this exciting?"

# 36

Cold Cut felt like he was always under the sword, and no matter what he did, or where he went, it was only a matter of time before he felt the sharp edge of it. This time he couldn't see what he had to barter with that might buy him a stay of execution, much less the chance for him to gather the power and status that he had allowed himself to daydream about over the past few days.

Everywhere he went he seemed to be in the company of killers. He had found a new way of living, but not the life of money clips and nodded respect. Instead a life where one wrong move or one failed test and he would vanish, left unloved and unmourned in an unmarked grave or lost in fresh concrete.

Barely hours after he had been attacked in his own flat, and wrenched into agonies by some mystery man asking questions about the Graces and the Starks, than he found himself pushed up against a wall, held by the throat, staring into the cold eyes of Parker. He had woken late after the terror of that interrogation, only to find Parker stood at the bottom of his bed, keen to show Cold Cut that his idea of an interrogation was fiercer, quicker and infinitely more direct.

Time sped up. The sand grains of his life fell through his fingers, too fast for him to stop. Parker hadn't listened to anything Cold Cut managed to say, letting him exhaust himself as he thrashed and squirmed, jumbling words out in a desperate attempt to find something – *anything* – that might see him safe. But Parker was impassive, his huge frame making Cold Cut's flat seem tiny simply by him being stood in it, a hand pressing Cold Cut back against a wall, unable to wriggle free. When the stream of words ran out, Parker simply leant forward, almost imperceptibly, and put one finger to his mouth.

"Shhhh," he said. "Plenty of time for that later."

Cold Cut knew that the one route that would lead to a very quick, or worse, a very, very slow end was antagonism. He did as he was told, and stopped talking. He shrank, defeated, completely docile.

"Out," Parker said, plainly. His huge hand relaxed the pressure, and pulled Cold Cut from the wall like peeling paper, indicating he should move towards the door, and out.

Cold Cut couldn't help himself. The fierce boil on his neck was red hot and pulsing, the blood that sped around his body only made it angrier and Parker had aggravated it by firmly grabbing him and pushing him forwards. Cold Cut squealed in pain, quickly strangling the yelp in his throat for fear of bringing some more chastening from Parker.

"Looks sore, that," Parker said. "You should get that looked at."

Cold Cut rubbed the back of his neck, dared himself to just half-glance over his shoulder, and walked down the stairs with the enthusiasm of one walking to the gallows.

Parker steered him out of his front door, onto the street, and around the corner to a side-road. A black car was parked against the kerb, with Solomon sat in the passenger seat, impassively staring ahead, not acknowledging Parker and Cold Cut as they approached the car. Parker, simply by applying a slight pressure with two of his fingers to the small of Cold Cut's back, moved him to the back of the car.

"Wait," Parker said, and Cold Cut froze.

Cold Cut quickly crashed calculations into each other – should he run? Could he get away? Where could he go? Who would help him? Whatever he decided, it had to be now. He had to do something now. He had to...

Parker grabbed Cold Cut by the scruff of the neck, from behind. With his other hand, he grabbed one of Cold Cut's arms, then the other, and quickly and smoothly bound them together with cable ties. A button was pressed, the boot opened, and Cold Cut was bundled inside.

"Don't make me open this again. One more to pick up."

And with that, Cold Cut was closed into the dark.

TIME EBBED AND FLOWED, in the back of that car. He had no idea if he was there for minutes or hours or days or all of them at once. It made no sense. He knew he wanted to be out of the car, but also knew that when the boot was opened he would be in real danger. He was Schrodinger's Gobshite.

Eventually, the boot *did* open. His eyes adjusted to the light, as best as they could, but no sooner was his view filled with colours and shapes again, before another huge shape filled the space. Cold Cut was forced further into the boot, as the heavy shape was dropped unceremoniously inside, and then any hint of the outside was lost to him again as the boot was slammed shut.

Cold Cut wasn't exactly sure what had just happened. Something had been thrown in with him. Something big and unwieldy. Something breathing.

Someone else.

COLD CUT STAYED conscious the entire time he was trapped in that tiny space, now smaller thanks to the giant body slammed in there with him. Low, shallow breaths huffed out of the person in there with him, but the body didn't move. The car moved this way and that, as it navigated through streets to wherever it was headed. For long periods, the car simply sat stationary, the slam of car door the only clue that the occupants were active. Cold Cut couldn't hear anything other than the breathing, and the muffled, indistinct sounds of the road traffic, and definitely nothing that would help him orientate himself, for all the good that would do him.

Hours must have passed. The boot opened one more time, this time revealing the wife of Jim Stark, looking down at him with a look of both shock and disgust, like someone looks at a backed-up toilet. Cold Cut was prepared for the boot opening that time, thanks to the sound of heels on concrete as Jackie Stark approached the car. Using that sound as a cue, Cold Cut scrunched his eyes closed, starving them of even the prospect of light and sight, and then opening them when the boot was opened, his eyes hungry for whatever they could get. As he focussed, he was able to see Stark, and Parker, and also, finally, to identify Connor, who was his impromptu bunkmate. It gave him a new reason to panic.

He knew who Connor was to Stark – a rival. If he was in there with him, then was he seen as an accomplice to Connor's crimes? Had he been found guilty before the chance to defend himself? Guilt by association?

The boot shut again. The light went. Cold Cut felt his neck throb.

THE FINAL PIECES on the chessboard were revealed to him in that huge, empty factory. Tony and Eleanor Grace. Two people who had dragged him along to hell in their slipstream. He hated them. If they had just died, all the way back in Norfolk, then he wouldn't be here. He glared at them as he was pressed forwards, by Parker behind him. If he took anything from his current situation – spared any moments for thoughts not devoted to his self-preservation – it was relief that at least those fuckers were going to get what was coming to them. And judging by the manic, giggling woman, perched on an old desk, swinging her legs and playing with knives, then it was going to be slow, painful and sharp. He took some solace from that as he left the factory floor and entered the side room that opened up from it.

He was right to be scared. Even knowing it was fruitless, he tried to push his feet back and resist the final step into the room because of what he saw as he reached the doorway. The room was smaller than the one he had just left, and darker too, being more towards the rear of the building, away from any streetlights, but even so, he could see more than enough. Parker was unyielding, and simply pushed him more firmly. The reality was unavoidable – there, in the middle of the room, gagged and hanging by the hands from a car tow rope thrown over a ceiling joist, was Connor. Hung like a pig in an abattoir.

Cold Cut couldn't take his eyes off that huge body, toes just barely reaching the floor. Was this his fate too? The end of him? Another sharp stab of pain burned into him from his neck, sending a jolt up and down his spine. A reminder that there was still agonies to be had, even if death was at the end of it.

Connor was the focus, but the periphery sharpened, and Cold Cut understood who he was here with, in this crucible. Parker behind him, a closed door to any escape, and standing quietly, waiting for him, Parker's more dangerous associate, Solomon, and their employer, Jackie Stark. Suddenly, a groan from Connor, and an uncertain lifting of the head, and then Cold Cut realised that everyone in this room was looking at him and him alone.

"We know everything," Solomon said. "Every tawdry little detail. We know how you and this gentleman here – " he indicated to Connor – "were looking to circumnavigate your betters, and invite unwanted competition into our employer's marketplace."

Solomon flexed his fingers, the squeal of stretched leather loud in the quiet room.

"This is not acceptable," Solomon continued. "I'm certain you are aware of this even as you explored this avenue. You were aware of the likely consequences. And here you are. Here you both are."

Cold Cut knew he had to say something.

"You're wrong," he managed to stammer out. "That's not what I was doing. I wanted to help."

Solomon smiled. It terrified Cold Cut.

"Help," Solomon said. It was not a question. Instead, it sounded like he was testing the word to see if it had some hitherto unknown meaning he hadn't considered.

"Help," Cold Cut repeated. "I had a hook-up, and thought since...since...Mr Stark...well, you know, since what happened happened, that it might be helpful if I could arrange something."

Jackie Stark just stared at him. Her lips were pursed, and her arms were crossed, and she radiated pure, complete contempt. Cold Cut tried not to look at her.

"Look, I'll be honest," Cold Cut continued. "I thought there might be something in all this for me. You know, if I could get some product in then maybe I could get myself on the payroll, somehow. Something permanent."

"That's an odd thing to say," Solomon replied. "Because why would you go to this man and try and facilitate some kind of coup, instead of presenting this offer to us directly? Forgive me, but I find this somewhat hard to believe."

"It's true," Cold Cut said. He felt Parker shift his weight slightly behind him, preparing for something, again emphasising how trapped he truly was. "I wanted to help. But..."

He couldn't help it. His throat dried, his Adam's apple bobbing vainly as he tried to maintain whatever composure he still had, his eyes stinging as the tears came close to spilling out.

"Look, I know what I am," he managed to say. "I'm a fucking loser. A fucking coward. I piss about on street corners looking for the scraps that you lot forget about. I wanted to get my foot in the door. And Connor, well, he fucking scared me."

"This man scared you? And we didn't?" Solomon said, pointing at Connor, pathetically turning this way and that as he hung from the rope, wide-eyed and sweating. Solomon had made Cold Cut's ogre small. In every life, there is always someone bigger, or more dangerous.

"Look, I know, right?" Cold Cut said. "But he was right there. He was *right there*. He found out about me, and the Argies, and he scared me. And lied to me. Made me think he wanted to talk to me so he could get the credit, and then he just made me think he'd fucking kill me if I didn't do as I was told."

"Prove it."

Everyone in the room turned and followed the voice. Jackie Stark had spoken.

"Mrs Stark?" Solomon asked.

"Let him prove it," Jackie said, her tone cold and level. "He says he was scared into this, and just wanted to get noticed by us – by *me* – so, let him show us, right now, just how loyal he is."

"I'm loyal. Of course I'm loyal," Cold Cut blustered. "But he was going to do me in if I didn't follow along. I wasn't going to go through with it. I would never – "

Jackie interrupted.

"So kill him," she said.

It seemed like the air and whatever light there was left was all sucked out of the room. Cold Cut felt his fingernails itch, the backs of his knees start sweating, and still, always, that perpetual drilling of the fucking boil or lesion or infection or whatever the hell it was, nagging away at the base of his skull.

The moment passed – a hundred years condensed into a heartbeat – and then Connor started thrashing. He was like a fish on a line. Fat and useless, cheeks puffing like he was asphyxiating. He had heard what was said, and didn't even have the chance to make a deal, or an appeal, or do anything that might mean he might stretch his life out a little longer.

"If you want to prove to me, right now, that you are loyal, and all of this is just some perfectly reasonable misunderstanding," Jackie said, "then I want you to prove it by killing him. Parker?"

Parker looked at Jackie, then to Solomon, then to Jackie again.

"Give him a knife, Parker," Jackie said, firmly.

Cold Cut looked at Parker, terrified. Solomon gave a tiny nod, and Parker reached inside his jacket, and pulled out a knife. He offered it, handle first, to Cold Cut, who had no choice but to take the six-inch blade, mesmerised by its sharp edge.

As soon as the knife was in his hand, Solomon reached inside his coat, and pulled out a small handgun, barely bigger than his palm, underlining for Cold Cut exactly the options available to him.

Cold Cut felt that he had been given a mighty broadsword, so heavy he could barely lift his arm. He looked at Connor, who looked back at him with wide, frantic eyes. Connor's pupils darted this way and that, his eyes blinking through the beads of sweat that were now pouring down from his forehead.

Cold Cut hissed his breath in and out through his teeth, searching for a way of convincing himself that this wasn't a human life he was faced with taking. No, no, this was just a trick. A dummy. Make-believe. All he had to do was slide this knife in and out of this phantom a few times, and he would wake up. Magicked back to his flat, small and dirty but, now, in his mind, a palace he wanted to retreat to. Just this one simple thing to do first.

A bang, the noise of which echoed around the empty

factory, as Solomon underlined the demand of his employer by firing one shot into the wall above Cold Cut's head, the plaster falling to the floorboards like hail. It was a sound that had many messages – it said "you are alone here, and no-one is close enough to care." It said "we have the power and you have none." It said "kill this man, or you will be killed."

He took a step towards Connor, the knife held out in front of him like it was pulling him on, eager for blood. Another step, then another, and then he was there, within arm's reach. Close enough to kill. He was concentrating on something over Connor's shoulder – an old safety poster that had somehow managed to remain stuck to the wall despite the damp and the cold of the deserted factory. Staring at cartoon images of stick men lifting boxes, and wearing hard hats. Anything to not remind himself that Connor was alive and breathing and real. The knife blade gently prodded into Connor's fleshy side, the skin creasing like an invitation.

Cold Cut dared himself to look over at Jackie; one last hope that this was enough to pass whatever test she was setting for him. She hadn't looked away from him at all. Hadn't moved. She reached inside her handbag, pulled out a cigarette from the pack within, and lit it with the lighter she had palmed at the same time. Cold Cut wanted to believe that he saw her fingers shake as she lit the cigarette. She couldn't be as cold as her husband. She just couldn't be.

"I believe Mrs Stark has been abundantly clear," Solomon said. "Now is the time."

A couple of movements. A couple of electrical pulses to run down muscles to jab an arm forward. Basic chemistry. Barely even a conscious thought needed. Come on, he thought. This is easy. This is easy.

Suddenly, another noise shattered the unbearable tension in the room. Loud, heavy thuds from elsewhere in the building. Loud voices and a scream followed, before the noises folded in on each other to just be commotion. The Graces.

"See to it," Solomon said to Parker, who immediately set off out of the room to investigate, powering from a standing start into a run.

"I am uncomfortable with you in this environment, Mrs Stark," Solomon said. "I think we should just take a step outside, and let Mr Parker do his work."

Jackie seemed to shrink. The impression of the cruel and determined ruler she had projected had been broken by the distraction, and she looked nervous. Cold Cut could see that things were in flux, and knew enough to know that when things became uncertain, decisions were made quickly. He knew he had to get away, and if he was going to manage that, now was his time.

"What about...?" Jackie said, the quavering of her voice leaving no doubt as to how precarious her stoicism was.

Solomon didn't let her finish her sentence. Instead, he aimed his gun, and without debate or discussion, shot Connor through the head.

Cold Cut didn't need a second warning. He only knew for sure that there was one way out of this place, and that was through the door he had come in through. It would mean he would have to make his way past Parker, the Graces and that woman summoned up from one of the circles of Hell, but surely they would all have enough to worry about with each other to worry about a no-mark like him?

But staying in here was a foot in the grave. He needed to run.

He ran for his life. All he could focus on was the

doorway – his escape into the light, and out of the dark of this room. He barely noticed that another shot was fired, more old plaster exploding like a firework above his head as he made it through the door.

Solomon was behind him. Chaos ahead of him. But he was still alive.

# 37

The woman put the knife down on the desk, gripped the edge with both hands, and levered herself to her feet. Picking up the knife with one hand, and the black bin liner with the other, she walked towards Tony and Eleanor, still with that loveless smile on her lips.

"Honey, it's just a job," she said to Tony. "You know that. You've both been around the block, right?"

Eleanor was quiet. Tony knew that she was doing what he was – thinking of some way, however unlikely, that she could find her way out of her bonds, or at worse, give him a few more minutes of life. He would keep this woman talking, and keep her attention away from Eleanor.

"Yeah, I've been in a chair like this before. More than once. Always got out, though."

"I'm not sure that's going to happen this time, my love," she said. "This lot have a real hard-on for you. I think killing her husband might be something of a faux-pas, you know."

"We had no choice," Tony said. "We were – "

The woman put her finger to her lips.

"Shhhhh," she said. "I'm not your judge. And I'm certainly not your priest."

She knelt down a metre away from Tony, and put the knife down in front of her, then the bin liner, before opening it up, as if she was giving out presents at Christmas. Her face winced, just for a moment, and she reached around to the back of her waistband, and pulled out the handgun she had tucked into her waistband.

The woman held it up to Tony, then Eleanor, and set it down on the floor next to her.

"It was digging right in," she said, almost to herself. "Really uncomfortable. Now, then. Let's have a look at what you came with. Dig for treasure."

She rustled the black bag, and started removing the contents, one at a time, studying each thing for a second, before carefully placing it in a pile to one side of her. She kept up a running commentary as she did so.

"Pretty standard jeans. Trim waist for an old fella, though. Well done, you. Not a big fan of the big labels, then? Supermarket special, was it?" the woman said, feeling around the waistband of Tony's trousers.

"Do you have to?" Tony said.

The woman looked up at Tony, head cocked to one side.

"Do I have to what?" she replied.

"The commentary. Why do people like you always feel you have to say something?"

"Just trying to pass the time. We've got all night. This is the easy part for you. I'd would've thought you'd want to keep this part going for as long as you can, because it's not going to be like this all night. Oh, and honey..."

The woman raised herself up and leaned in towards Tony. Close enough for a whisper.

"There aren't people like me," she said. Then she sat

back down on the floor, and continued searching through Tony's clothes, pulling out his wallet from the back pocket of his jeans.

She emptied it, laying out the cards in front of her like she was playing solitaire. Tony was happy for her to be distracted by this – he had no surprises in there, but her being thorough meant there was more time for maybe some miracle to enable him or Eleanor, quiet in the next chair, to find some way to change the balance of things.

The woman raised her eyebrows at Tony, put the cards back into the wallet, and put it to one side with the jeans. She went back to the bag, and pulled out his underwear.

"Don't worry," she said. "I've got a strong stomach."

Her fingers quickly ran the circumference of the waistband.

"What's this, now?" she said, playfully surprised. "Oh, now. This is naughty. What even *is* it?"

Her fingertips were probing and prodding at one particular area of the waistband, finally locating the cut in the material that Tony had made earlier. Finding purchase on whatever it was Tony had hidden in there, she worked it free to examine it closely.

"Now, I like this!" she said. This was a game to her. She was so certain of her position – the security of it, and the power she had over them. She held up what she had found, delighted with herself. It was the knife blade, wrapped in tape, that Tony had prepared earlier that night.

"What a good idea," the woman said. "Clever, clever, clever. Shame for you that we've left you in the altogether. A good attempt, though. I'll be careful when I'm checking your missus out, that's for sure."

"Do you ever shut up?" Eleanor said, breaking her silence.

"Speak when you're fucking spoken to," the woman snapped at Eleanor, the ferocity of it at odds with the matter-of-fact commentary of before.

Tony needed to do something. His idea of stashing the blade was bordering on ridiculous. Almost as ridiculous as him being in the position where it had been discovered. He stared at the woman, sat in front of him, who was still turning the wrapped blade over and over in her hands, amused at the conceit of it. There might still be a chance. His shoes were in the bag, and in the soles of those shoes he had hidden the hair-pins he had prepared earlier. If he could somehow get one of those pins in his hand, and find a way of distracting this woman for a few seconds, he might just be able to get out of the cable ties that had him bound to this chair.

Maybe there was a way to provoke her?

Tony managed to shift his weight to move his chair a few precious inches towards Eleanor. Straining as hard as he could, he turned to her, to see if he could get close to her – close enough to reassure her, or kiss her, or, at least, make it seem like that was what he was doing. Eleanor looked at him, confused, trying to understand why he was risking himself by doing this in front of their captor. But, despite that, she knew her husband, and she knew how his mind worked. She had to trust in that.

"I'm sorry. I love you," he said, nudging his forehead against hers.

"No, no, NO!" the woman said, quickly getting to her feet. "You can fucking pack that shit in. You don't deserve it. You don't deserve this."

The woman reached between them, pulling them apart with a hand on each shoulder. Tony pushed as hard as he could to resist, Eleanor doing the same, forcing the woman to pull harder, until suddenly he relented, the lack of resistance allowing him to use the woman's pressure to throw him to the floor, chair and all.

He was close to the bag, shoes inside, having fallen in front of it, between it and the woman, who was stood in front of Eleanor, looking down at him with a look that oscillated from confusion to amusement to anger and back again, all in an instant. He was so close. His fingers could touch the bag, and if he could reach the shoes, he could reach the hairpin and...

This was the moment. Eleanor knew something was happening, but she didn't know what, but there was no way she wasn't going to play her part in this.

The woman burst out laughing.

"Look at you," she said. "Stuck little pig, wriggling around with your cock out. I was going to let you have just a tiny bit of dignity, but I guess you've just seen to that, haven't you?"

"Go fuck yourself," Eleanor said.

"Don't test me, you fucking bitch," the woman said, bringing herself down to eye level with Eleanor, hatred and venom in every syllable. "I will fucking slice your face off and let you look at it, as I cut your old man into little pieces. Do not doubt me."

Tony's fingers stretched and clenched and stretched and clenched, pulling the bag, and its contents, closer to him inch by inch. Eleanor was playing her part perfectly. If this woman was angry, and distracted, then he had a chance of getting away with this.

A gunshot. Tony reacted first, taking advantage of the split-second distraction to pull the bag those final few inches closer to him, so he could finally feel one of the shoes at his finger-tips.

"Looks like things are warming up," the woman said. "I was so hoping to spend a bit of time with you both. Especially you." She ran her finger down the line of Eleanor's face, from forehead to brow to cheek, sizing her up like a surgeon.

Every word she said was a moment Tony could use to get closer to his goal. Only now did he realise that the wrapped blade had another possible purpose. The idea of it was so outlandish and unlikely that it made the prospect of there being more things hidden away seem impossible. If someone would go *this* far, then why would they try anything else? This was how you win at cards – bluff your hand one way or the other.

The hairpin slid out of the rubber sole quietly and smoothly. He palmed it quickly, and with it hidden away in the fold of his hand, he could manoeuvre it so he could try and work it between the teeth of the cable tie.

"I would have you counting your teeth with one eye shut in a heartbeat," Eleanor said. She saw that Tony was working on something, and knew she had to keep the woman distracted, just for a little longer. "I've done shits bigger."

"I'm going to beg," the woman said. "I'm going to beg and squeal and sob until they let me spend a few hours with you. Your man can get fucked. Shot through the head, see if I care. But you? You I want to spend time with."

The cable tie slid loose quietly. Tony could get his hands free. He – they – had a chance.

The woman had lost it. That was obvious. The facade she had built had crumbled, and all that was left, under the rubble of her self-control was a desperate need to hurt. She trembled with what might be anger, or might be anticipation, and turned away from Eleanor, back towards Tony, where she knelt down to pick up the gun and the knife that she had set down on the floor. Maybe he could somehow find a way of getting free of the bonds that still tied his feet to the chair with the hair pin, but he needed that knife. And if she got hold of the gun, they were both dead.

The woman put the gun back in her waistband, just below the small of her back, then flourished the knife at Eleanor like she was about to perform a party piece.

"I just can't wait," the woman said. "I was always the same. It was so hard pretending when I went to see some of your friends. What was his name? Johnny? Sweet guy. Ended up with this blade through his eye. Too quick for my liking."

Eleanor lurched forward in the chair, any pretence lost as her emotions got the better of her. She didn't even form words, instead making a sound that could only be described as a growl. Animalistic and desperate. This was the time.

Tony slid his hands free of the bounds, and with the woman's attention distracted, grabbed her by both of her ankles and pulled back, as hard as he could, taking her from her feet and down to the hard, wooden floorboards face first.

His legs were useless to him, with the chair tightly bound to them still, but his arms were strong, and free. He swarmed over the woman, pulling himself on top of her as quickly as he could, desperate to reach the gun and the knife.

The woman was stunned – her head had bounced off the floor, but she was by no means incapacitated. She thrashed like a landed fish, screaming with a viciousness that pierced.

His right hand reached towards her right hand, which held the knife. At the same time, his left hand managed to close around the handle of the gun in the woman's waistband. So close. So close.

The woman bucked and twisted just as Tony had pulled at the gun, it slipping out of his grip and onto the floor, where the woman's kicking and flailing legs managed to connect with it and send it cartwheeling across the floor away from both of them. It simplified things. He needed to concentrate on the knife, and with his left hand free now, he had two hands to try and wrench it free.

Another thud. As they were wrestling, Eleanor had rocked her chair this way and that, until she managed to over-balance, and send herself to the floor, close to them. He needed the knife. Quickly. They wouldn't be alone for long.

He managed to prise the woman's fingers from the handle of the knife, and wrap his own fingers around it. The woman understood the desperation of her situation now, and dug her nails into his arm, and then, as hard as she could, she sunk her teeth into the soft flesh of the hand holding the knife.

The pain was incredible, and it caused him to loosen his grip on the knife, which fell to the floor. Eleanor kicked her legs, and rotated her position, chair and all, until she could grasp the fallen knife in her hands. They were so close to freedom now. And so close to disaster. All he could do was wrap his arms around the flailing woman, and hold on for as long as he could, hoping that it would give Eleanor enough time to use that knife to get herself free.

The woman bit and scratched and kicked, a rabid animal furious and murderous. The pain was incredible, but he had no choice – tied to a chair, fighting for an extra second.

"Let her go, Tony."

Eleanor was free, stood tall, knife in hand. The sound of

her voice was a distraction for both Tony and the woman, and as Tony relaxed his grip in response to hearing his wife speak, so the woman scuttled clear, and with one hand on the floor to balance her, she got to her feet. She looked at Eleanor, then down at Tony, blood spattered and smeared on the dirty floorboards around him, then down at the gun a few metres away from all of them. She moved towards it first.

Tony knew his wife well. He had only rarely seen her like this, in these situations, but he understood why her unit respected her as much as they did. As she moved towards the woman, knife in hand, he knew there was no-one else he wanted to be here with him.

Tony scrabbled around on the floor, until his slippery, gnawed fingers managed to find the hairpin on the floor. With free hands, he was able to use it to free his legs, quickly, and get himself to his feet. His legs burned – a combination of the efforts of the last few minutes, and the blood properly finding its way again after so long tied up.

Eleanor had closed the distance to the woman – one good stride forward and she could attack, but the woman had a gun.

"You're fucking dead," the woman said. "You're both fucking dead."

"Wait," another voice said, from the other side of the room. Parker had made his way into the room, and had slowed from a run as he saw the scene in front of him.

It was the killing time now, Tony knew. They had managed to create options where a few minutes ago they had only one – oblivion – but everything came down to what happened now. This was the deep breath before the leap. The pause.

Tony felt small all of a sudden. Ridiculous. Stood naked

in this room of killers. He reached down, picked up his underwear, and slid them on.

"Our employer wants to take their time with them, Ruth," Parker said, closing the distance. "This won't take long. Earn your money."

Ruth dared a look at Parker, who was now walking more slowly, sizing up Tony as he approached. It was the quickest of glances, her pupils just flicking away from Eleanor for an instant, but it was enough.

Eleanor jabbed the knife forwards with her right hand, at Ruth's torso. Ruth blocked this with her left, flat-palm onto Eleanor's forearm, deflecting the blow. But this was the feint – Eleanor had another target. Spinning around, with her left hand, she grabbed the gun barrel and twisted it back, as hard and as quickly as she could. Eleanor screamed, her finger on the trigger had nowhere to go but to be bent back and broken. The gun fell to the floor, too near to the other for either one of them to risk picking it up.

"Amateur," Eleanor hissed.

Ruth growled, baring her teeth. She circled Eleanor, poised, and without making the mistake of breaking her stare, held her hand out behind her. Parker was walking directly to Tony, fists balled and ready, but without slowing his stride, reached inside his jacket, and placed a knife, handle-first, into Ruth's palm.

"We'll see, won't we?" Ruth said.

Parker didn't stop. Tony sprang towards him, as soon as he was close enough, fist cocked. Parker was quick, though. The man was huge, but the speed was the most frightening thing about him. A massive fist arced through the air, pain exploding in Tony's head as it connected with his jaw. He fell to the floor with a thud.

Parker reached down and heaved Tony back to his feet,

then with one hand wrapped around the back of his head, the other rained down blow after blow, Tony's legs failing beneath him. Muscle memory would have to do, and somehow, he managed to throw a few punches of his own into Parker's midriff. It made no difference.

Parker levered his left arm under Tony's right armpit, and heaved, sending Tony spiralling through the air, landing in a heap a few metres away, momentum carrying him across the floor until he was close to the main door out of the room – the one that could take him outside, and freedom. But Eleanor was still here, and she needed him. Parker knew that. He closed off the distance relentlessly, but without urgency.

Tony was breaking, and bleeding. He couldn't beat this man, he knew. But once Parker was finished with him, as was surely inevitable, then Eleanor would be next. All he had was the power to delay. Breathing was difficult – hard wheezes forced themselves out of his body, past ribs which surely must be broken. He put a palm down onto the floor to try and lever himself up, conscious enough to avoid the sharp edges of broken glass that littered this part of the room. Then, almost as quickly as the impulse to mind the glass occurred to him, another idea took hold. A gunshot from somewhere else in the building gave him the distraction he needed.

He had no weapons. His faintly ludicrous idea with the hidden blades had been shown up as the long shot that it was, but the seed of that idea had grown new roots. As Parker paused his approach to look over his shoulder, back towards the sound of the shot, he pushed his other palm onto the floor, looking to all the world like he was just getting to his feet. The pain on his face from his injuries made it easy to hide another agony, as he ground his palm into small, sharp shards of glass on the floor. A fistful of glass.

This brutal and relentless beatdown was impossible for Eleanor to ignore, despite the dangers in front of her. She knew that any distraction would only give Ruth an advantage, but every blow or gasp from the other side of the room just made her hurry, risking making a mistake that would be the end of her. Ruth saw Eleanor pause, or hesitate, and revelled in the superiority it gave her.

"Won't be long now," Ruth said. "He's done well to last this long."

She smiled, as another thought occurred to her.

"Longer than some of the friends of yours I've visited."

Eleanor had realised that her unit would become a target, but hearing this woman say as much, making it real and definite, added yet more to the sins Eleanor would have to answer for.

"One of them even killed himself to avoid helping you. That knife there – " she pointed at Eleanor's blade with her own – "he jammed right into his eye. Never seen that done before."

That was enough for Eleanor. She might lose this fight. Tony might die. But if she could only do one thing, she was going to shut this bitch up once and for all.

Eleanor knew a knife fight might need only one wound to end it. The long preamble – circling and feinting, shifting weight to move away from the enemy, but still close enough to strike – would culminate in a burst of movement, and then blood on the floor, and an expression losing light and life. Everything was about timing. But waiting for the perfect moment was a luxury to her, her husband surely close to death on the other side of the room. She stepped forward, within touching distance. Another gunshot was the impetus Eleanor needed.

Ruth reacted, instantly. Her knife jabbed forward – a cobra strike. Eleanor tried to bat the arm away with her free hand, but she had overstepped. Her white skin cut red, and a pain burned, as Ruth made her mark on her forearm. Eleanor grunted, but refused to cry out. The dance continued.

COLD CUT ENTERED the room running, but was shocked still by what he found. The Graces had gotten free, and were now at odds with the two killers that Jackie Stark had brought here with her, with another one, Solomon, at his back. He didn't care about anyone here. He didn't care about anyone but himself. All he wanted was to get out of here and get away. Away to hide, to scheme, and to rage.

The two women were just off to his left, eyes locked on each other, knives occasionally jabbing forward as they negotiated the end of their opponent. Worse, though, were the two men – Grace, broken on the floor, and Parker ready to deliver a coup de grace, blocking the only way out of the room. Once he had finished with Grace, then the Grace woman would be next, and then all eyes would turn to Cold Cut.

He needed something, and he needed it fast. The windows were too high to risk jumping from, even if they hadn't weren't vicious mouths with sharp, glass teeth. No, all he had was one door – the one Parker and Grace were blocking. Then he saw it. On the floor, by the two women – a gun. If he was quick, he could snatch it, and then he would have his way out.

He needed to be careful. Quick, precise and nimble, or risk being pulled into the middle of that knife fight, especially if one or other of the combatants realised what he was doing. He saw Eleanor Grace cut, and recoil, and as the other woman pressed forward, looking to make good on her advantage, he made his move. One, two, three quick strides and he crouched low, scooping up the gun.

Cold Cut had never held a gun before. It was heavier than he expected. It would be even heavier if he had to point it at someone. Solomon would be here soon. There was no doubt that Solomon was much more comfortable with a gun in his hand. There would be no hesitation. Cold Cut pointed the gun at the ceiling and fired.

"Get out of the fucking way," he shouted.

Parker turned away from Tony Grace and looked at Cold Cut. Cold Cut felt Parker was looking at him like he was a monkey that was wielding a bone club for the first time – a distraction now becoming an irritation. He took a stride towards Cold Cut, who was stood in the middle of the room, the women to Cold Cut's left, and Solomon and Stark soon to be behind him. He had Parker's full attention now. It was what gave Tony Grace the chance to attack.

Tony had made his way back to his feet, blood mingling with sweat as it fell from him, a dark flood in particular dripping from his left hand. With gritted teeth and a grunt, Tony leapt onto Parker's back.

Tony thought about the hidden blade he had prepared, and he thought about Steaky, and where that whole idea had come from. "The forehead bleeds like a bastard," Steaky had said. He wrapped his right arm around Parker's neck, and then, with his left hand, glass ground into his palm, he mashed it back and forth across Parker's forehead as hard as he could bear. Maybe he couldn't beat this man, but he could blind him.

Parker's huge arms reached around his back to try and get purchase on Tony. As the blood started to flow from the patchwork of gashes Tony had made, instinctively, Parker put a hand to his eyes to try and clear them. Parker whirled and shook, trying to get this man off his back. Tony fell to the floor, his one good hand not strong enough to maintain his hold. He looked up at Cold Cut, who was trembling with the gun in his hand.

"You're dead if you don't kill him," Tony said to Cold Cut. "You know that, right?"

"Shut up," Cold Cut said.

"After us, they are going to hurt you, then they are going to kill you," Tony said. "They'll make it last all night if they have to."

"Stop talking," Cold Cut screamed. Then another voice spoke.

"Put the gun down, and step away," Solomon said, from the other side of the room.

Cold Cut took a step back as he turned slightly, so he could keep everyone in sight. Solomon had entered the room, gun raised, and pointing directly at Cold Cut.

"You still have an opportunity to prove yourself to us," Solomon said. "Don't be foolish."

Cold Cut looked at Solomon, then at Jackie Stark who was behind him. Solomon was calm and measured, as he always was. Cold Cut thought of how easily Solomon had killed Connor, as if he was stepping on a bug, and knew he would have the same ease in killing him as well. Jackie looked haunted. This was not her world. Not really. Jim Stark swum in these waters. Now everything was becoming too real.

The two women had paused their lethal waltzing, and were instead inching this way and that to keep all the players on this stage in view, without leaving each other open to attack from the other.

Cold Cut looked back at Parker, then Grace on the floor. Parker had turned back to Grace and was closing the distance to him, inching forward through his near-blindness to deliver the killing blow.

"I just want to go," Cold Cut said. "Just let me be."

Tony Grace was pushing himself backwards with his feet, sliding on the blood on the floor with slick feet.

"They will kill you, man," Grace shouted at Cold Cut. "You know they will."

Cold Cut hated Tony Grace. He was the cause of all of this. If Grace hadn't come into his world, bringing his wife with him, then he wouldn't be here. Jim Stark wouldn't be dead, and he would still be where he had always been – scratching a living from the street corners and the underpasses, however he could. He always wanted more than that. He always believed he deserved more than that, but right now, a gun in his hand and another pointed at him, he promised whichever god was foolish enough to listen, that he would go back to that life in a heartbeat and never complain about it again, if only he could get out of this room. With Tony Grace on the floor, ready to die, the root of all his problems, one shot was all it would take.

The back of his neck throbbed into cruel life as time slowed. That evil boil that was squatting at the top of his spine chose now to jangle fierce pain from his scalp to his toes. The pulse of his heart a call and response to the fire that ran around his body. His eyes watered, and all he could see was Tony Grace. Then Parker. Then Solomon. Then Jackie Stark. He fired the gun.

Parker had cleared most of the blood from his eyes, and looked down at Tony, his face a crimson mask. Anger had bubbled up, and he was ready to put an end to this old fool once and for all. The look of anger on his face was replaced by a look of confusion. He managed to take one more stride before his mind and body caught up with each other, and it realised that he had a hole in the side of his head. Parker looked perplexed as he drop to his knees, then from there, face forwards, on top of Tony.

Tony Grace had been right. Cold Cut knew that. It didn't matter how he had gotten here. There was no way Solomon would let him leave. Parker needed to die, and then he could escape. He ran for the door.

Eleanor knew what happened at times like this. This was the killing time – where each second slowed until it almost broke under the strain, and every move was vital. She had been in firefights, bullets flying from all sides. She knew the tiny cues someone made before they decided whether to let you live or die. She knew that to hesitate was to die.

All she needed to do was focus on Ruth. One at a time. Eleanor ducked low, and pushed forward, dropping her knife at the same time. Ruth surprised by Eleanor's decision to move, could only manage a wild swipe with her knife, but Eleanor now had two free hands. Her foot was planted, her hands grabbed Ruth's wrist, and then as Eleanor's weight shifted, she turned Ruth around, driving Ruth's own knife towards herself from behind her.

Eleanor was pulling Ruth's hand towards her face as hard as she could. Ruth was doing the opposite, her eyes fixed on the sharp point of her own knife.

"You're a fucking hobbyist," Eleanor said. "You can't hold

a gun properly, and you're only good when it's sport. You've never had to push yourself to live, have you?"

Ruth didn't speak. She screamed. A banshee wail of anger, that came from deep within her, until the whole room was filled with her fury. The knife was getting closer, inexorably.

"I might be as good as dead," Eleanor said, for Ruth's ears only, "but you're going to die first."

Ruth dug her sharp nails into Eleanor's wrists. The knife moved closer, still.

Eleanor didn't need to think about her friends. She didn't even need to think about her husband, lying close to death on the floor a few yards from her. She didn't need anything to motivate her – to dig deep for some anger or some injustice to give her some kind of advantage. She just let herself find that part of her that thrived at times like this. The part of her she would otherwise refuse to acknowledge. She was a killer. And she let herself truly become that part of her once again.

Eleanor let Ruth's body drop to the floor, the knife hilt-deep in her eye-socket. Parker and Ruth dead. Two less in her way.

SOLOMON FIRED HIS GUN.

Cold Cut had made just a few metres before he realised that his neck didn't hurt anymore. The realisation of it slowed him, the sudden relief a shock to his system. His hand reached around the back of his neck to feel what had happened. He stared at the red on his palm when he looked at his hand to see what had made it warm and wet. He looked up at Tony, as his legs failed, and opened his mouth to speak, his expression one of confusion. No sound came out, other than a wretched gurgle. He fell to the floor, mouth still opening and closing.

Solomon's bullet had sliced through Cold Cut from the back of his neck to the front, perfectly piercing him as he looked to escape. As he fell forwards, his elbow jarring against the floor as he hit the ground, the gun Cold Cut was holding jarred itself free from his grip, and slid towards Tony.

This was his way out. He reached for it, trying to wriggle free of Parker's huge weight. Solomon saw Tony stretch, fingers clutching, and fired. Then he fired again.

The two bullets hit Parker's body with dull thuds. Solomon was walking towards Tony now, his pace quickening, knowing that killing Tony, so close to a weapon, was of the utmost importance. Then he could kill the woman, and he and Jackie could get away from this embarrassment and regroup.

Eleanor was not to be ignored. As the shots rang out, she reached down for the knife she had discarded earlier in her fight with Ruth. In one smooth movement, she threw it at Solomon with as much accuracy as her haste would allow her. She didn't need to kill him. She just needed to delay him.

The knife missed. The chair that followed did not, crashing against Solomon's shoulder, knocking him off-balance.

It was all the delay Tony needed. He managed to find purchase on the floor with his bare feet, digging against a raised floorboard, pushing himself free of Parker's body and finally, within reach of the gun. Stretched out against the floor, he aimed up at Solomon from halfway across the room, and shot.

Solomon wheezed quietly as the bullet hit him, his gloved hand grasping at his chest, a vain attempt at stemming the flow of the blood now blooming from the wound. The gasp sounded like someone letting air out of tyre, and he collapsed to his knees, empty. Solomon raised his arm one last time taking aim, before the life left him completely, and his arm dropped to his side, the gun skittering out of his hand.

The room was silent, except for Tony's laboured breathing, broken ribs making every breath agony. Tony and Eleanor looked at each other, just glad to be alive, and finally safe. Almost.

Jackie took a few hurried steps forward, unsure whether she was going to run or try and pick up Solomon's gun, until the stares from Eleanor and Tony froze her to the spot.

"No," said Eleanor. "Don't try anything. You don't get away from this."

Eleanor walked towards Jackie, wiping blood on her legs as she walked, but not once taking her eyes from Jackie. Tony was heaving himself to his feet, slowly and painfully.

"Eleanor," he said. "Wait."

Jackie looked at them both. She felt like she was at the bottom of a well, looking up, the possibilities available to her now narrowed to a point. She had failed completely. Her husband was dead, the men he had sent to her were dead, and in a moment, she was to be dead.

"Why couldn't you let us be?" Eleanor said. "This – *this* – is all your fault."

Jackie still stood still, frozen to the spot. She looked smaller. Older. Like all her spirit had been forced out of her.

"Eleanor," Tony said, again, but Eleanor wasn't listening.

"You and your fucking husband couldn't just leave it, could you? We didn't have anything to do with that fucking robbery, but you chased us across the country, killed friends of ours, and what? Expected us to just fucking line up to die?"

Eleanor grabbed Jackie by the throat, and pushed her until her back was against the wall. Eleanor's eyes were wide. This had been a long time coming.

"How many of our friends have you killed?" Eleanor said. Her arm stiffened, and her grip tightened. Jackie could only feebly grip onto Eleanor's wrist, but Eleanor was not to be stopped.

"...I don't..." Jackie managed to say. "I don't know what they did."

"Don't you fucking dare," Eleanor said. "This is on you. All of it."

Tony had made it to the two women, and put a hand on Eleanor's shoulder. She shook it off, her focus total, and her fury undimmed.

"No," Jackie said, finding some indignation of her own. "You killed him. You killed my husband."

"He came at us, with his fucking mob, to do what? Apologise for the misunderstanding?"

"You killed him," Jackie said again, quietly.

"You'll never stop, will you?" Eleanor continued. "We can never relax. Ever. You'll just buy some more thugs, dress them up in suits all you fucking well want, and then send them at us. Well, that has to stop."

Eleanor started to squeeze Jackie's neck with both hands now. Jackie's heels scraped against the floorboards as she tried to do anything to break free, but Eleanor was too strong for her.

"Eleanor," Tony said, one more time.

He put his hand on her shoulder again, softly. Eleanor squeezed harder, then relaxed, and let go. Jackie slumped to the floor, her hand on her throat, gasping for breath, tears streaming down her face.

"If we kill her, then what?" Tony said. "Someone else feels they have to come after us? More revenge?"

"We can't just let her go," Eleanor said. "Not after what she's done."

Jackie was sobbing now. Deep, painful sobs that shook her whole body. She had lost completely and totally. Her husband was dead. He was a gangster, a murderer and a villain, but she loved him, and now he was gone. She had pushed her family away. Her daughter was scared of her, and her grandchildren – her beloved grandkids – looked at her with confusion and fear. What did she have left? All she had was her vengeance, and here, in a cold, gutted factory, surrounded by blood and murder, that vengeance seemed tiny and cheap.

Tony crouched down with a wince. He was eye-level with Jackie. She looked at him, wide-eyed, with her make-up running down her face.

"Jackie, I'm going to talk to you one last time, as honestly as I can. We're going to leave now. If we kill you, which, trust me, would be really easy for us, then I'm pretty sure that all this bullshit will never, ever stop. Someone will come after us, and then we'll come after them, and around and around we go."

Jackie was still sobbing, but quieter now. Tony continued.

"So, we're going to let you go. And you're going to go back to Liverpool, and never think about us again. And – this is the most important thing – if we ever feel like there is someone over our shoulder, then we are going to find you, and I'm not even going to try to persuade my wife to take it easy. I want you to think about your family, Jackie. Think really hard."

When Tony mentioned "family", Jackie broke down into heavy sobs again.

"She can't just..." Eleanor started.

"Think about it," Tony said. "I'm right. You know I'm right. And you know we're good for it, don't you, Jackie?"

Tony stood up, slowly and painfully, and walked over to the pile of his belongings that Ruth had left on the floor. He started pulling clothes on, as carefully as he could. Eleanor stared at him for a moment, then down at Jackie, pitiful and beaten, then back at Tony. The anger broke, like oil on water, looking at her husband. He was right, she knew. She wanted to kill Jackie Stark so much it burned, but who knew who would come after them to fill the gap with her dead? And that's why she loved her husband – the quiet practicality of him, even now.

Tony groaned again, as he struggled to pull his jeans on. Eleanor's shoulders softened, as she watched him. She went over to him, put his arm over her shoulder, and helped him pull his trousers on, one leg at a time, then his shoes.

Together, they made their way to the doorway that led to the outside, slowly but steadily. Tony looked at the bodies as they crossed the floor. Ruth, a look of surprise on her face, the knife hilt-deep in her eye, Solomon slumped like a marionette with its strings cut, and there, by the door, the huge body of Parker. The thin man was face down on the floor, his long fingers stretched out like he was hanging onto something. Tony never knew his name. No reason now. Just another casualty drawn into this murderous orbit.

A few more steps and this was all behind them. Tony looked back over his shoulder at Jackie. She was still sobbing, her knees pulled tight to her, lost and broken. Let her deal with all this death. Let that be her punishment. And if she talked? It didn't matter. They would be gone, reborn somewhere else in a new life.

A cold wind blew outside, bouncing off the steep walls of these deserted buildings. It felt like it was blowing right through them, cleansing them, the chill reminding them that there were still things to feel. Still ways to know they were alive.

"How are we going to get to Steaky's?" Tony said. His face dropped. "Oh fuck. Steaky. What have they done to him?"

"We need to walk. We can't risk anything else. Can you make it?" Eleanor said. She pointed, up at the city centre, sat atop its hill. "He's all the way up there."

Tony slipped his arm around Eleanor's waist, pulling her close to him for support. She put an arm around his shoulder. They were together.

"I can make it."

# 38

The walk took hours. To begin with, Tony found himself needing to stop every so often, to catch his breath, and to let the pain ease, before daring himself to start again. But, in time, he felt it was better to just push on and push through, finding strength from his wife, and using the determination to get back to Steaky as motivation to put one foot in front of the other.

They both looked like shit. As they walked, any last trace of night was chased away by dawn, the sun dragging itself up with the same weariness that Tony was feeling. No-one looked at them more than twice – walking these streets at these hours meant you had a story to tell, but more than that, you had a reason to be out here. And whatever that reason was, it was never good for someone to ask about it. Even a passing glance was met with fire from Eleanor.

The day woke up as they walked. People scurried past, adjusting clothes thrown on in the morning panic, or taking quick sips from too-hot coffee as they made their way to work. Vans parked themselves half-on, half-off pavements, with couriers starting their long day of battling the clock and the traffic. As the pavements filled, Tony and Eleanor felt like they were driftwood, carried along by the hectic mundanity of the morning. It helped. The colours of the day gave them distraction, and helped them along to their destination. To the house of their friend, and whatever they were going to find within.

Neither of them spoke to each other with anything more than an encouraging word. They both knew that Steaky was likely dead – if he was alive and had avoided Stark and her people when they came for Tony and Eleanor, then he would've come after them, surely. This was Steaky, after all. They wanted to get to him, prepared for yet another of their friends killed because of them. But at the same time, with each step forward, they still hoped.

The road to Steaky's house fell away from the main road like a tributary. It wound down from the higher ground and then banked up again, into the maze of streets and brown earth that made up the estates. As they walked down, they could see Steaky's house for a moment, before it hid itself behind other houses. It looked serene – like nothing had changed.

They made their way onto the street, and walked up to Steaky's front door. Still no sign of movement or activity inside. The curtains were pulled, but a lamp was on, even this far into the morning. Eleanor felt Tony sag next to her when he noticed it, making the same conclusion she had reached.

She slowly turned the door handle, and opened the door. It opened into a quiet house. Eleanor crouched slightly, from the doorstep, so Tony could use her as a lever to pull himself up and in. Neither said a word, concentrating on listening for the tiniest sound, or wanting to make their fears real by saying them out loud.

They made their way into the front room, and there, collapsed in the chair was Steaky.

"Oh god," Tony said. "Oh god, no."

Steaky was lifeless, his head flopped back in the chair. Each arm was resting on an arm of the chair he was collapsed in.

"Oh, Eleanor, I can't fucking stand –" Tony said, until Eleanor held a hand up suddenly.

"Wait a minute," she said.

"What?"

"Wait," she said again.

Eleanor was smiling. Tony looked at her, baffled.

"Richard Pye!" Eleanor shouted. "To. Your. Feet."

A sandpaper snort escaped from somewhere within Steaky's body. His eyes flicked open, wide and frantic, and he slammed his feet on the floor. A glass left on a plate was catapulted across the room as his foot came down on the plate rim.

"Fucking hell!" Steaky said. "What the fuck are you playing at?"

"What? He's not...?" Tony looked at Steaky, then to Eleanor, and then back to Steaky again. "How?"

"You pair look like shit," Steaky said. "Bad night?"

"You don't know?" Tony said. "They didn't...?"

"Who?" Steaky replied.

Eleanor had sat down on the arm of the sofa, and was shaking, head in hands. She looked up from her hands, and her face was creased, tears rolling down her face as she laughed so hard no sound came.

He'd slept through it. A joint the size of a baby's arm had put paid to him, and he had missed everything. The Starks snatching Tony, then finding Eleanor and dragging her along as well. Why risk going into the house at all, if they didn't have to bother? They'd only wanted Tony and Eleanor, after all.

Tony started laughing as well, and before long, all three of them were laughing, Steaky looking at both of them incredulously, unable to understand exactly what was happening. Tony winced every so often, his ribs furious with him, but the stabs of pain only made him laugh longer.

"Wait a minute..." Tony said, finally. "Who the fuck is Richard Pye?"

"That's my name, brother," Steaky said. "Steaky Pye."

"I thought it was because...because of all the knives," Tony said. "Steak Knife, or something."

Steaky roared with laughter. Eleanor was still doubled over, laughing uncontrollably.

"My mate," Steaky said, a hand on Tony's shoulder. "This is Stoke. When you're born, they hand you a steak pie. My little brother is called..."

"Oh no," Tony said. "Don't tell me. He's called 'Kidney' isn't he?"

Steaky patted Tony on the cheek, and winked.

"I'll put the kettle on," he said, and walked out of the room, to the kitchen.

# EPILOGUE

"Keep this line open during the search."

"Yes, sir."

"Survivors?"

"Checking now. There's a lot of blood."

"Police?"

"We've paid our man. He's running interference with the local force. We have time."

"Good."

"There's a woman, definitely dead."

"Confirm?"

"She has a knife in her eye, sir. A big guy, dead from gunshot wounds. One to the head, plus shots to the body."

"Anyone else?"

"An older guy. He's...hold on, sir."

"We might have time, but not that much time. Expedite your search."

"Understood, sir. It's just I think I know this one."

"You can identify?"

"It's Solomon. Freelance fixer. London-based, but gets around."

"So, with the one in the back, and these three, that's it. No sign of the Stark woman?"

"No, sir. She is not on the scene."

"No matter. She is irrelevant now, anyway."

"Sir? I think there's something else."

"Explain."

"In the corner. Someone else. Dragged himself. Shot in the neck, I think, but there's a lot of blood. His blood."

"Do we know him?"

"Oh, I think we do, sir. I think this is the man who you interviewed. In the safe house. The street corner dealer."

"Really. Fascinating. Is he dead?"

"Checking, sir. He is not moving, and his neck is a mess."

"Very well. Leave the scene. I know what I need to know."

"Sir?"

"Yes."

"This man. The dealer. I think I saw his fingers twitch."

## ABOUT THE AUTHOR

More information about Craig Dawson can be found at his website: craigdawsonwrites.com

Please visit to sign up to the mailing list for updates. If you enjoyed this book, please consider leaving a review.

First published in Great Britain in 2020 Ebook first published in 2020

Printed in Great Britain
by Amazon